W9-CZT-871

THE BREAD-WINNERS

THE BREAD-WINNERS

A Social Study

by
JOHN HAY

THE GREGG PRESS / RIDGEWOOD, N. J.

First published in ·1883 by Harper & Brothers
Republished in 1967 by
The Gregg Press Incorporated
171 East Ridgewood Avenue
Ridgewood, New Jersey, U.S.A.

Copyright© 1967 by
The Gregg Press, Inc.

Library of Congress Catalog Card Number: 67-29270

Printed in United States of America

AMERICANS
IN
FICTION

INTRODUCTION BY PROFESSOR CLARENCE GOHDES
Editor of *American Literature* Magazine

In the domain of literature the play may once have been the chief abstract and chronicle of the times, but during the nineteenth and twentieth centuries the novel has usurped the chief place in holding the mirror up to the homely face of society. On this account, if for no other, the Gregg Press series of reprints of American fiction merits the attention of all students of Americana and of librarians interested in building up adequate collections dealing with the social and literary history of the United States. Most of the three score and ten novels or volumes of short stories included in the series enjoyed considerable fame in their day but have been so long out of print as to be virtually unobtainable in the original editions.

Included in the list are works by writers not presently fashionable in critical circles — but nevertheless well known to literary historians — among them Joel Chandler Harris, Harriet Beecher Stowe, Thomas Bailey Aldrich, and William Gilmore Simms. A substantial element in the list consists of authors who are known especially for their graphic portrayal of a particular American setting, such as Gertrude Atherton (California), Arlo Bates (Boston), Alice Brown (New England), Edward Eggleston (Indiana), Mary Wilkins Freeman (New England), Henry B. Fuller (Chicago), Richard M. Johnston (Georgia), James Lane Allen (Kentucky), Mary N. Murfree (Tennessee), and Thomas Nelson Page (Virginia). There is even a novel by Frederic Remington, one of the most popular painters of the Western cowboy and Indian — and another, an impressive minor classic on the early mining region of Colorado, from the pen of Mary Hallock Foote. The professional student of American literature will rejoice in the opportunity afforded by the collection to extend his reading of fiction belonging to what is called the "local-color movement" — a major current in the development of the national belles-lettres.

Among the titles in the series are also a number of famous historical novels. Silas Weir Mitchell's *Hugh Wynne* is one of the best fictional treatments of the American Revolution. John Esten Cooke is the foremost Southern writer of his day who dealt with the Civil War. The two books by Thomas Dixon are among the most famous novels on the Reconstruction Era, with sensational disclosures of the original Ku Klux Klan in action. They supplied the grist for the first great movie "spectacular" — *"The Birth of a Nation* (1915).

Paul Leicester Ford's *The Honorable Peter Stirling* is justly ranked among the top American novels which portray American politics in action — a subject illuminated by other novelists in the Gregg list — A. H. Lewis, Frances H. Burnett, and Alice Brown, for example. Economic problems are forcefully put before the reader in works by Aldrich, Mrs. Freeman, and John Hay, whose novels illustrate the ominous concern over the early battles between labor and capital. From the sweatshops of Eastern cities in which newly arrived immigrants toiled for pittances, to the Western mining camps where the laborers packed revolvers, the working class of the times enters into various other stories in the Gregg list. The capitalist class, also, comes in for attention, with an account of a struggle for the ownership of a railroad in Samuel Merwin's *The Short-Line War* and with the devastating documentation of the foibles of the newly rich and their wives in the narratives of David Graham Phillips. It was Phillips whose annoying talent for the exposure of abuses led Theodore Roosevelt to put the term "muck-raker" into currency.

While it is apparent that local-color stories, the historical novel, and the economic novel have all been borne in mind in choosing the titles for this important series of reprints, it is evident that careful consideration has also been given to treatments of various minority elements in the American population. The Negro, especially, but also the Indian, the half-breed, Creoles, Cajuns — and even the West Coast Japanese — appear as characters in various of these novels or volumes of short stories and sketches. Joel Chandler Harris's *Free Joe* will open the eyes of readers who know that author solely as the creator of humorous old Uncle Remus. And there is a revelatory volume of dialect tales, written by a Negro author, *The Conjure Woman* by Charles W. Chesnutt.

In literary conventions and the dominating attitudes toward life, the works in the Gregg series range from the adventurous romance illustrated so well by Mayne Reid or the polite urbanity of Owen Wister to the mordant irony of Kate Chopin and the grimmer realism of Joseph Kirkland's own experiences on bloody Civil War battlefields or the depressing display of New York farm life by Harold Frederic. In short, the series admirably illustrates the general qualities of the fiction produced in the United States during the era covered, just as it generously mirrors the geographical regions, the people, and the problems of the times.

THE BREAD-WINNERS.

I.

A MORNING CALL.

A FRENCH clock on the mantel-piece, framed of
brass and crystal, which betrayed its inner structure
as the transparent sides of some insects betray their
vital processes, struck ten with the mellow and
lingering clangor of a distant cathedral bell. A
gentleman, who was seated in front of the fire reading a newspaper, looked up at the clock to see what
hour it was, to save himself the trouble of counting
the slow, musical strokes. The eyes he raised were
light gray, with a blue glint of steel in them,
shaded by lashes as black as jet. The hair was also
as black as hair can be, and was parted near the
middle of his forehead. It was inclined to curl,
but had not the length required by this inclination.
The dark brown mustache was the only ornament
the razor had spared on the wholesome face, the
outline of which was clear and keen. The face
suited the hands—it had the refinement and gentleness of one delicately bred, and the vigorous lines
and color of one equally at home in field and court;

and the hands had the firm, hard symmetry which
showed they had done no work, and the bronze
tinge which is the imprint wherewith sky and air
mark their lovers. His clothes were of the fashion
seen in the front windows of the Knickerbocker
Club in the spring of the year 187-, and were worn
as easily as a self-respecting bird wears his feathers.
He seemed, in short, one of those fortunate natures,
who, however born, are always bred well, and come
by prescription to most of the good things the
world can give.

He sat in a room marked, like himself, with a
kind of serious elegance—one of those apartments
which seem to fit the person like a more perfect
dress. All around the walls ran dwarf book-cases
of carved oak, filled with volumes bound in every
soft shade of brown and tawny leather, with only
enough of red and green to save the shelves from
monotony. Above these the wall space was covered
with Cordovan leather, stamped with gold *fleurs-de-
lis* to within a yard of the top, where a frieze of
palm-leaves led up to a ceiling of blue and brown
and gold. The whole expression of the room was
of warmth and good manners. The furniture was
of oak and stamped leather. The low book-cases
were covered with bronzes, casts, and figurines, of
a quality so uniformly good that none seemed to
feel the temptation either to snub or to cringe to its
neighbor. The Owari pots felt no false shame
beside the royal Satsuma; and Barbédienne's
bronzes, the vases of Limoges and Lambeth and
bowls from Nankin and Corea dwelt together in
the harmony of a varied perfection.

It was an octagon room, with windows on each
side of the fire-place, in which a fire of Ohio coal
was leaping and crackling with a cheerful and unctuous noisiness. Out of one window you could see
a pretty garden of five or six acres behind the house,
and out of the other a carefully kept lawn, extend-
ing some hundred yards from the front door to the
gates of hammered iron which opened upon a wide-
paved avenue. This street was the glory of Buffland, a young and thriving city on Lake Erie, which
already counted a population of over two hundred
thousand souls. The people of Clairfield, a rival
town, denied that there was anything like so many
inhabitants, and added that "the less we say about
'souls' the better." But this was pure malice;
Buffland was a big city. Its air was filled with the
smoke and odors of vast and successful trade, and
its sky was reddened by night with the glare of its
furnaces, rising like the hot breath of some prostrate Titan, conquered and bowed down by the
pitiless cunning of men. Its people were, as a rule,
rich and honest, especially in this avenue of which
I have spoken. If you have ever met a Bufflander,
you have heard of Algonquin Avenue. He will
stand in the Champs Elysées, when all the vice and
fashion of Europe are pouring down from the
Place of the Star in the refluent tide that flows from
Boulogne Wood to Paris, and calmly tell you that
"Algonquin Avenue in the sleighing season can
discount this out of sight." Something is to be
pardoned to the spirit of liberty; and the avenue is
certainly a fine one. It is three miles long and has
hardly a shabby house in it, while for a mile or two

the houses upon one side, locally called "the Ridge," are unusually fine, large, and costly. They are all surrounded with well-kept gardens and separated from the street by velvet lawns which need scarcely fear comparison with the emerald wonders which centuries of care have wrought from the turf of England. The house of which we have seen one room was one of the best upon this green and park-like thoroughfare. The gentleman who was sitting by the fire was Mr. Arthur Farnham. He was the owner and sole occupant of the large stone house—a widower of some years' standing, although he was yet young. His parents had died in his childhood. He had been an officer in the army, had served several years upon the frontier, had suffered great privations, had married a wife much older than himself, had seen her die on the Plains from sheer want, though he had more money than he could get transportation for; and finally, on the death of his grandfather he had resigned, with reluctance, a commission which had brought him nothing but suffering and toil, and had returned to Buffland, where he was born, to take charge of the great estate of which he was the only heir. And even yet, in the midst of a luxury and a comfort which anticipated every want and gratified every taste, he often looked longingly back upon the life he had left, until his nose inhaled again the scent of the sage-brush and his eyes smarted with alkali dust. He regretted the desolate prairies, the wide reaches of barrenness accursed of the Creator, the wild chaos of the mountain cañons, the horror of the Bad Lands, the tingling cold of winter in the Black Hills. But the

Republic holds so high the privilege of serving her that, for the officer who once resigns—with a good character—there is no return forever, though he seek it with half the lobby at his heels. So Captain Farnham sat, this fine May morning, reading a newspaper which gave the stations of his friends in the "Tenth" with something of the feeling which assails the exile when he cons the court journal where his name shall appear no more.

But while he is looking at the clock a servant enters.

"That same young person is here again."

"What young person?"

There was a slight flavor of reproach in the tone of the grave Englishman as he answered:

"I told you last night, sir, she have been here three times already; she doesn't give me her name nor yet her business; she is settin' in the drawin'-room, and says she will wait till you are quite at leisure. I was about to tell her," he added with still deeper solemnity, "that you were hout, sir, but she hinterrupted of me and said, 'He isn't gone, there's his 'at,' which I told her you 'ad several 'ats, and would she wait in the drawin'-room and I'd see."

Captain Farnham smiled.

"Very well, Budsey, you've done your best—and perhaps she won't eat me after all. Is there a fire in the drawing-room?"

"No, sir."

"Let her come in here, then."

A moment afterward the rustle of a feminine step made Farnham raise his head suddenly from his paper. It was a quick, elastic step, accompanied by

that crisp rattle of drapery which the close clinging
garments of ladies produced at that season. The
door opened, and as the visitor entered Farnham
rose in surprise. He had expected to see the usual
semi-mendicant, with sad-colored raiment and dole-
ful whine, calling for a subscription for a new "Cen-
tennial History," or the confessed genteel beggar
whose rent would be due to-morrow. But there
was nothing in any way usual in the young person
who stood before him. She was a tall and robust
girl of eighteen or nineteen, of a singularly fresh
and vigorous beauty. The artists forbid us to look
for physical perfection in real people, but it would
have been hard for the coolest-headed studio-rat to
find any fault in the slender but powerful form of
this young woman. Her color was deficient in
delicacy, and her dark hair was too luxuriant to be
amenable to the imperfect discipline to which it had
been accustomed; but the eye of Andrea, sharpened
by criticising Raphael, could hardly have found a
line to alter in her. The dress of that year was
scarcely more reticent in its revelations than the
first wet cloth with which a sculptor swathes his
kneaded clay; and pretty women walked in it with
almost the same calm consciousness of power which
Phryne displayed before her judges. The girl who
now entered Farnham's library had thrown her
shawl over one arm, because the shawl was neither
especially ornamental nor new, and she could not
afford to let it conceal her dress of which she was
innocently proud; for it represented not only her
beautiful figure with few reserves, but also her skill
and taste and labor. She had cut the pattern out

of an illustrated newspaper, had fashioned and
sewed it with her own hands; she knew that it
fitted her almost as well as her own skin; and
although the material was cheap and rather flimsy,
the style was very nearly the same as that worn the
same day on the Boulevard of the Italians. Her
costume was completed by a pair of eyeglasses with
steel rims, which looked odd on her rosy young
face.

"I didn't send in my name," she began with a
hurried and nervous utterance, which she was evidently trying to make easy and dashing, "because
you did not know me from Adam—— I have been
trying to see you for some time," she continued.

"It has been my loss that you have not succeeded.
Allow me to give you a chair."

She flushed and seemed not at all comfortable.
This grave young man could not be laughing at
her; of course not; she was good-looking and had
on a new dress; but she felt all her customary assurance leaving her, and was annoyed. She tried to
call up an easy and gay demeanor, but the effort
was not entirely successful. She said, "I called this
morning—it may surprise you to receive a visit from
a young lady——"

"I am too much pleased to leave room for surprise."

She looked sharply at him to see if she were being
derided, but through her glasses she perceived no
derision in his smile. He was saying to himself,
"This is a very beautiful girl who wants to beg or
to borrow. I wonder whether it is for herself or
for some 'Committee'? The longer she talks the

more I shall have to give. But I do not believe she is near-sighted."

She plucked up her courage and said:

"My name is Miss Maud Matchin."

Farnham bowed, and rejoined:

"My name is——"

She laughed outright, and said:

"I know well enough what your name is, or why should I have come here? Everybody knows the elegant Mr. Farnham."

The smile faded from his face.

"She is more ill-bred than I suspected," he thought; "we will condense this interview."

He made no reply to her compliment, but looked steadily at her, waiting to hear what she wanted, and thinking it was a pity she was so vulgar, for she looked like the huntress Diana.

Her eyes fell under his glance, which was not at all reassuring. She said in almost a humble tone:

"I have come to ask a great favor of you. I am in a good deal of trouble."

"Let us see what it is, and what we can do," said Farnham, and there was no longer any banter in his voice.

She looked up with sudden pleasure, and her glasses fell from her eyes. She did not replace them, but, clasping her hands tightly together, exclaimed:

"Oh, sir, if you can do anything for me—— But I don't want to make you think——" She paused in evident confusion, and Farnham kindly interposed.

"What I may think is not of any consequence

just now. What is it you want, and how can I be of service to you?"

"Oh, it is a long story, and I thought it was so easy to tell, and I find it isn't easy a bit. I want to do something—to help my parents—I mean they do not need any help—but they can't help me. I have tried lots of things." She was now stammering and blushing in a way that made her hate herself mortally, and the innocent man in front of her tenfold more, but she pushed on manfully and concluded, "I thought may be you could help me get something I would like."

"What would you like?"

"Most anything. I am a graduate of the high school. I write a good hand, but I don't like figures well enough to clerk. I hear there are plenty of good places in Washington."

"I could do nothing for you if there were. But you are wrong: there are no good places in Washington, from the White House down."

"Well, you are president of the Library Board, ain't you?" asked the high-school graduate. "I think I would like to be one of the librarians."

"Why would you like that?"

"Oh, the work is light, I suppose, and you see people, and get plenty of time for reading, and the pay is better than I could get at anything else. The fact is," she began to gain confidence as she talked, "I don't want to go on in the old humdrum way forever, doing housework and sewing, and never getting a chance at anything better. I have enough to eat and to wear at home, but the soul has some claims too, and I long for the contact of higher natures than those by whom I am now surrounded. I want opportunities for self-culture, for intercourse with kindred spirits, for the attainment of a higher destiny."

She delivered these swelling words with great fluency, mentally congratulating herself that she had at last got fairly started, and wishing she could have struck into that vein at the beginning. Farnham was listening to her with more of pain than amusement, saying to himself: "The high school has evidently spoiled her for her family and friends, and fitted her for nothing else."

"I do not know that there is a vacancy in the library."

"Oh, yes, there is," she rejoined, briskly; "I have been to see the librarian himself, and I flatter myself I made a favorable impression. In fact, the old gentleman seemed really smitten."

"That is quite possible," said Farnham. "But I hope you will not amuse yourself by breaking his heart."

"I can't promise. He must look out for his own heart." She had regained her saucy ease, and evidently enjoyed the turn the conversation was taking. "I find my hands full taking care of myself."

"You are quite sure you can do that?"

"Certingly, sir!" This was said with pouting lips, half-shut eyes, the head thrown back, the chin thrust forward, the whole face bright with smiles of provoking defiance. "Do you doubt it, Monsieur?" She pronounced this word Moshoor.

Farnham thought in his heart "You are about as fit to take care of yourself as a plump pigeon at a

shooting match." But he said to her, "Perhaps
you are right—only don't brag. It isn't lucky. I
do not know what are the chances about this place.
You would do well to get some of your friends to
write a letter or two in your behalf, and I will see
what can be done at the next meeting of the
Board."

But her returning fluency had warmed up Miss
Maud's courage somewhat, and instead of taking her
leave she began again, blushingly, but still boldly
enough:

"There is something I would like much better
than the library."

Farnham looked at her inquiringly. She did not
hesitate in the least, but pushed on energetically,
"I have thought you must need a secretary. I
should be glad to serve you in that capacity."

The young man stared with amazement at this
preposterous proposal. For the first time, he asked
himself if the girl's honest face could be the ambush
of a guileful heart; but he dismissed the doubt in
an instant, and said, simply:

"No, thank you. I am my own secretary, and
have no reason for displacing the present incum-
bent. The library will suit you better in every
respect."

In her embarrassment she began to feel for her
glasses, which were lying in her lap. Farnham
picked up a small photograph from the table near
him, and said:

"Do you recognize this?"

"Yes," she said. "It is General Grant."

"It is a photograph of him, taken in Paris,

which I received to-day. May I ask a favor of
you ?"

"What is it?" she said, shyly.

"Stop wearing those glasses. They are of no use
to you, and they will injure your eyes."

Her face turned crimson. Without a word of
reply she seized the glasses and put them on, her
eyes flashing fire. She then rose and threw her
shawl over her arm, and said, in a tone to which her
repressed anger lent a real dignity:

"When can I learn about that place in the
library?"

"Any time after Wednesday," Farnham answered.

She bowed and walked out of the room. She
could not indulge in tragic strides, for her dress
held her like a scabbard, giving her scarcely more
freedom of movement than the high-born maidens
of Carthage enjoyed, who wore gold fetters on
their ankles until they were married. But in spite
of all impediments her tall figure moved, with that
grace which is the birthright of beauty in any circumstances, out of the door, through the wide hall
to the outer entrance, so rapidly that Farnham
could hardly keep pace with her. As he opened
the door she barely acknowledged his parting salutation, and swept like a huffy goddess down the steps.

Farnham gazed after her a moment, admiring the
undulating line from the small hat to the long and
narrow train which dragged on the smooth stones of
the walk. He then returned to the library. Budsey was mending the fire.

"If you please, sir," he said, "Mrs. Belding's man

came over to ask, would you dine there this evening, quite informal."

"Why didn't he come in?"

"I told him you were engaged."

"Ah, very well. Say to Mrs. Belding that I will come, with pleasure."

II.

A HIGH-SCHOOL GRADUATE.

Miss Matchin picked up her train as she reached the gate, and walked down the street in a state of mind by no means tranquil. If she had put her thoughts in words they would have run like this :

"That was the meanest trick a gentleman ever played. How did he dare know I wasn't near-sighted ? And what a fool I was to be caught by that photograph—saw it as plain as day three yards off. I had most made up my mind to leave them off anyway, though they are awful stylish ; they pinch my nose and make my head ache. But I'll wear them now," and here the white teeth came viciously together, "if they kill me. Why should he put me down that way ? He made me shy for the first time in my life. It's a man's business to be shy before me. If I could only get hold of him somehow ! I'd pay him well for making me feel so small. The fact is, I started wrong. I did not really know what I wanted ; and that graven image of an English butler set me back so ; and then I never saw such a house as that. It is sinful for one man to live there all alone. Powers alive ! How well that house would suit my complexion ! But I don't believe I'd take it with *him* thrown in."

It is doubtful whether young girls of Miss Matchin's kind are ever quite candid in their soliloquies.

It is certain she was not when she assured herself that she did not know why she went to Farnham's house that morning. She went primarily to make his acquaintance, with the hope also that by this means she might be put in some easy and genteel way of earning money. She was one of a very numerous class in large American towns. Her father was a carpenter, of a rare sort. He was a good workman, sober, industrious, and unambitious. He was contented with his daily work and wage, and would have thanked Heaven if he could have been assured that his children would fare as well as he. He was of English blood, and had never seemed to imbibe into his veins the restless haste and hunger to rise which is the source of much that is good and most that is evil in American life. In the dreams of his early married days he created a future for his children, in the image of his own decent existence. The boys should succeed him in his shop, and the daughters should go out to service in respectable families. This thought sweetened his toil. When he got on well enough to build a shop for himself, he burdened himself with debt, building it firmly and well, so as to last out his boys' time as well as his own. When he was employed on the joiner-work of some of those large houses in Algonquin Avenue, he lost himself in reveries in which he saw his daughters employed as house-maids in them. He studied the faces and the words of the proprietors, when they visited the new buildings, to guess if they would make kind and considerate employers. He put many an extra stroke of fine work upon the servants' rooms he finished, thinking:

"Who knows but my Mattie may live here some-
time?"

But Saul Matchin found, like many others of us,
that fate was not so easily managed. His boys
never occupied the old shop on Dean Street, which
was built with so many sacrifices and so much of
hopeful love. One of them ran away from home
on the first intimation that he was expected to learn
his father's trade, shipped as a cabin-boy on one of
the lake steamers, and was drowned in a storm which
destroyed the vessel. The other, less defiant or less
energetic, entered the shop and attained some pro-
ficiency in the work. But as he grew toward manhood, he became, as the old man called it, "trifling";
a word which bore with it in the local dialect no
suggestion of levity or vivacity, for Luke Matchin
was as dark and lowering a lout as you would readily find. But it meant that he became more and
more unpunctual, did his work worse month by
month, came home later at night, and was continually seen, when not in the shop, with a gang of low
ruffians, whose head-quarters were in a den called
the "Bird of Paradise," on the lake shore. When
his father remonstrated with him, he met everything
with sullen silence. If Saul lost his temper at this
mute insolence and spoke sharply, the boy would
retort with an evil grin that made the honest man's
heart ache.

"Father," he said one day, "you'd a big sight
better let me alone, if you don't want to drive me
out of this ranch. I wasn't born to make a nigger
of myself in a free country, and you can just bet
your life I ain't a-going to do it."

These things grieved Saul Matchin so that his anger would die away. At last, one morning, after a daring burglary had been committed in Buffland, two policemen were seen by Luke Matchin approaching the shop. He threw open a back window, jumped out and ran rapidly down to the steep bluff overlooking the lake. When the officers entered, Saul was alone in the place. They asked after his boy, and he said:

"He can't be far away. What do you want of him? He hain't been doing nothing, I hope."

"Nothing, so far as we know, but we are after two fellows who go by the names of Maumee Jake and Dutch George. Luke runs with them sometimes, and he could make a pile of money by helping of us get them."

"I'll tell him when he comes in," said Saul, but he never saw or heard of his son again.

With his daughters he was scarcely more successful. For, though they had not brought sorrow or shame to his house, they seemed as little amenable to the discipline he had hoped to exert in his family as the boys were. The elder had married, at fifteen years of age, a journeyman printer; and so, instead of filling the place of housemaid in some good family, as her father had fondly dreamed, she was cook, housemaid, and general servant to a man aware of his rights, and determined to maintain them, and nurse and mother (giving the more important function precedence) to six riotous children. Though his child had thus disappointed his hopes, she had not lost his affection, and he even enjoyed the Sunday afternoon romp with his six grandchildren, which ordinarily took place in the shop among the shavings. Wixham, the son-in-law, was not prosperous, and the children were not so well dressed that the sawdust would damage their clothes.

The youngest of Matchin's four children was our acquaintance Miss Maud, as she called herself, though she was christened Matilda. When Mrs. Matchin was asked, after that ceremony, " Who she was named for ?" she said, " Nobody in partic'lar. I call her Matildy because it's a pretty name, and goes well with Jurildy, my oldest gal." She had evolved that dreadful appellation out of her own mind. It had done no special harm, however, as Miss Jurildy had rechristened herself Poguy at a very tender age, in a praiseworthy attempt to say " Rogue," and the delighted parents had never called her anything else. Thousands of comely damsels all over this broad land suffer under names as revolting, punished through life, by the stupidity of parental love, for a slip of the tongue in the cradle. Matilda got off easily in the matter of nicknames, being called Mattie until she was pretty well grown, and then having changed her name suddenly to Maud, for reasons to be given hereafter.

She was a hearty, blowzy little girl. Her father delighted in her coarse vigor and energy. She was not a pretty child, and had not a particle of coquetry in her, apparently ; she liked to play with the boys when they would allow her, and never presumed upon her girlhood for any favors in their rough sport ; and good-natured as she was, she was able to defend herself on occasion with tongue and fists. She was so full of life and strength that, when

she had no playing to do, she took pleasure in helping her mother about her work. It warmed Saul
Matchin's heart to see the stout little figure sweep-
ing or scrubbing. She went to school but did not
"learn enough to hurt her," as her father said; and
he used to think that here, at least, would be one
child who would be a comfort to his age. In fancy
he saw her, in a neat print dress and white cap,
wielding a broom in one of those fine houses he had
helped to build, or coming home to keep house for
him when her mother should fail.

But one day her fate came to her in the shape of
a new girl, who sat near her on the school-bench.
It was a slender, pasty young person, an inch taller
and a year or two older than Mattie, with yellow
ringlets, and more pale-blue ribbons on her white
dress than poor Mattie had ever seen before. She
was a clean, cold, pale, and selfish little vixen, whose
dresses were never rumpled, and whose temper was
never ruffled. She had not blood enough in her
veins to drive her to play or to anger. But she
seemed to poor Mattie the loveliest creature she had
ever seen, and our brown, hard-handed, blowzy tom-
boy became the pale fairy's abject slave. Her first
act of sovereignty was to change her vassal's name.

"I don't like Mattie; it ain't a bit romantic. I
had a friend in Bucyrus whose name was Mattie,
and she found out somehow—I believe the teacher
told her—that Queen Matilda and Queen Maud was
the same thing in England. So you're Maud!"
and Maud she was henceforward, though her tyrant
made her spell it Maude. "It's more elegant with
an *e*," she said.

Maud was fourteen and her school-days were end-
ing when she made this new acquaintance. She
formed for Azalea Windom one of those violent
idolatries peculiar to her sex and age, and in a fort-
night she seemed a different person. Azalea was
rather clever at her books, and Maud dug at her
lessons from morning till night to keep abreast of
her. Her idol was exquisitely neat in her dress,
and Maud acquired, as if by magic, a scrupulous
care of her person. Azalea's blonde head was full
of pernicious sentimentality, though she was saved
from actual indiscretions by her cold and vaporous
temperament. In dreams and fancies, she was
wooed and won a dozen times a day by splendid cava-
liers of every race and degree ; and as she was thoroughly false and vain, she detailed these airy adven-
tures, part of which she had imagined and part read
in weekly story-papers, to her worshipper, who listened with wide eyeballs, and a heart which was
just beginning to learn how to beat. She initiated
Maud into that strange world of vulgar and unhealthy sentiment found in the cheap weeklies which
load every news-stand in the country, and made her
tenfold more the child of dreams than herself.

Miss Windom remained but a few months at the
common school, and then left it for the high school.
She told Maud one day of her intended flitting, and
was more astonished than pleased at the passion of
grief into which the announcement threw her friend.
Maud clung to her with sobs that would not be stilled,
and with tears that reduced Miss Azalea's dress to
limp and moist wretchedness, but did not move the
vain heart beneath it. "I wonder if she knows,"

thought Azalea, "how ugly she is when she bawls
like that. Few brunettes can cry stylishly anyhow."
Still, she could not help feeling flattered by such
devotion, and she said, partly from a habit of careless kindness and partly to rescue the rest of her
raiment from the shower which had ruined her neck-
ribbon,—

"There, don't be heart-broken. You will be in
the high school yourself in no time."

Maud lifted up her eyes and her heart at these
words.

"Yes, I will, darling!"

She had never thought of the high school before.
She had always expected to leave school that very
season, and to go into service somewhere. But
from that moment she resolved that nothing should
keep her away from those walls that had suddenly
become her Paradise.

Her mother was easily won over. She was a
woman of weak will, more afraid of her children
than of her husband, a phenomenon of frequent occurrence in that latitude. She therefore sided naturally with her daughter in the contest which, when
Maud announced her intention of entering the high
school, broke out in the house and raged fiercely
for some weeks. The poor woman had to bear the
brunt of the battle alone, for Matchin soon grew shy
of disputing with his rebellious child. She was
growing rapidly and assuming that look of maturity
which comes so suddenly and so strangely to the
notice of a parent. When he attacked her one
day with the brusque exclamation, "Well, Mattie,
what's all this blame foolishness your ma's being

tellin' me ?" she answered him with a cool decision and energy that startled and alarmed him. She stood straight and terribly tall, he thought. She spoke with that fluent clearness of girls who know what they want, and used words he had never met with before out of a newspaper. He felt himself no match for her, and ended the discussion by saying : " That's all moonshine—you shan't go ! D'ye hear me ?" but he felt dismally sure that she would go, in spite of him.

Even after he had given up the fight, he continued to revenge himself upon his wife for his defeat. " We've got to have a set of gold spoons, I guess. These will never do for highfliers like us." Or, "Drop in at Swillem's and send home a few dozen champagne; I can't stummick such common drink as coffee for breakfast." Or, "I must fix up and make some calls on Algonkin Av'noo. Sence we've jined the Upper Ten, we mustn't go back on Society." But this brute thunder had little effect on Mrs. Matchin. She knew the storm was over when her good-natured lord tried to be sarcastic.

It need hardly be said that Maud Matchin did not find the high school all her heart desired. Her pale goddess had not enough substantial character to hold her worshipper long. Besides, at fifteen, a young girl's heart is as variable as her mind or her person ; and a great change was coming over the carpenter's daughter. She suddenly gained her full growth ; and after the first awkwardness of her tall stature passed away, she began to delight in her own strength and beauty. Her pride waked at the same time with her vanity, and she applied herself closely to her books, so as to make a good appearance in her classes. She became the friend instead of the vassal of Azalea, and by slow degrees she found their positions reversed. Within a year, it seemed perfectly natural to Maud that Azalea should do her errands and talk to her about her eyes; and Miss Windom found her little airs of superiority of no avail in face of the girl who had grown prettier, cleverer, and taller than herself. It made no difference that Maud was still a vulgar and ignorant girl —for Azalea was not the person to perceive or appreciate these defects. She saw her, with mute wonder, blooming out before her very eyes, from a stout, stocky, frowzy child, with coarse red cheeks and knuckles like a bootblack, into a tall, slender girl, whose oval face was as regular as a conic section, and whose movements were as swift, strong, and graceful, when she forgot herself, as those of a race-horse. There were still the ties of habit and romance between them. Azalea, whose brother was a train-boy on the Lake Shore road, had a constant supply of light literature, which the girls devoured in the long intervals of their studies. But even the romance of Miss Matchin had undergone a change. While Azalea still dreamed of dark-eyed princes, lords of tropical islands, and fierce and tender warriors who should shoot for her the mountain eagle for his plumes, listen with her to the bulbul's song in valleys of roses, or hew out a throne for her in some vague and ungeographical empire, the reveries of Miss Maud grew more and more mundane and reasonable. She was too strong and well to dream much; her only visions were of a rich man who

should love her for her fine eyes. She would meet
him in some simple and casual way ; he would fall
in love at sight, and speedily prosper in his wooing ; they would be married,—privately, for Maud
blushed and burned to think of her home at such
times,—and then they would go to New York to
live. She never wasted conjecture on the age, the
looks, the manner of being of this possible hero.
Her mind intoxicated itself with the thought of his
wealth. She went one day to the Public Library
to read the articles on Rothschild and Astor in the
encyclopedias. She even tried to read the editorial
articles on gold and silver in the Ohio papers.

She delighted in the New York society journals.
She would pore for hours over those wonderful
columns which described the weddings and the re-
ceptions of rich tobacconists and stock-brokers, with
lists of names which she read with infinite gusto.
At first, all the names were the same to her, all
equally worshipful and happy in being printed,
black on white, in the reports of these upper-worldly
banquets. But after a while her sharp intelligence
began to distinguish the grades of our republican
aristocracy, and she would skip the long rolls of ob-
scure guests who figured at the " coming-out parties"
of thrifty shop-keepers of fashionable ambition, to
revel among the genuine swells whose fathers were
shop-keepers. The reports of the battles of the
Polo Club filled her with a sweet intoxication. She
knew the names of the combatants by heart, and had
her own opinion as to the comparative eligibility of
Billy Buglass and Tim Blanket, the young men most
in view at that time in the clubs of the metropolis.

Her mind was too much filled with interests of this kind to leave any great room for her studies. She had pride enough to hold her place in her classes, and that was all. She learned a little music, a little drawing, a little Latin, and a little French— the French of "Stratford-atte-Bowe," for French of Paris was not easy of attainment at Buffland. This language had an especial charm for her, as it seemed a connecting link with that elysium of fashion of which her dreams were full. She once went to the library and asked for "a nice French book." They gave her "La Petite Fadette." She had read of George Sand in newspapers, which had called her a "corrupter of youth." She hurried home with her book, eager to test its corrupting qualities, and when, with locked doors and infinite labor, she had managed to read it, she was greatly disappointed at finding in it nothing to admire and nothing to shudder at. "How could such a smart woman as that waste her time writing about a lot of peasants, poor as crows, the whole lot!" was her final indignant comment.

By the time she left the school her life had become almost as solitary as that of the bat in the fable, alien both to bird and beast. She made no intimate acquaintances there; her sordid and selfish dreams occupied her too completely. Girls who admired her beauty were repelled by her heartlessness, which they felt, but could not clearly define. Even Azalea fell away from her, having found a stout and bald-headed railway conductor, whose adoration made amends for his lack of romance. Maud knew she was not liked in the

school, and being, of course, unable to attribute it to
any fault of her own, she ascribed it to the fact that
her father was a mechanic and poor. This thought
did not tend to make her home happier. She passed
much of her time in her own bedroom, looking out
of her window on the lake, weaving visions of
ignoble wealth and fashion out of the mists of the
morning sky and the purple and gold that made
the north-west glorious at sunset. When she sat
with her parents in the evening, she rarely spoke.
If she was not gazing in the fire, with hard bright
eyes and lips, in which there was only the softness
of youth, but no tender tremor of girlhood's dreams,
she was reading her papers or her novels with rapt
attention. Her mother was proud of her beauty
and her supposed learning, and loved, when she
looked up from her work, to let her eyes rest upon
her tall and handsome child, whose cheeks were
flushed with eager interest as she bent her graceful
head over her book. But Saul Matchin nourished
a vague anger and jealousy against her. He felt
that his love was nothing to her; that she was too
pretty and too clever to be at home in his poor
house ; and yet he dared not either reproach her or
appeal to her affections. His heart would fill with
grief and bitterness as he gazed at her devouring
the brilliant pages of some novel of what she imagined high life, unconscious of his glance, which
would travel from her neatly shod feet up to her
hair, frizzed and banged down to her eyebrows,
"making her look," he thought, " more like a Scotch
poodle-dog than an honest girl." He hated those
books which, he fancied, stole away her heart from

her home. He had once picked up one of them
where she had left it; but the high-flown style
seemed as senseless to him as the words of an incan-
tation, and he had flung it down more bewildered
than ever. He thought there must be some strange
difference between their minds when she could delight in what seemed so uncanny to him, and he
gazed at her, reading by the lamp-light, as over a
great gulf. Even her hands holding the book made
him uneasy; for since she had grown careful of
them, they were like no hands he had ever seen on
any of his kith and kin. The fingers were long and
white, and the nails were shaped like an almond,
and though the hands lacked delicacy at the articu-
lations, they almost made Matchin reverence his
daughter as his superior, as he looked at his own.

One evening, irritated by the silence and his own
thoughts, he cried out with a sudden suspicion :

" Where do you git all them books, and what do
they cost ?"

She turned her fine eyes slowly upon him and
said :

" I get them from the public library, and they
cost nothing."

He felt deeply humiliated that he should have
made a blunder so ridiculous and so unnecessary.

After she had left the school—where she was
graduated as near as possible to the foot of the class
—she was almost alone in the world. She rarely
visited her sister, for the penury of the Wixham
household grated upon her nerves, and she was not
polite enough to repress her disgust at the affection-
ate demonstrations of the Wixham babies. " There,

there! get along, you'll leave me not fit to be
seen!" she would say, and Jurilda would answer in
that vicious whine of light-haired women, too early
overworked and overprolific: " Yes, honey, let your
aunt alone.   She's too tiffy for poor folks like us";
and Maud would go home, loathing her lineage.

The girls she had known in her own quarter were
by this time earning their own living: some in the
manufactories, in the lighter forms of the iron
trade, some in shops, and a few in domestic service.
These last were very few, for the American blood
revolts against this easiest and best-paid of all occu-
pations, and leaves it to more sensible foreigners.
The working bees were clearly no company for this
poor would-be butterfly.   They barely spoke when
they met, kept asunder by a mutual embarrassment.
One girl with whom she had played as a child had
early taken to evil courses.   Her she met one day
in the street, and the bedraggled and painted creature called her by her name.

" How dare you?" said Maud, shocked and frightened.

" All right!" said the shameless woman.   " You
looked so gay, I didn't know."

Maud, as she walked away, hardly knew whether
to be pleased or not.   "She saw I looked like a
lady, and thought I could not be one honestly.   I'll
show them!"

She knew as few men as women.   She sometimes
went to the social gatherings affected by her father's
friends, Odd Fellows' and Druids' balls and the
festivities with which the firemen refreshed themselves after their toils and dangers.   But her un-

deniable beauty gained her no success. She seemed
to take pains to avoid pleasing the young carpenters,
coachmen, and journeyman printers she met on
these occasions. With her head full of fantastic
dreams, she imagined herself a mere visitor at these
simple entertainments of the common people, and
criticised the participants to herself with kindly
sarcasm. If she ever consented to dance, it was
with the air with which she fancied a duchess might
open a ball of her servants. Once, in a round game
at a "surprise" party, it came her turn to be kissed
by a young blacksmith, who did his duty in spite
of her struggles with strong arms and a willing
heart. Mr. Browning makes a certain queen, mourning over her lofty loneliness, wish that some common soldier would throw down his halberd and
clasp her to his heart. It is doubtful if she would
really have liked it better than Miss Maud did, and
she was furious as a young lioness. She made herself so disagreeable about it that she ceased to be
invited to those lively entertainments; and some of
the most eligible of the young "Cariboos"—a social
order of a secret and mysterious rite, which met
once a week in convenient woodsheds and stable-
lofts—took an oath with hands solemnly clasped in
the intricate grip of the order, that "they would
never ask Miss Matchin to go to party, picnic, or
sleigh-ride, as long as the stars gemmed the blue
vault of heaven," from which it may be seen that
the finer sentiments of humanity were not unknown
to the Cariboos.

Maud came thus to be eighteen, and though she
was so beautiful and so shapely that no stranger

3

ever saw her without an instant of glad admiration, she had had no suitor but one, and from him she never allowed a word of devotion. Samuel Sleeny, a carpenter who worked with her father, and who took his meals with the family, had fallen in love with her at first sight, and, after a year of dumb hopelessness, had been so encouraged by her father's evident regard that he had opened his heart to Saul and had asked his mediation. Matchin undertook the task with pleasure. He could have closed his eyes in peace if he had seen his daughter married to so decent a man and so good a joiner as Sleeny. But the interview was short and painful to Matchin. He left his daughter in possession of the field, and went to walk by the lake shore to recover his self-possession, which had given way beneath her firm will and smiling scorn. When he returned to the shop Sleeny was there, sitting on a bench and chewing pine shavings.

"What did she say?" asked the young fellow. "But never mind—I see plain enough it's no use. She's too good for me, and she knows it."

"Too good!" roared Saul. "She's the goldern dest——"

"Hold on there," said Sleeny. "Don't say nothin' you'll have to take back. Ef you say anything ag'in her, you'll have to swaller it, or whip me."

Saul looked at him with amazement.

"Well! you beat me, the pair of you! You're crazy to want her, and she's crazy not to want you. She liked to a' bit my head off for perposin' you, and you want to lick me for calling her a fool."

"She ain't no fool," said Sleeny with sullen resignation; "she knows what she's about," and he picked up another shaving and ruminated upon it.

The old man walked to and fro, fidgeting with his tools. At last he came back to the young man and said, awkwardly dusting the bench with his hand:

"Sam, you wasn't 'lowin' to leave along o' this here foolishness?"

"That's just what I was 'lowin' to do, sir."

"Don't you be a dern fool, Sam!" and Saul followed up this judicious exhortation with such cogent reasons that poor Sleeny was glad to be persuaded that his chance was not over yet, and that he would much better stay where he was.

"How'll *she* like it?"

"Oh! it won't make a mite o' difference to her," said the old man airily, and poor Sam felt in his despondent heart that it would not.

He remained and became like the least of her servants. She valued his attachment much as a planter valued the affection of his slaves, knowing they would work the better for it. He did all her errands; fetched and carried for her; took her to church on evenings when she did not care to stay at home. One of the few amusements Saul Matchin indulged in was that of attending spiritualist lectures and séances, whenever a noted medium visited the place. Saul had been an unbeliever in his youth, and this grotesque superstition had rushed in at the first opportunity to fill the vacuum of faith in his mind. He had never succeeded, however, in thoroughly indoctrinating his daughter. She regarded her father's religion with the same contempt

she bestowed upon the other vulgar and narrow circumstances of her lot in life, and so had preferred
her mother's sober Presbyterianism to the new and
raw creed of her sire. But one evening, when she
was goaded by more than usual restlessness, Sleeny
asked her if she would go with him to a "sperritual
lectur." To escape from her own society, she accepted, and the wild, incoherent, and amazingly
fluent address she heard excited her interest and admiration. After that, she often asked him to take
her, and in the long walk to and from the Harmony
Hall, where the long-haired brotherhood held their
sessions, a sort of confidential relation grew up between them, which meant nothing to Maud, but
bound the heart of Sleeny in chains of iron. Yet
he never dared say a word of the feeling that was
consuming him. He feared he should lose her forever, if he opened his lips.

Of course, she was not at ease in this life of
dreamy idleness. It did not need the taunts of her
father to convince her that she ought to be doing
something for herself. Her millionaire would
never come down to the little house on Dean Street
to find her, and she had conscience enough to feel
that she ought to earn her own clothes. She tried
to make use of the accomplishments she had learned
at school, but was astonished to find how useless
they were. She made several attempts to be a
teacher, but it was soon found that her high-school
diploma covered a world of ignorance, and no board,
however indulgent, would accept her services. She
got a box of colors, and spoiled many fans and dis-
figured many pots by decorations which made the

eyes of the beholder ache; nobody would buy them, and poor Maud had no acquaintances to whom she might give them away. So they encumbered the mantels and tables of her home, adding a new tedium to the unhappy household. She answered the advertisements of several publishing companies, and obtained agencies for the sale of subscription books. But her face was not hard enough for this work. She was not fluent enough to persuade the undecided, and she was too proud to sue *in forma pauperis;* she had not the precious gift of tears, by which the travelling she-merchant sells so many worthless wares. The few commissions she gained hardly paid for the wear and tear of her high-heeled boots.

One day at the public library she was returning a novel she had read, when a gentleman came out of an inner room and paused to speak to the librarian's assistant, with whom Maud was at the moment occupied—a girl whom she had known at school, and with whom she had renewed acquaintance in this way. It was about a matter of the administration of the library, and only a few words were exchanged. He then bowed to both the ladies, and went out.

"Who was that?" Maud asked.

"Don't you know?" rejoined the other. "I thought everybody knew the elegant Captain Farnham. He is president of our board, you know, and he is just lovely. I always manage to stop him as he leaves a board meeting and get a word or two out of him. It's worth the trouble if I only get a bow."

"I should think so," assented Maud. "He is as sweet as a peach. Is there any chance of getting

one of those places? I should like to divide those
bows with you."

"That would be perfectly splendid," said her
friend, who was a good-natured girl. "Come, I
will introduce you to the old Doctor now."

And in a moment Maud was in the presence of
the librarian.

She entered at a fortunate moment. Dr. Buchlieber was a near-sighted old gentleman who read
without glasses, but could see nothing six feet away.
He usually received and dismissed his visitors without bothering himself to discover or imagine what
manner of people they were. "I do not care
how they look," he would say. "They probably
look as they talk, without form and void." But at
the moment when Maud entered his little room, he
had put on his lenses to look out of the window,
and he turned to see a perfect form in a closely fit-
ting dress, and a face pretty enough to look on with
a critical pleasure. He received her kindly, and encouraged her to hope for an appointment, and it
was in accordance with his suggestion that she called
upon Farnham, as we have related.

She did not go immediately. She took several
days to prepare what she called "a harness" of sufficient splendor, and while she was at work upon it
she thought of many things. She was not even yet
quite sure that she wanted a place in the library.
The Doctor had been very kind, but he had given
her clearly to understand that the work required of
her would be severe, and the pay very light. She
had for a long time thought of trying to obtain a
clerkship at Washington,—perhaps Farnham would

help her to that,—and her mind wandered off among the possibilities of chance acquaintance with bachelor senators and diplomats. But the more she thought of the coming interview, the more her mind dwelt upon the man himself whom she was going to see—his bow and his smile, his teeth and his mustache, and the perfect fit of his clothes. One point in regard to him was still vague in her mind, and as to that her doubts were soon resolved. One evening she said to her father:

"Did you ever see Captain Farnham?"

"Now, what a foolish question that is! I'd like to know who built his greenhouses, ef I didn't?"

"He is pretty well off, ain't he?"

Saul laughed with that satisfied arrogance of ignorant men when they are asked a question they can answer easily.

"I rather guess he is; that is, ef you call three, four, five millions well off. I don't know how it strikes you" (with a withering sarcasm), "but *I* call Arthur Farnham pretty well fixed."

These words ran in Maud's brain with a ravishing sound. She built upon them a fantastic palace of mist and cloud. When at last her dress was finished and she started, after three unsuccessful attempts, to walk to Algonquin Avenue, she was in no condition to do herself simple justice. She hardly knew whether she wanted a place in the library, a clerkship at Washington, or the post of amanuensis to the young millionaire. She was confused by his reception of her; his good-natured irony made her feel ill at ease; she was nervous and flurried; and she felt, as she walked away, that the battle had gone against her.

III.

THE WIDOW AND HER DAUGHTER.

MRS. BELDING's house was next to that of Mr. Farnham, and the neighborly custom of Algonquin Avenue was to build no middle walls of partition between adjoining lawns. A minute's walk, therefore, brought the young man to the door of Mrs. Belding's cottage. She called it a cottage, and so we have no excuse for calling it anything else, though it was a big three-storied house, built of the soft creamy stone of the Buffland quarries, and it owed its modest name to an impression in the lady's mind that gothic gables and dormer windows were a necessary adjunct of cottages. She was a happy woman, though she would have been greatly surprised to hear herself so described. She had not been out of mourning since she was a young girl. Her parents, as she sometimes said, " had put her into black"; and several children had died in infancy, one after the other, until at last her husband, Jairus Belding, the famous bridge-builder, had perished of a malarial fever caught in the swamps of the Wabash, and left her with one daughter and a large tin box full of good securities. She never afterward altered the style of her dress, and she took much comfort in feeling free from all further allegiance to milliners. In fact, she had a nature which was predisposed to comfort. She had been fond of her husband, but she had been a little afraid of him, and, when she had wept her grief into tranquillity, she felt a certain satisfaction in finding herself the absolute mistress of her income and her bedroom. Her wealth made her the object of matrimonial ambition once or twice, and she had sufficient beauty to flatter herself that she was loved more for her eyes than her money; but she refused her suitors with an indolent good-nature that did not trouble itself with inquiries as to their sincerity. "I have been married once, thank you, and that is enough"; this she said simply without sighing or tears. Perhaps the unlucky aspirant might infer that her heart was buried in the grave of Jairus. But the sober fact was that she liked her breakfast at her own hours. Attached to the spacious sleeping-room occupied in joint tenancy by herself and the bridge-builder were two capacious closets. After the funeral of Mr. Belding, she took possession of both of them, hanging her winter wardrobe in one and her summer raiment in the other, and she had never met a man so fascinating as to tempt her to give up to him one of these rooms.

She was by no means a fool. Like many easy-going women, she had an enlightened selfishness which prompted her to take excellent care of her affairs. As long as old Mr. Farnham lived, she took his advice implicitly in regard to her investments, and after his death she transferred the same unquestioning confidence to his grandson and heir, although he was much younger than herself and comparatively inexperienced in money matters. It seemed to her only natural that some of the Farnham wisdom should have descended with the Farnham millions. There was a grain of good sense in this reasoning, founded as it was upon her knowledge of Arthur's good qualities ; for upon a man who is neither a sot nor a gambler the possession of great wealth almost always exercises a sobering and educating influence. So, whenever Mrs. Belding was in doubt in any matter of money, she asked Arthur to dine with her, and settle the vexing questions somewhere between the soup and the coffee. It was a neighborly service, freely asked and willingly rendered.

As Farnham entered the widow's cosey library, he saw a lady sitting by the fire whom he took to be Mrs. Belding; but as she rose and made a step toward him, he discovered that she was not in mourning. The quick twilight was thickening into night, and the rich glow of the flaming coal in the grate, deepening the shadows in the room, while it prevented him from distinguishing the features of her face, showed him a large full form with a grace of movement which had something even of majesty in it.

" I see you have forgotten me," said a voice as rich and full as the form from which it came. " I am Alice Belding."

" Of course you are, and you have grown as big and beautiful as you threatened to," said Farnham, taking both the young girl's hands in his, and turning until she faced the fire-light. It was certainly a bonny face which the red light shone upon, and quite uncommon in its beauty. The outline was very pure and noble ; the eyes were dark-brown and the hair was of tawny gold, but the complexion

was of that clear and healthy pallor so rarely met
with among blonde women. The finest thing about
her face was its expression of perfect serenity.
Even now, as she stood looking at Farnham, with
her hands in his, her cheek flushed a little with the
evident pleasure of the meeting, she received his
gaze of unchecked admiration with a smile as quiet
and unabashed as that of a mother greeting a
child.

"Well, well!" said Farnham, as they seated themselves, "how long has it taken you to grow to that
stature? When did I see you last?"

"Two years ago," she answered, in that rich and
gentle tone which was a delight to the ear. "I was
at home last summer, but you were away—in Ger-
many, I think."

"Yes, and we looked for you in vain at Christ-
mases and Thanksgivings."

"Mamma came so often to New York that there
seemed no real necessity of my coming home until
I came for good. I had so much to learn, you know.
I was quite old and very ignorant when I started
away."

"And you have come back quite young and very
learned, I dare say."

She laughed a little, and her clear and quiet laugh
was as pleasant as her speech.

Mrs. Belding came in with gliding footsteps and
cap-strings gently fluttering.

"Why, you are all in the dark! Arthur, will you
please light that burner nearest you?"

In the bright light Miss Alice looked prettier
than ever; the jet of gas above her tinged her crisp

hair with a lustre of twisted gold wire and threw
tangled shadows upon her low smooth forehead.

"We have to thank Madame de Veaudrey for
sending us back a fine young woman," said Farnham.

"Yes, she *is* improved," the widow assented
calmly. "I must show you the letter Madame de
Veaudrey wrote me. Alice is first in languages,
first——"

"In peace, and first in the hearts of her country-
women," interrupted Miss Alice, not smartly, but
with smiling firmness. "Let Mr. Farnham take
the rest of my qualities for granted, please."

"There will be time enough for you two to get
acquainted. But this evening I wanted to talk to
you about something more important. The 'Tri-
bune' money article says the Dan and Beersheba
Railroad is not really earning its dividends. What
am I to do about that, I should like to know?"

"Draw your dividends, with a mind conscious
of rectitude, though the directors rage and the 'Tri-
bune' imagine a vain thing," Farnham answered,
and the talk was of stocks and bonds for an hour
afterward.

When dinner was over, the three were seated
again in the library. The financial conversation
had run its course, and had perished amid the arid
sands of reference to the hard times and the gloomy
prospects of real estate. Miss Alice, who took no
part in the discussion, was reading the evening
paper, and Farnham was gratifying his eyes by gazing at the perfect outline of her face, the rippled
hair over the straight brows, and the stout braids

that hung close to the graceful neck in the fashion affected by school-girls at that time.

A servant entered and handed a card to Alice. She looked at it and passed it to her mother.

"It is Mr. Furrey," said the widow. "He has called upon *you*."

"I suppose he may come in here?" Alice said, without rising.

Her mother looked at her with a mute inquiry, but answered in an instant, "Certainly."

When Mr. Furrey entered, he walked past Mrs. Belding to greet her daughter, with profuse expressions of delight at her return, "of which he had just heard this afternoon at the bank; and although he was going to a party this evening, he could not help stopping in to welcome her home." Miss Alice said "Thank you," and Mr. Furrey turned to shake hands with her mother.

"You know my friend Mr. Farnham?"

"Yes, ma'am—that is, I see him often at the bank, but I am glad to owe the pleasure of his acquaintance to you."

The men shook hands. Mr. Furrey bowed a little more deeply than was absolutely required. He then seated himself near Miss Alice and began talking volubly to her about New York. He was a young man of medium size, dressed with that exaggeration of the prevailing mode which seems necessary to provincial youth. His short fair hair was drenched with pomatum and plastered close to his head. His white cravat was tied with mathematical precision, and his shirt-collar was like a wall of white enamel from his shoulders to his ears. He wore white kid gloves, which he secured from spot or blemish as much as possible by keeping the tips of the fingers pressed against each other. His speech was quicker than is customary with Western people, but he had their flat monotone and their uncompromising treatment of the letter R.

Mrs. Belding crossed over to where Farnham was seated and began a conversation with him in an undertone.

"You think her really improved ?"

"In every way. She has the beauty and stature of a Brunhild; she carries herself like a duchess, I was going to say—but the only duchess I ever knew was at Schwalbach, and she was carried in a wicker hand-cart. But mademoiselle is lovely, and she speaks very pretty English; and knows how to wear her hair, and will be a great comfort to you, if you can keep the boys at bay for awhile."

"No danger there, I imagine; she will keep them at bay herself. Did you notice just now? Mr. Furrey called especially to see her. He was quite attentive to her last summer. Instead of going to the drawing-room to see him, she wants him to come in here, where he is in our way and we are in his. That is one of Madame de Veaudrey's notions."

"I should fancy it was," said Farnham, dryly; "I have heard her spoken of as a lady of excellent principles and manners."

"Now you are going to side against me, are you ? I do not believe in importing these European ideas of surveillance into free America. I have confidence in American girls."

"But see where your theories lead you. In Algonquin Avenue, the young ladies are to occupy the drawing-room, while the parents make themselves comfortable in the library. But the houses in Dean Street are not so spacious. Most citizens in that quarter have only two rooms below stairs. I understand the etiquette prevailing there is for parents, when their daughters receive calls, to spend the evening in the kitchen."

"Oh, dear! I see I'm to get no help from you. That's just the way Alice talks. When she came home to-day, there were several invitations for her, and some notes from young gentlemen offering their escort. She told me in that quiet way of hers, that reminds me of Mr. Belding when he was dangerous, that she would be happy to go with me when I cared to go, and happy to stay at home if I stayed. So I imagine I am booked for a gay season."

"Which I am sure you will greatly enjoy. But this Madame de Veaudrey must be a very sensible woman."

"Because I disagree with her? I am greatly obliged. But she *is* a saint, although you admire her," pursued the good-tempered woman. "She was a Hamilton, you know, and married Veaudrey, who was secretary of legation in Washington. He was afterward minister in Sweden, and died there. She was returning to this country with her three girls, and was shipwrecked and they all three perished. She was picked up unconscious and recovered only after a long illness. Since then she has gone very little into the world, but has devoted herself to the education of young ladies. She never has more than three or four at a time, and these she selects herself.

Alice had heard of her from Mrs. Bowman, and we ventured to write to ask admission to her household, and our request was civilly but peremptorily declined. This was while we were in New York two years ago. But a few days afterward we were at church with Mrs. Bowman, and Madame de Veaudrey saw us. She called the next day upon Mrs. Bowman and inquired who we were, and then came to me and begged to withdraw her letter, and to take Alice at once under her charge. It seems that Alice resembled one of her daughters—at all events, she was completely fascinated by her, and Alice soon came to regard her in return as the loveliest of created beings. I must admit I found her a little stiff—though she *was* lovely and, of course, being a Hamilton, a perfect lady. But still, I cannot help being afraid that she has made Alice a little too particular; you know, the young gentlemen don't like a girl to be too stiff."

Farnham felt his heart grow hot with something like scorn for the worthy woman, as she prattled on in this way. He could hardly trust himself to reply and soon took his leave. Alice rose and gave him her hand with frank and winning cordiality. As he felt the warm soft pressure of her strong fingers, and the honest glance of her wide young eyes, his irritation died away for a moment, but soon came back with double force.

"Gracious heavens!" he exclaimed, as he closed the door behind him, and stepped into the clear spring starlight, hardly broken as yet by the budding branches of the elms and limes. "What a crazy woman that mother is! Her daughter has come home to her a splendid white swan, and she is waddling and quacking about with anxiety and fear lest the little male ducklings that frequent the pond should find her too white and too stately."

Instead of walking home he turned up the long avenue, and went rapidly on, spurred by his angry thoughts.

" What will become of that beautiful girl ? She cannot hold out forever against the universal custom. She will be led by her friends and pushed by her mother, until she drops to the level of the rest and becomes a romping flirt; she will go to parties with young Furrey, and to church with young Snevel. I shall see her tramping the streets with one, and waltzing all night with another, and sitting on the stairs with a third. She is too pretty to be let alone, and her mother is against her. She is young and the force of nature is strong, and women are born for sacrifice—she will marry one of these young shrimps, and do her duty in the sphere whereto she has been called."

At this thought so sharp a pang of disgust shot through him, that he started with surprise.

" Oh, no, this is not jealousy; it is a protest against what is probable in the name of the eternal fitness of things."

Nevertheless, he went on thinking very disagreeably about Mr. Furrey.

" How can a nice girl endure a fellow who pomatums his hair in that fashion, and sounds his R's in that way, and talks about Theodore Thommus and Cinsunnatta ? Still, they do it, and Providence must be on the side of that sort of men. But what

4

business is all this of mine ?   I have half a mind to
go to Europe again."

He stopped, lighted a cigar, and walked briskly
homeward. As he passed by the Belding cottage,
he saw that the lower story was in darkness, and in
the windows above the light was glowing behind
the shades.

"So Furrey is gone, and the tired young traveller
is going early to rest."

He went into his library and sat down by the
dying embers of the grate. His mind had been full
of Alice and her prospects during his long walk in
the moonlight; and now as he sat there, the image
of Maud Matchin suddenly obtruded itself upon
him, and he began to compare and contrast the two
girls, both so beautiful and so utterly unlike; and
then his thoughts shifted all at once back to his own
early life. He thought of his childhood, of his
parents removed from him so early that their memory was scarcely more than a dream; he wondered
what life would have been to him if they had been
spared. Then his school-days came up before him;
his journey to France with his grandfather; his
studies at St. Cyr; his return to America during
the great war, his enlistment as a private in the
regular cavalry, his promotion to a lieutenancy
three days afterward, his service through the terrible campaign of the Peninsula, his wounds at
Gettysburg, and at last the grand review of the veterans in front of the White House when the war
was over.

But this swift and brilliant panorama did not
long delay his musing fancy. A dull smart like

that of a healing wound drew his mind to a succession of scenes on the frontier. He dwelt with that
strange fascination which belongs to the memory of
hardships—and which we are all too apt to mistake
for regret—upon his life of toil and danger in the
wide desolation of the West. There he met, one
horrible winter, the sister-in-law of a brother captain, a tall, languid, ill-nourished girl of mature
years, with tender blue eyes and a taste for Byron.
She had no home and no relatives in the world except her sister, Mrs. Keefe, whom she had followed
into the wilderness. She was a heavy burden on
the scanty resources of poor Keefe, but he made
her cordially welcome like the hearty soldier that
he was. She was the only unmarried white woman
within a hundred miles, and the mercury ranged
from zero to −20° all winter. In the spring, she
and Farnham were married; he seemed to have lost
the sense of there being any other women in the
world, and he took her, as one instinctively takes to
dinner the last lady remaining in a drawing-room,
without special orders. He had had the consolation
of reflecting that he made her perfectly proud and
happy every day of her life that was left. Before the autumn ended, she died, on a forced march
one day, when the air was glittering with alkali,
and the fierce sun seemed to wither the dismal plain
like the vengeance of heaven. Though Farnham
was even then one of the richest men in the army,
so rigid are the rules imposed upon our service, by
the economy of an ignorant demagogy, that no
transportation could be had to supply this sick lady
with the ordinary conveniences of life, and she died

in his arms, on the hot prairie, in the shade of an overloaded baggage wagon. He mourned her with the passing grief one gives to a comrade fallen on the field of honor. Often since he left the army, he reproached himself for not having grieved for her more deeply. "Poor Nellie," he would sometimes say, "how she would have enjoyed this house, if she had lived to possess it." But he never had that feeling of widowhood known to those whose lives have been torn in two.

IV.

PROTECTOR AND PROTÉGÉE.

A FEW days later, Mr. Farnham attended a meeting of the library board, and presented the name of Miss Matchin as a candidate for a subordinate place in the library. There were several such positions, requiring no special education or training, the duties of which could be as well filled by Miss Maud as by any one else. She had sent several strong letters of recommendation to the board, from prominent citizens who knew and respected her father, for when Maud informed him of her new ambition, Matchin entered heartily into the affair, and bestirred himself to use what credit he had in the ward to assist her.

Maud had not exaggerated the effect of her blandishments upon Dr. Buchlieber. The old gentleman spoke in her favor with great fluency; "she was young, healthy, active, intelligent, a graduate of the high school."

"And very pretty, is she not?" asked a member of the board, maliciously.

The Doctor colored, but was not abashed. He gazed steadily at the interrupter through his round glasses, and said:

"Yes, she is very fine looking—but I do not see that that should stand in her way."

Not another word was said against her, and a

ballot was taken to decide the question. There
were five members of the board, three besides
Farnham and Buchlieber. Maud had two votes,
and a young woman whose name had not been
mentioned received the other three. Buchlieber
counted the ballots, and announced the vote. Farnham flushed with anger. Not only had no attention been paid to his recommendation, but he had
not even been informed that there was another
candidate. In a few sarcastic words he referred
to the furtive understanding existing among the
majority, and apologized for having made such a
mistake as to suppose they cared to hear the merits
of appointees discussed.

The three colleagues sat silent. At last, one of
them crossed his legs anew and said:

"I'm sure nobody meant any offence. We
agreed on this lady several days ago. I know
nothing about her, but her father used to be one
of our best workers in the seventh ward. He is
in the penitentiary now, and the family is about
down to bedrock. The reason we didn't take part
in the discussion was we wanted to avoid hard
feelings."

The other two crossed their legs the other way,
and said they " concurred."

Their immovable phlegm, their long, expression-
less faces, the dull, monotonous twang of their
voices, the oscillation of the three large feet hung
over the bony knees had now, as often before, a
singular effect upon Farnham's irritation. He felt
he could not irritate them in return; they could
not appreciate his motives, and thought too little of

his opinion to be angry at his contempt. He was thrown back upon himself now as before. It was purely a matter of conscience whether he should stay and do what good he could, or resign and shake the dust of the city hall from his feet. Whatever he recommended in regard to the administration of the library was always adopted without comment; but, whenever a question of the sort which the three politicians called " practical " arose, involving personal patronage in any form, they always arranged it for themselves, without even pretending to ask his or Buchlieber's opinion.

The very fact of his holding the position ot chairman of the board was wounding to his self-love, as soon as he began to appreciate the purpose with which the place had been given him. He and some of his friends had attempted a movement the year before, to rescue the city from the control of what they considered a corrupt combination of politicians. They had begun, as such men always do, too late, and without any adequate organization, and the regular workers had beaten them with ridiculous ease. In Farnham's own ward, where he possessed two thirds of the real estate, the candidates favored by him and his friends received not quite one tenth of the votes cast. The leader of the opposing forces was a butcher, one Jacob Metzger, who had managed the politics of the ward for years. He was not a bad man so far as his lights extended. He sold meat on business principles, so as to get the most out of a carcass; and he conducted his political operations in the same way. He made his bargains with aspirants and office-holders, and kept them religiously. He had been a little alarmed at the sudden irruption of such men as Farnham and his associates into the field of ward politics; he dreaded the combined effect of their money and their influence. But he soon found he had nothing to fear—they would not use their money, and they did not know how to use their influence. They hired halls, opened committee-rooms, made speeches, and thundered against municipal iniquities in the daily press; but Jacob Metzger, when he discovered that this was all, possessed his soul in peace, and even got a good deal of quiet fun out of the canvass. He did not take the trouble to be angry at the men who were denouncing him, and supplied Farnham with beefsteaks unusually tender and juicy, while the young reformer was seeking his political life.

"Lord love you," he said to Budsey, as he handed him a delicious rib-roast the day before election. "There's nothing I like so much as to see young men o' property go into politics. We need 'em. Of course, I wisht the Cap'n was on my side; but anyhow, I'm glad to see him takin' an interest."

He knew well enough the way the votes would run; that every grog-shop in the ward was his recruiting station; that all Farnham's tenants would vote against their landlord; that even the respectable Budsey and the prim Scotch gardener were sure for him against their employer. Farnham's conscience which had roused him to this effort against Metzger's corrupt rule, would not permit him to ask for the votes of his own servants and tenants, and he would have regarded it as simply infamous to spend money to secure the floating crowd of publicans and sinners who formed the strength of Jacob.

His failure was so complete and unexpected that there seemed to him something of degradation in it, and in a fit of uncontrollable disgust he sailed for Europe the week afterward. Metzger took his victory good-naturedly as a matter of course, and gave his explanation of it to a reporter of the "Bale-Fire" who called to interview him.

"Mr. Farnham, who led the opposition to our organize-ation, is a young gen'l'man of fine talents and high character. I ain't got a word to say against him. The only trouble is, he lacks practical experience, and he ain't got no pers'nal magn't-ism. Now I'm one of the people, I know what they want, and on that line I carried the ward against a combine-ation of all the wealth and aristocracy of Algonkin Av'noo."

Jacob's magnanimity did not rest with merely a verbal acknowledgment of Farnham's merits. While he was abroad some of the city departments were reorganized, and Farnham on his return found himself, through Metzger's intervention, chairman of the library board. With characteristic sagacity the butcher kept himself in the background, and the committee who waited upon Farnham to ask him to accept the appointment placed it entirely upon considerations of the public good. His sensitive conscience would not permit him to refuse a duty thus imposed, and so with many inward qualms he assumed a chair in the vile municipal government he had so signally failed to overthrow. He

had not long occupied it, when he saw to what his
selection was attributable. He was a figure-head
and he knew it, but he saw no decent escape from
the position. As long as they allowed him and the
librarian (who was also a member of the board) to
regulate the library to their liking, he could not inquire into their motives or decline association with
them. He was perfectly free to furnish what mental food he chose to two hundred thousand people,
and he felt it would be cowardice to surrender that
important duty on any pitiful question of patronage
or personal susceptibility.

So once more he stifled the impulse to resign his
post, and the meeting adjourned without further
incident. As he walked home, he was conscious of
a disagreeable foreboding of something in the future
which he would like to avoid. Bringing his mind
to bear upon it, it resolved itself into nothing more
formidable than the coming interview with Miss
Matchin. It would certainly be unpleasant to tell
her that her hopes were frustrated, when she had
seemed so confident. At this thought, he felt the
awakening of a sense of protectorship; she had
trusted in him; he ought to do something for her,
if for nothing else, to show that he was not de-
pendent upon those ostrogoths. But what could be
done for such a girl, so pretty, so uncultivated, so
vulgarly fantastic? Above all, what could be done
for her by a young and unmarried man? Providence and society have made it very hard for single
men to show kindness to single women in any way
but one.

At his door he found Sam Sleeny with a kit of

tools; he had just rung the bell. He turned, as Farnham mounted the steps, and said :

"I come from Matchin's—something about the greenhouse."

"Yes," answered Farnham. "The gardener is over yonder at the corner of the lawn. He will tell you what is to be done."

Sam walked away in the direction indicated, and Farnham went into the house. Some letters were lying on the table in the library. He had just begun to read them when Budsey entered and announced :

"That young person."

Maud came in flushed with the fresh air and rapid walking. Farnham saw that she wore no glasses, and she gained more by that fact in his good-will than even by the brilliancy of her fine eyes which seemed to exult in their liberation. She began with nervous haste :

"I knew you had a meeting to-day, and I could not wait. I might as well own up that I followed you home."

Farnham handed her a chair and took her hand with a kindly earnestness, saying,

"I am very glad to see you."

"Yes, yes," she continued ; "but have you any good news for me ?"

The anxious eagerness which spoke in her sparkling eyes and open lips touched Farnham to the heart. "I am sorry I have not. The board appointed another person."

The tears sprang to her eyes.

"I really expected it. I hoped you would interest yourself."

"I did all I possibly could," said Farnham. "I have never tried so hard for anybody before, but a majority were already pledged to the other applicant."

She seemed so dejected and hopeless that Farnham, forgetting for a moment how hard it is for a young man to assist a young woman, said two or three fatal words, "We must try something else."

The pronoun sounded ominous to him as soon as he had uttered it. But it acted like magic upon Maud. She lifted a bright glance through her tears and said, like a happy child to whom a new game has been proposed, "What shall we try?"

Simple as the words were, both of them seemed to feel that a certain relation—a certain responsibility—had been established between them. The thought exhilarated Maud; it seemed the beginning of her long-expected romance; while the glow of kind feeling about the heart of Farnham could not keep him from suspecting that he was taking a very imprudent step. But they sat a good while, discussing various plans for Maud's advantage, and arriving at nothing definite; for her own ideas were based upon a dime-novel theory of the world, and Farnham at last concluded that he would be forced finally to choose some way of life for his protégée, and then persuade her to accept it.

He grew silent and thoughtful with this reflection, and the conversation languished. He was trying to think how he could help her without these continued interviews at his house, when she disposed of the difficulty by rising briskly and saying, "Well, I will call again in a day or two, about this hour?"

" Yes, if it suits you best," he answered, with a troubled brow. He followed her to the door. As she went out, she said, "May I pick a flower as I go ?"

He seized his hat, and said, "Come with me to the rose-house in the garden, and you shall have something better."

They walked together down the gravel paths, through the neat and well-kept garden, where the warm spring sunshine was calling life out of the tender turf, and the air was full of delicate odors. She seemed as gay and happy as a child on a holiday. Her disappointment of an hour ago was all gone in the feeling that Arthur was interested in her, was caring for her future. Without any definite hopes or dreams, she felt as if the world was suddenly grown richer and wider. Something good was coming to her certainly, something good had come ; for was she not walking in this lovely garden with its handsome proprietor, who was, she even began to think, her friend ? The turf was as soft, the air as mild, the sun as bright as in any of her romances, and the figure of Farnham's wealth which she had heard from her father rang musically in her mind.

They went into the rose-house, and he gave her two or three splendid satiny Maréchal Niels, and then a Jacqueminot, so big, so rich and lustrous in its dark beauty, that she could not help crying out with delight. He was pleased with her joy, and gave her another, "for your hair," he said. She colored with pleasure till her cheek was like the royal flower. "Hallo!" thought Farnham to him-

self, "she does not take these things as a matter of
course." When they came into the garden again,
he made the suggestion which had been in his mind
for the last half hour.

"If you are going home, the nearest way will be
by the garden gate into Bishop's Lane. It is only a
minute from there to Dean Street."

"Why, that would be perfectly lovely. But
where is the gate?"

"I will show you. They walked together to the
lower end of the lawn, where a long line of glass
houses built against the high wall which separated
the garden from the street called Bishop's Lane,
sheltered the grapes and the pine-apples. At the
end of this conservatory, in the wall, was a little
door of thin but strong steel plates, concealed from
sight by a row of pear trees. Farnham opened it,
and said, "If you like, you can come in by this
way. It is never locked in the daytime. It will
save you a long walk."

"Thanks," she replied. "That will be perfectly
lovely."

Her resources of expression were not copious,
but her eyes and her mouth spoke volumes of joy
and gratitude. Her hands were full of roses, and
as she raised her beautiful face to him with pleasure flashing from her warm cheeks and lips and
eyes, she seemed to exhale something of the vigorous life and impulse of the spring sunshine. Farnham felt that he had nothing to do but stoop and
kiss the blooming flower-like face, and in her exalted
condition she would have thought little more of it
than a blush-rose thinks of the same treatment.

But he refrained, and said "Good morning," because she seemed in no mood to say it first.

"Good-by, for a day or two," she said, gayly, as she bent her head to pass under the low lintel of the gate.

Farnham walked back to the house not at all satisfied with himself. "I wonder whether I have mended matters? She is certainly too pretty a girl to be running in and out of my front door in the sight of all the avenue. How much better will it be for her to use the private entrance, and come and go by a sort of stealth! But then she does not regard it that way. She is so ignorant of this wicked world that it seems to her merely a saving of ten minutes' walk around the block. Well! all there is of it, I must find a place for her before she domesticates herself here."

The thought of what should be done with her remained persistently with him and kept him irritated by the vision of her provoking and useless beauty. "If she were a princess," he thought, "all the poets would be twanging their lyres about her, all the artists would be dying to paint her; she would have songs made to her, and sacred oratorios given under her patronage. She would preside at church fairs and open the dance at charity balls. If I could start her in life as a princess, the thing would go on wheels. But to earn her own living—that is a trade of another complexion. She has not breeding or education enough for a governess: she is not clever enough to write or paint; she is not steady enough to keep accounts,—by the Great Jornada! I have a grievous contract on my hands."

He heard the sound of hoofs outside his window, and, looking out, saw his groom holding a young brown horse by the bridle, the well-groomed coat of the animal shining in the warm sunlight. In a few moments Farnham was in the saddle and away. For awhile he left his perplexities behind, in the pleasure of rapid motion and fresh air. But he drew rein half an hour afterward at Acland Falls, and the care that had sat on the crupper came to the front again. "As a last resort," he said, "I can persuade her she has a voice, and send her to Italy, and keep her the rest of her life cultivating it in Milan."

All unconscious of the anxiety she was occasioning, Maud walked home with her feet scarcely aware of the pavement. She felt happy through and through. There was little thought, and we may say little selfishness in the vague joy that filled her. The flowers she held in her hands recalled the faint odors she had inhaled in Farnham's house; they seemed to her a concrete idea of luxury. Her mind was crowded and warmed with every detail of her visit: the dim, wide hall; the white cravat of Budsey; the glimpse she caught of the dining-room through the open door; the shimmer of cut glass and porcelain; the rich softness of the carpets and rugs, the firelight dancing on the polished brass, the tender glow of light and repose of shadow on the painted walls and ceilings; the walk in the trim garden, amid the light and fragrance of the spring; the hot air of the rose-house, which held her close, and made her feel faint and flushed, like a warm embrace; and through all the ever-present image of

the young man, with his pleasant, unembarrassed
smile, the white teeth shining under the dark mustache; the eyes that seemed to see through her, and
yet told her nothing; and more than all this to poor
Maud, the perfect fit and fashion of his clothes,
filled her with a joyous trouble. She could not
dwell upon her plans for employment. She felt as
if she had found her mission, her true trade,—which
was to walk in gardens and smell hot-house roses.
The perplexities which filled Farnham's head as to
what he should do with her found no counterpart
in hers. She had stopped thinking and planning;
things were going very well with her as it was. She
had lost the place she had wished and expected,
and yet this was the pleasantest day of her life.
Her responsibility seemed shifted to stronger hands.
It had become Farnham's business to find something
nice for her: this would be easy for him; he belonged to the class to whom everything is easy. She
did not even trouble herself to think what it would
be as she loitered home in the sunshine. She saw
her father and informed him in a few words of her
failure; then went to her room and sat down by
her window, and looked for hours at the sparkling
lake.

She was called to supper in the midst of her
reverie. She was just saying to herself, "If there
was just one man and one woman in the world, and
I had the picking out of the man and the woman,
this world would suit me pretty well." She re-
sented being called into other society than that of
her idle thoughts, and sat silent through supper, trying to keep the thread of her fancies from breaking.

5

But she was not allowed to go back undisturbed to her fool's paradise.

Sleeny, who had scarcely removed his eyes from her during the meal, rose with a start as she walked into the little sitting-room of the family, and followed her. She went to the window with a novel to make use of the last moments of daylight. He stood before her without speaking, until she raised her eyes, and said sharply :

"Well, Sam, what's the matter?"

He was not quick either of thought or speech. He answered :

"Oh! nothin'. Only——"

"Only what?" she snapped.

"Won't you go and take a walk by the Bluff?"

She threw down her book at once. She liked exercise and fresh air, and always walked with pleasure by the lake. Sam was to her such a nullity that she enjoyed his company almost as much as being alone. She was ready in a moment, and a short walk brought them to the little open place reserved for public use, overlooking the great fresh-water sea. There were a few lines of shade trees and a few seats, and nothing more; yet the plantation was called Bluff Park, and it was much frequented on holidays and Sundays by nurses and their charges. It was in no sense a fashionable resort, or Maud would never have ventured there in company with her humble adorer. But among the jovial puddlers and brakemen that took the air there, it was well enough to have an escort so devoted and so muscular. So pretty a woman could scarcely have walked alone in Bluff Park without insulting approaches. Maud

would hardly have nodded to Sleeny on Algonquin
Avenue, for fear some millionaire might see it casu-
ally, and scorn them both. But on the Bluff she
was safe from such accidents, and she sometimes
even took his arm, and made him too happy to talk.
They would walk together for an hour, he dumb
with audacious hopes that paralyzed his speech, and
she dreaming of things thousands of miles away.

This evening he was even more than usually silent. Maud, after she had worn her reverie threadbare, noticed his speechlessness, and, fearing he was
about to renew the subject which was so tiresome,
suddenly stopped and said :

"What a splendid sunset ! Did you ever see anything like it ?"

"Yes," he said, with his gentle drawl. "Less set
here, and look at it."

He took his seat on one of the iron benches
painted green, and decorated with castings of grapes
and vine leaves. She sat down beside him and
gazed out over the placid water, on which the crimson clouds cast a mellow glory. The sky seemed
like another sea, stretching off into infinite distance,
and strewn with continents of fiery splendor. Maud
looked straight forward to the clear horizon line,
marking the flight of ships whose white sails were
dark against the warm brightness of the illumined
water. But no woman ever looked so straight before her as not to observe the man beside her, and
she knew, without moving her eyes from the spec-
tacle of the sunset, that Sam was gazing fixedly at
her, with pain and trouble in his face. At last, he
said, in a timid, choking voice,

" Mattie !"

She did not turn her face, but answered :

" If it ain't too much trouble, I'd like to have you call me Miss when we're alone. You'll be forgetting yourself, and calling me Mattie before other people, before you know it."

" Hold on," he burst out. " Don't talk to me that way to-night—I can't stand it."

She glanced at him in surprise. His face was pale and disordered ; he was twisting his fingers as if he would break them.

" Your temper seems to be on the move, Mr. Sleeny. We'd better go home," she said quietly, drawing her shawl about her.

" Don't go till I tell you something," he stammered hastily.

" I have no curiosity to hear what you have to say," she said, rising from her seat.

" It ain't what you think—it aint about me !"

Her curiosity awoke, and she sat down again. Sleeny sat twisting his fingers, growing pale and red by turns. At last, in a tremulous voice, he said :

" *I* was there to-day."

She stared at him an instant and said :

" Where ?"

" Oh, I was there, and I seen you. I was at work at the end of the greenhouse there by the gate when you come out of the rose-house. I was watchin' for you. I was on the lawn talkin' with the gardener when you went in the house. About an hour afterward I seen you comin' down the garden with him to the rose-house. If you had 'a' stayed there a minute more, I would ha' went in there. But out you

come with your hands full o' roses, and him and
you come to the gate. I stopped workin' and kep'
still behind them pear trees, and I heard everything."

He uttered each word slowly, like a judge delivering sentence. His face had grown very red and
hot, and as he finished his indictment he drew a
yellow handkerchief from his pocket and mopped
the sweat from his forehead, his chin, and the back
of his neck.

"Oh!" answered Maud, negligently, "you heard
everything, did you? Well, you didn't hear much."

"I tell you," he continued, with a sullen rage,
"I heard every word. Do you hear me? I heard
every word."

The savage roughness of his voice made her
tremble, but her spirits rose to meet his anger, and
she laughed as she replied :

"Well, you heard 'Thank you, sir,' and 'Good-
morning.' It wasn't much, unless you took it as a
lesson in manners, and goodness knows you need it."

"Now, look'ye here. It's no use foolin' with me.
You know what I heard. If you don't, I'll tell
you !"

"Very well, Mr. Paul Pry, what was it?" said
the angry girl, who had quite forgotten that any
words were spoken at the gate.

"I heard him tell you you could come in any
time the back way," Sam hoarsely whispered, watching her face with eyes of fire. She turned crimson
as the sunset she was gazing at, and she felt as if
she could have torn her cheeks with her finger-
nails for blushing. She was aware of having done

nothing wrong, nothing to be ashamed of. She had been all day cherishing the recollection of her visit to Farnham as something too pleasant and delicate to talk about. No evil thought had mingled with it in her own mind. She had hardly looked beyond the mere pleasure of the day. She had not given a name or a form to the hopes and fancies that were fluttering at her heart. And now to have this sweet and secret pleasure handled and mauled by such a one as Sam Sleeny filled her with a speechless shame. Even yet she hardly comprehended the full extent of his insinuation. He did not leave her long in doubt. Taking her silence and her confusion as an acknowledgment, he went on, in the same low, savage tone :

" I had my hammer in my hand. I looked through the pear trees to see if he kissed you. If he had 'a' done it, I would have killed him as sure as death."

At this brutal speech she turned pale a moment, as if suddenly struck a stunning blow. Then she cried out :

" Hold your vile tongue, you——"

But she felt her voice faltering and the tears of rage gushing from her eyes. She buried her face in her hands and sat a little while in silence, while Sam was dumb beside her, feeling like an awkward murderer. She was not so overcome that she did not think very rapidly during this moment's pause. If she could have slain the poor fellow on the spot, she would not have scrupled to do so; but she required only an instant to reflect that she had better appease him for the present, and reserve her vengeance for a more convenient season.

She dried her eyes and turned them on him with an air of gentle, almost forgiving reproach.

"Sam! I could not have believed you had such a bad, wicked heart. I thought you knew me better. I won't make myself so cheap as to explain all that to you. But I'll ask you to do one thing for me. When we go home this evening, if you see my father alone, you tell him what you saw—and if you've got any shame in you you'll be ashamed of yourself."

He had been irritated by her anger, but he was completely abashed by the coolness and gentleness which followed her burst of tears. He was sorely confused and bewildered by her command, but did not dream of anything but obeying it, and as they walked silently home, he was all the time wondering what mysterious motive she could have in wishing him to denounce her to her father. They found Saul Matchin sitting by the door, smoking a cob-pipe. Maud went in and Sam seated himself beside the old man.

"How'd you get along at Farnham's ?" said Saul.

Sam started, as if "the boss" had read his uneasy conscience. But he answered in his drawling mono-tone :

"All right, I guess. That doggoned Scotchman thinks he knows it all ; but it'll take nigh on to a week to do what I could ha' done in a day or two, if I worked my way."

"Well," said Saul, "that ain't none o' your look-out. Do what Scotchee tells you, and I'll keep the time on 'em. We kin stand it, ef they kin," and the old carpenter laughed with the foolish pleasure

of a small mind aware of an advantage. " Ef Art.
Farnham wants to keep a high-steppin' Scotchman
to run his flowers, may be he kin afford it. I ain't
his gardeen."

Now was Sleeny's chance to make his disclosure;
but his voice trembled in spite of him, as he said :

" I seen Mattie up there."

" Yes," said the old man, tranquilly. " She went
up to see about a place in the library. He said there
wasn't none, but he'd try to think o' somethin' else
that 'ud suit her. He was mighty polite to Mat—
give her some roses, and told her to run in and out
when she liked, till he got somethin' fixed. Fact
is, Mat is a first-rate scholar, and takes with them
high-steppers, like fallin' off a log." Saul had begun to feel a certain pride in his daughter's accomplishments which had so long been an affliction to
him. The moment he saw a possibility of a money
return, he even began to plume himself upon his
liberality and sagacity in having educated her. " I've
spared nothin'—Sam—in giving her a——" he
searched an instant for a suitable adjective, "a com-
modious education." The phrase pleased him so
well that he smoked for awhile contemplatively, so
as not to mar the effect of his point.

Sam had listened with a whirling brain to the old
man's quiet story, which anticipated his own in
every point. He could not tell whether he felt
more relieved or disquieted by it. It all seemed
clear and innocent enough ; but he felt, with a sinking heart, that his own hopes were fading fast, in
the flourishing prospects of his beloved. He hated
Farnham not less in his attitude of friendly protec-

tion than in that which he had falsely attributed to him. His jealousy, deprived of its specific occasion, nourished itself on vague and torturing possibilities. He could not trust himself to talk further with Matchin, but went away with a growing fire in his breast. He hated himself for having prematurely spoken. He hated Maud for the beauty that she would not give him, and which, he feared, she was ready to give to another. He hated Saul, for his stolid ignorance of his daughter's danger. He hated most of all Farnham, for his handsome face, his easy smile, his shapely hands, his fine clothes, his unknown and occult gifts of pleasing.

"'Tain't in natur," he growled. "She's the prettiest woman in the world. If he's got eyes, he knows it. But I spoke first, and he shan't have her, if I die for it."

V

A PROFESSIONAL REFORMER.

SLEENY walked moodily down the street, engaged
in that self-torture which is the chief recreation of
unhappy lovers. He steeped his heart in gall by
imagining Maud in love with another. His passion
stimulated his slow wits into unwonted action, until
his mind began to form exasperating pictures of in-
timacies which drove him half mad. His face grew
pale, and his fists were tightly clinched as he walked.
He hardly saw the familiar street before him; he
had a far clearer vision of Maud and Farnham by the
garden gate : her beautiful face was turned up to the
young man's with the winning sweetness of a flower,
and Sam's irritated fancy supplied the kisses he had
watched for in the shadow of the pear-trees. "I
'most wish't he'd 'a' done it," he growled to himself.
"I had my hammer in my hand, and I could 'a'
finished him then and had no more bother."

He felt a hand on his shoulder, and, turning, saw
a face grinning a friendly recognition. It was a face
whose whole expression was oleaginous. It was
surmounted by a low and shining forehead covered
by reeking black hair, worn rather long, the ends
being turned under by the brush. The mustache
was long and drooping, dyed black and profusely
oiled, the dye and the grease forming an inharmo-
nious compound. The parted lips, which were coarse

and thin, displayed an imperfect set of teeth, much discolored with tobacco. The eyes were light green, with the space which should have been white suffused with yellow and red. It was one of those gifted countenances which could change in a moment from a dog-like fawning to a snaky venomousness.

The man wore a black hat of soft felt; his clothes were black and glistening with use and grease. He was of medium height, not especially stout, but still strong and well knit; he moved too briskly for a tramp, and his eyes were too sly and furtive to belong to an honest man.

"Well, Samivel!" he began, with a jolly facetiousness, "what's your noble game this evenin'? You look like you was down on your luck. Is the fair one unkind?"

Sam turned upon him with an angry gesture.

"Hold your jaw, or I'll break it for you! Ever since I was fool enough to mention that thing to you, you've been cacklin' about it. I've had enough of it."

"Go slow, Quaker!" the man rejoined. "If you can't take a joke, I'll stop jokin'—that settles it. Come along and get a glass of beer, and you'll feel better."

They soon came to a garden near the lake, and sat down by a little table at their beer. The consumers were few and silent. The garden was dimly lighted, for the spring came slowly up that way, and the air was not yet conducive to out-door idling. The greasy young man laid a dirty hand on the arm of Sleeny, and said:

"Honor bright, now, old fellow, I didn't mean to rough you when I said that. I don't want to hurt your feelings or lose your confidence. I want you to tell me how you are gettin' along. You ain't got no better friend than me nowhere."

"Oh," said Sam, sulkily, "I got nothin' to say. She don't no more care for me than that there mug."

The expression that came over his friend's face at these discouraged words was not one of sympathetic sorrow. But he put some sympathy into his voice as he said:

"Jest think of that! Such a fine young fellow as you are, too. Where can her eyes be? And I seen you walking this evenin' by the lake just like two robins. And yet you don't get ahead any!"

"Not a step," said Sam.

"Anybody in your light, you think? Hullo there, Dutchy, swei glass. Any other fellow takin' your wind?" and his furtive eyes darted a keen interrogation. Sam did not answer at once, and his friend went on: "Why, she don't hardly know anybody but me and you, and, he-he! I wouldn't stand no chance at all against you—hum?"

"Of course you wouldn't," said Sam, with slow contempt, which brought the muddy blood into the sallow cheek in front of him. "She wouldn't look at you. I'm not afraid of no man, Andy Offitt,—I'm afraid of money."

He flattered his jealous heart by these words. It was too intolerable to think that any mere man should take his sweetheart away from him; and though he felt how hopeless was any comparison between himself and Farnham, he tried to soothe himself by the lie that they were equal in all but money.

His words startled his friend Offitt. He exclaimed, "Why, who does she know that's got money?"

But Sleeny felt a momentary revolt against delivering to even his closest confidant the name of the woman he loved coupled with the degrading suspicions by which he had been tormented all day. He gruffly answered: "That's none of your business; you can't help me in this thing, and I ain't agoin' to chin about it any more."

They sat for awhile in silence, drank their beer, and ordered more. Offitt at last spoke again:

"Well, I'll be hanged if you ain't the best grit of any fellow I know. If you don't want to talk, a team of Morgan horses couldn't make you. I like a man that can hold his tongue."

"Then I'm your huckleberry," said Sleeny, whose vanity was soothed by the compliment.

"That's so," said Offitt, with an admiring smile. "If I wanted a secret kept, I'd know where to come." Then changing his manner and tone to an expression of profound solemnity, and glancing about to guard against surprise, he said: "My dear boy, I've wanted to talk to you a long time,—to talk serious. You're not one of the common kind of cattle that think of nothin' but their fodder and stall—are you?"

Now, Sam was precisely of the breed described by his friend, but what man ever lived who knew he was altogether ordinary? He grinned uneasily and answered:

"I guess not."

"Exactly!" said Offitt. "There are some of us laboring men that don't propose to go on all our lives working our fingers off to please a lot of vampires; we propose to have a little fairer divide than heretofore; and if there is any advantage to be gained, we propose to have it on the side of the men who do the work. What do you think of that?"

"That's all solid," said Sleeny, who was indifferently interested in these abstractions. "But what you goin' to do about it?"

"Do!" cried Offitt. "We are goin' to make war on capital. We are goin' to scare the blood-suckers into terms. We are goin' to get our rights—peaceably, if we can't get them any other way. We are goin' to prove that a man is better than a money-bag." He rattled off these words as a listless child says its alphabet without thinking of a letter. But he was closely watching Sam to see if any of these stereotyped phrases attracted his attention. Sleeny smoked his cigar with the air of polite fatigue with which one listens to abstract statements of moral obligations.

"What are we, anyhow?" continued the greasy apostle of labor. "We are slaves; we are Roosian scurfs. We work as many hours as our owners like; we take what pay they choose to give us; we ask their permission to live and breathe."

"Oh, that's a lie!" Sleeny interrupted, with unbroken calmness. "Old Saul Matchin and me come to an agreement about time and pay, and both of us was suited. Ef he's got his heel onto me, I don't feel it."

Offitt darted a glance of scorn upon the ignoble soul who was content with his bondage; but the mention of Matchin reminded him that he had a final shot in reserve, and he let it off at once.

"Yes, Saul Matchin is a laborin' man himself; but look at his daughter. She would die before she would marry a workman. Why?" and his green eyes darted livid fire as they looked into the troubled ones of Sleeny.

"Well, why?" he asked, slowly.

"Because she loves money more than manhood. Because she puts up her beauty for a higher bidder than any——"

"Now, shet up, will you?" cried Sam, thoroughly aroused. "I won't set here and hear her abused by you or any other man. What business is it of yours, anyway?"

Offitt felt that his shot had gone home, and pursued his advantage.

"It's my business, Sam, because I'm your friend; because I hate to see a good fellow wronged; because I know that a man is better than a money-bag. Why, that girl would marry you in a minute if you was rich. But because you're not she will strike for one of them rose-water snobs on Algonquin Avenue." Sam writhed, and his wheedling tormentor continued, watching him like a ferret. "Perhaps she has struck for one of them already— perhaps—oh, I can't say what may have happened. I hate the world when I see such doin's. I hate the heartless shams that give labor and shame to the toilers and beauty and luxury to the drones. Who is the best man," he asked, with honest frankness,

"you, or some high-steppin' snob whose daddy has
left him the means to be a loafer all his days? And
who would the prettiest girl in Buffland prefer, you
or the loafer? And you intend to let Mr. Loafer
have it all his own way?"

"No, I don't!" Sam roared, like a baited bull.
"Ef any man crosses my path, he can find out
which is the best man."

"There, that's more like you. But what can you
do alone? That's where they get us foul. The er-
ristocrats, the money power, all hang together. The
laborin' men fight singly, and alwuz get whipped.
Now, we are goin' to change that. We are goin' to
organize. Look here, Sam, I am riskin' my head
in tellin' you this—but I trust you, and I like you,
and I'll tell you. We *have* organized. We've got
a society in this town pledged to the cause of honest
labor and against capital—for life or death. We
want you. We want men of sand and men of
sense, and you've got both. You must join."

Sam Sleeny was by this time pretty well filled
with beer and wrath. He felt himself in a certain
sense bound by the weighty secret which Offitt had
imparted to him and flattered by his invitation. A
few touches more of adroit flattery, and the agita-
tor's victory was complete. Sleeny felt sore and
tired to the very heart. He had behaved like a
brute to the girl he loved; he had been put clearly
in the wrong in his quarrel with her, and yet he
was certain that all was not well with either of
them. The tormenting syllogism ran continually
through his head: "She is the prettiest woman in
the world—rich fellows like pretty women,—there-

fore—death and curses on him!" Or sometimes the form of it would change to this: "He is rich and handsome—girls like men who are rich and handsome,—therefore——," the same rage and imprecations, and the same sense of powerless fury. He knew and cared nothing about Offitt's Labor Reform. He could earn a good living by his trade no matter who went to Congress, and he hated these "chinny bummers," as he called them, who talked about "State help and self-help" over their beer. But to-night he was tormented and badgered to such a point that he was ready for anything which his tempter might suggest. The words of Offitt, alternately wheedling and excoriating, had turned his foolish head. His hatred of Farnham was easily extended to the class to which he belonged, and even to the money which made him formidable.

He walked away from the garden with Offitt, and turned down a filthy alley to a squalid tenement house,—called by its proprietor Perry Place, and by the neighbors Rook's Ranch,—to the lodge-room of the Brotherhood of Bread-winners, which proved to be Offitt's lodging. They found there a half dozen men lounging about the entrance, who scowled and swore at Offitt for being late, and then followed him sulkily up two flights of ill-smelling stairs to his room. He turned away their wrath by soft answers, and hastily lighting a pair of coal-oil lamps, which gave forth odor more liberally than illumination, said briskly:

"Gentlemen, I have brought you a recruit this evenin' that you will all be glad to welcome to our **brotherhood.**"

6

The brothers, who had taken seats where they could find them, on a dirty bed, a wooden trunk, and two or three chairs of doubtful integrity, grunted a questionable welcome to the new-comer. As he looked about him, he was not particularly proud of the company in which he found himself. The faces he recognized were those of the laziest and most incapable workmen in the town—men whose weekly wages were habitually docked for drunkenness, late hours, and botchy work. As the room gradually filled, it seemed like a roll-call of shirks. Among them came also a spiritual medium named Bott, as yet imperfectly developed, whose efforts at making a living by dark séances too frequently resulted in the laughter of skeptics and the confusion of his friends. His forehead and cheek were even then purple with an aniline dye, which some cold-blooded investigator had squirted in his face a few nights before while he was gliding through a twilight room impersonating the troubled shade of Pocahontas. This occurrence gave, for the moment, a peculiarly sanguinary and sinister character to his features, and filled his heart with a thirst for vengeance against an unbelieving world.

After the meeting had been called to order, and Sam had taken an oath of a hot and lurid nature, in which he renounced a good many things he had never possessed, and promised to do a lot of things of which he had no idea, Mr. Offitt asked "if any brother had anything to offer for the good of the order." This called Mr. Bott to his feet, and he made a speech, on which he had been brooding all day, against the pride of so-called science, the arro-

gance of unrighteous wealth, and the grovelling superstition of Christianity. The light of the kerosene lamp shone full on the decorated side of his
visage, and touched it to a ferocious purpose. But
the brotherhood soon wearied of his oratory, in
which the blasphemy of thought and phrase was
strangely contrasted with the ecclesiastical whine
which he had caught from the exhorters who were
the terror of his youth. The brothers began to guy
him without mercy. They requested him to "cheese
it"; they assisted him with uncalled-for and inap-
propriate applause, and one of the party got behind
him and went through the motion of turning a
hurdy-gurdy. But he persevered. He had joined
the club to practise public speaking, and he got a
good half hour out of the brothers before they
coughed him down.

When he had brought his speech to a close, and
sat down to wipe his streaming face, a brother rose
and said, in a harsh, rasping voice, "I want to ask
a question."

"That's in order, Brother Bowersox," said Offitt.

The man was a powerful fellow, six feet high.
His head was not large, but it was as round as
an apple, with heavy cheek-bones, little eyes, close-
cut hair, and a mustache like the bristles of a
blacking-brush. He had been a driver on a street-
car, but had recently been dismissed for insolence
to passengers and brutality to his horses.

"What I want to ask is this: I want to know if
we have joined this order to listen to chin-music the
rest of our lives, or to do somethin'. There is some
kind of men that kin talk tell day of jedgment, let-

tin' Gabrel toot and then beginnin' ag'in. I ain't that
kind; I j'ined to do somethin';—what's to be done?"

He sat down with his hand on his hip, squarely
facing the luckless Bott, whose face grew as purple
as the illuminated side of it. But he opened not
his mouth. Offitt answered the question:

"I would state," he said glibly, "the objects we
propose to accomplish: the downfall of the money
power, the rehabitation of labor, the——"

"Oh, yes!" Bowersox interrupted, "I know all
about that,—but what are we goin' to *do*?"

Offitt paled a little, but did not flinch at the savage tone of the surly brute. He began again in his
smoothest manner:

"I am of the opinion that the discussion of sound
principles, such as we have listened to to-night, is
among the objects of our order. After that, organization for mutual profit and protection against the
minions of the money power,—for makin' our influence felt in elections,—for extendin' a helpin'
hand to honest toil,—for rousin' our bretheren from
their lethargy, which, like a leaden pall——"

"I want to know," growled Bowersox, with sullen
obstinacy, "what's to be done."

"Put your views in the form of a motion, that
they may be properly considered by the meetin',"
said the imperturbable president.

"Well, I motion that we stop talkin' and com-
mence doin'——"

"Do you suggest that a committee be appointed
for that purpose?"

"Yes, anything." And the chairman appointed
Bowersox, Bott, and Folgum such a committee.

All breathed more freely and felt as if something practical and energetic had been accomplished. The committee would, of course, never meet nor report, but the colloquy and the prompt action taken upon it made every one feel that the evening had been interesting and profitable. Before they broke up, Sleeny was asked for his initiation fee of two dollars, and all the brethren were dunned for their monthly dues.

"What becomes of this money?" the neophyte bluntly inquired of the hierophant.

"It pays room rent and lights," said Offitt, with unabashed front, as he returned his greasy wallet to his pocket. "The rest goes for propagatin' our ideas, and especially for influencin' the press."

Sleeny was a dull man, but he made up his mind on the way home that the question which had so long puzzled him—how Offitt made his living—was partly solved.

VI.

TWO MEN SHAKE HANDS.

SLEENY, though a Bread-winner in full standing, was not yet sufficiently impressed with the wrongs of labor to throw down his hammer and saw. He continued his work upon Farnham's conservatory, under the direction of Fergus Ferguson, the gardener, with the same instinctive fidelity which had always characterized him. He had his intervals of right feeling and common sense, when he reflected that Farnham had done him no wrong, and probably intended no wrong to Maud, and that he was not answerable for the ill luck that met him in his wooing, for Maud had refused him before she ever saw Farnham. But, once in a while, and especially when he was in company with Offitt, an access of jealous fury would come upon him, which found vent in imprecations which were none the less fervid for being slowly and haltingly uttered. The dark-skinned, unwholesome-looking Bread-winner found a singular delight in tormenting the powerful young fellow. He felt a spontaneous hatred for him, for many reasons. His shapely build, his curly blond hair and beard, his frank blue eye, first attracted his envious notice; his steady, contented industry excited in him a desire to pervert a workman whose daily life was a practical argument against the doctrines of socialism, by which Offitt made a part of

his precarious living; and after he had met Maud
Matchin and had felt, as such natures will, the force
of her beauty, his instinctive hate became an active,
though secret, hostility. She had come one evening
with Sleeny to a spiritualist conference frequented
by Offitt, and he had at once inferred that Sleeny
and she were either engaged to be married or on the
straight road toward it. It would be a profanation
of the word to say that he loved her at first sight.
But his scoundrel heart was completely captivated
so far as was possible to a man of his sort. He was
filled and fired with a keen cupidity of desire to
possess and own such beauty and grace. He railed
against marriage, as he did against religion and
order, as an invention of priests and tyrants to en-
slave and degrade mankind; but he would gladly
have gone to any altar whatever in company with
Maud Matchin. He could hardly have said whether
he loved or hated her the more. He loved her
much as the hunter loves the fox he is chasing to its
death. He wanted to destroy anything which kept
her away from him : her lover, if she had one ; her
pride, her modesty, her honor, if she were fancy-
free. Aware of Sleeny's good looks, if not of his
own ugliness, he hated them both for the comeli-
ness that seemed to make them natural mates for
each other. But it was not in his methods to pro-
ceed rashly with either. He treated Maud with
distant respect, and increased his intimacy with
Sleeny until he found, to his delight, that he was
not the prosperous lover that he feared. But he
still had apprehensions that Sleeny's assiduity might
at last prevail, and lost no opportunity to tighten

the relations between them, to poison and pervert the man who was still a possible rival. By remaining his most intimate friend, he could best be informed of all that occurred in the Matchin family.

One evening, as Sam was about leaving his work, Fergus Ferguson said :

"You'll not come here the morn. You're wanted till the house—a bit o' work in the library. They'll be tellin' you there."

This was faithfully reported by Sam to his confessor that same night.

"Well, you are in luck. I wish I had your chance," said Offitt.

Sam opened his blue eyes in mute wonder.

"Well, what's the chance, and what would you do with it, ef you had it?"

Offitt hesitated a moment before replying.

"Oh, I was just a jokin'. I meant it was such an honor for common folks like us to git inside of the palace of a high-toned cuss like Farnham; and the fact is, Sammy," he continued, more seriously, "I *would* like to see the inside of some of these swell places. I am a student of human nature, you know, in its various forms. I consider the lab'rin' man as the normal healthy human—that is, if he don't work too hard. I consider wealth as a kind of disease ; wealth and crristocracy is a kind of dropsy. Now, the true reformer is like a doctor,—he wants to know all about diseases, by sight and handlin'! I would like to study the symptoms of erristocracy in Farnham's house—right in the wards of the hospital."

"Well, that beats me," said Sam. " I've been

in a lot of fine houses on Algonquin Avenue, and I never seen anything yet that favored a hospital."

This dense stupidity was almost more than Offitt could bear. But a ready lie came to his aid.

"Looky here!" he continued, "I'll tell you a secret. I'm writin' a story for the 'Irish Harp,' and I want to describe the residence of jess such a vampire as this here Farnham. Now, writin', as I do, in the cause of humanity, I naturally want to git my facts pretty near right. You kin help me in this. I'll call to-morrow to see you while you're there, and I'll get some p'ints that'll make Rome howl when they come out."

Sam was hardly educated up to the point his friend imagined. His zeal for humanity and the "rehabitation" of labor was not so great as to make him think it a fine thing to be a spy and a sneak in the houses of his employers. He was embarrassed by the suggestion, and made no reply, but sat smoking his pipe in silence. He had not the diplomatist's art of putting a question by with a smile. Offitt had tact enough to forbear insisting upon a reply.

He was, in fact, possessed of very considerable natural aptitude for political life. He had a quick smile and a ready tongue; he liked to talk and shake hands; he never had an opinion he was not willing to sell; he was always prepared to sacrifice a friend, if required, and to ask favors from his worst enemies. He called himself Andrew Jackson Offitt— a name which, in the West, is an unconscious brand. It generally shows that the person bearing it is the

son of illiterate parents, with no family pride or affections, but filled with a bitter and savage partisan-
ship which found its expression in a servile worship
of the most injurious personality in American history. But Offitt's real name was worse than Andrew
Jackson—it was Ananias, and it was bestowed in
this way: When he was about six years old, his father, a small farmer in Indiana, who had been a
sodden, swearing, fighting drunkard, became converted by a combined attack of delirium tremens
and camp-meeting, and resolved to join the church,
he and his household. The morning they were
going to the town of Salem for that purpose, he
discovered that his pocket had been picked, and the
money it contained was found on due perquisition
in the blue jeans trousers of his son Andrew Jackson. The boy, on being caught, was so nimble and
fertile in his lies that the father, in a gust of rage, de-
clared that he was not worthy the name of the great
President, but that he should be called Ananias;
and he was accordingly christened Ananias that
morning in the meeting-house at Salem. As long
as the old man lived, he called him by that dreadful name; but when a final attack of the trembling
madness had borne him away from earth, the widow
called the boy Andrew again, whenever she felt
careless about her spiritual condition, and the youth
behaved himself, but used the name of Sapphira's
husband when the lad vexed her, or the obligations
of the christening came strongly back to her super-
stitious mind. The two names became equally familiar to young Offitt, and always afterward he was
liable to lapses of memory when called on suddenly

to give his prenomen; and he frequently caused hateful merriment among his associates by signing himself Ananias.

When Sam presented himself at Captain Farnham's house the next morning, he was admitted by Budsey, who took him to the library and showed him the work he was to do. The heat of the room had shrunk the wood of the heavy doors of carved oak so that the locks were all out of position. Farnham was seated by his desk, reading and writing letters. He did not look up as Sam entered, and paid no attention to the instructions Budsey was giving him. For the first time in his life, Sleeny found that this neglect of his presence was vaguely offensive to him. A week before, he would no more have thought of speaking to Farnham, or being spoken to by him, than of entering into conversation with one of the busts on the book-cases. Even now he had no desire to talk with the proprietor of the house. He had come there to do certain work which he was capable of doing well, and he preferred to do it and not be bothered by irrelevant gossip. But, in spite of himself, he felt a rising of revolt in his heart, as he laid out his tools, against the quiet gentleman who sat with his back to him, engaged in his own work and apparently unconscious of Sleeny's presence. A week before, they had been nothing to each other, but now a woman had come between them, and there is no such powerful conductor in nature. The quiet in which Farnham sat seemed full of insolent triumph to the luckless lover, and scraps of Offitt's sounding nonsense went through his mind: "A man is more

than a money-bag"; "the laborer is the true gentleman"; but they did not give him much comfort.
Not until he became interested in his work did he
recover the even beat of his pulse and the genuine
workmanlike play of his faculties. Then he forgot
Farnham's presence in his turn, and enjoyed himself
in a rational way with his files and chisels and screw-
drivers.

He had been at work for an hour at one door, and
had finished it to his satisfaction, and sat down before another, when he heard the bell ring, and Budsey immediately afterward ushered a lady through
the hall and into the drawing-room. His heart
stood still at the rustle of the dress,—it sounded so
like Maud's; he looked over his shoulder through the
open door of the library and saw, to his great relief,
that there were two female figures taking their seats
in the softly lighted room beyond. One sat with
her back to the light, and her features were not distinctly visible; the other was where he could see
three-quarters of her face clearly relieved against
the tapestry portière. There is a kind of beauty
which makes glad every human heart that gazes on
it, if not utterly corrupt and vile, and it was such a
face as this that Sam Sleeny now looked at with a
heart that grew happier as he gazed. It was a
morning face, full of the calm joy of the dawn, of
the sweet dreams of youth untroubled by love, the
face of Aurora before she met Tithonus. From the
little curls of gold on the low brow to the smile that
hovered forever, half formed, on the softly curving
lips and over the rounded chin, there was a light of
sweetness, and goodness, and beauty, to be read of

all men, and perhaps in God's good time to be worshipped by one.

Budsey announced "Mrs. Belding and Miss Halice," and Farnham hastened to greet them.

If Sam Sleeny had few happy hours to enjoy, he could at least boast himself that one was beginning now. The lovely face bore to his heart not only the blessing of its own beauty, but also a new and infinitely consoling thought. He had imagined till this moment, in all seriousness, that Maud Matchin was the prettiest woman in the world, and that therefore all men who saw her were his rivals, the chief of whom was Farnham. But now he reflected, with a joyful surprise, that in this world of rich people there were others equally beautiful, and that here, under Farnham's roof, on terms of familiar acquaintance with him, was a girl as faultless as an angel,—one of his own kind. "Why, of course," he said to himself, with a candid and happy self-contempt, "that's *his* girl—you dunderheaded fool —what are you botherin' about ?"

He took a delight which he could not express in listening to the conversation of these friends and neighbors. The ladies had come over, in pursuance of an invitation of Farnham's, to see the additions which had recently arrived from Europe to his collection of bronzes and pottery, and some little pictures he had bought at the English water-color exhibition. As they walked about the rooms, expressing their admiration of the profusion of pretty things which filled the cabinets and encumbered the tables, in words equally pretty and profuse, Sleeny listened to their voices as if it were music played to cheer him at his work. He knew nothing of the things they were talking about, but their tones were gentle and playful; the young lady's voice was especially sweet and friendly. He had never heard such voices before; they are exceptional everywhere in America, and particularly in our lake country, where the late springs develop fine high sopranos, but leave much to be desired in the talking tones of women. Alice Belding had been taught to use her fine voice as it deserved and Cordelia's intonations could not have been more "soft, gentle, and low,—an excellent thing in woman."

After awhile, the voices came nearer, and he heard Farnham say:

"Come in here a moment, please, and see my new netsukes; I got them at a funny little shop in Ostend. It was on a Sunday afternoon, and the man of the house was keeping the shop, and I should have got a great bargain out of him, but his wife came in before we were through, and scolded him for an imbecile and sent him into the back room to tend the baby, and made me pay twice what he had asked for my little monsters."

By this time they were all in the library, and the young lady was laughing, not loudly, but musically, and Mrs. Belding was saying:

"Served you right for shopping on Sunday. But they are adorable little images, for all that."

"Yes," said Farnham, "so the woman told me, and she added that they were authentic of the twelfth century. I asked her if she could not throw off a century or two in consideration of the hard,

times, and she laughed, and said I blagued, and
honestly she didn't know how old they were, but it
was *drôle, tout de même, qu'on pût adorer un petit
bon Dieu d'une laideur pareille.*"

"Really, I don't see how they can do it," said
Mrs. Belden, solemnly; at which both the others
laughed, and Miss Alice said, "Why, mamma, you
have just called them adorable yourself."

They went about the room, admiring, and touching, and wondering, with the dainty grace of ladies
accustomed to rare and beautiful things, until the
novelties were exhausted and they turned to go.
But Budsey at that moment announced luncheon,
and they yielded to Farnham's eager importunity,
and remained to share his repast.

They went to the dining-room, leaving Sleeny
more than content. He still heard their voices, too
distant to distinguish words; but he pleased himself
by believing that there was a tender understanding
in the tones of Farnham and Miss Belding when
they addressed each other, and that it was altogether
a family party. He had no longer any feeling of
slight or neglect because none of them seemed aware
of his presence while they were in the room with
him. There was, on the contrary, a sort of comfort
in the thought that he belonged to a different world
from them; that he and Maud were shut out—shut
out together—from the society and the interests
which claimed the Beldings and the Farnhams.
"You was a dunderheaded fool," he said, cheerfully
apostrophizing himself again, "to think everybody
was crazy after your girl."

He was brought down to a lower level by hearing

the door open, and the voice of Offitt asking if **Mr.** Sleeny was in.

"No one of that name here," said Budsey.

"I was told at Matchin's he was here."

"Oh! the young man from Matchin's. He is in the library," and Offitt came in, looking more disreputable than usual, as he had greased his hair inordinately for the occasion. Budsey evidently regarded him with no favorable eye; he said to Sleeny, "This person says he comes from Matchin's; do you know him?"

"Yes, it's all right," said Sam, who could say nothing less; but when Budsey had left them, he turned to Offitt with anything but welcome in his eye.

"Well, you've come, after all."

"Yes," Offitt answered, with an uneasy laugh. "Curiosity gets us all, from Eve down. What a lay-out this is, anyhow," and his small eyes darted rapidly around the room. "Say, Sam, you know Christy Fore, that hauls for the Safe Company? He was telling me about the safe he put into this room—said nobody'd ever guess it *was* a safe. Where the devil is it?"

"I don't know. It's none of my business, nor yours either."

"I guess you got up wrong foot foremost, Sam, you're so cranky. Where can the —— thing be? Three doors and two winders and a fire-place, and all the rest book-cases. By Jinx! there it is, I'll swear." He stepped over to one of the cases where a pair of oaken doors, rich with arabesque carving, veiled a sort of cabinet. He was fingering at them when Sam seized him by the shoulder, and said:

"Look here, Andy, what *is* your game, anyhow? I'm here on business, and I ain't no fence, and I'll just trouble you to leave."

Offitt's face turned livid. He growled:

"Of all Andylusian jacks, you're the beat. I ain't agoin' to hurt you nor your friend Farnham. I've got all the p'ints I want for my story, and devilish little thanks to you, neither. And say, tell me, ain't there a back way out? I don't want to go by the dinin'-room door. There's ladies there, and I ain't dressed to see company. Why, yes, this fits me like my sins," and he opened the French window, and stepped lightly to the gravel walk below, and was gone.

Sleeny resumed his work, ill content with himself and his friend. "Andy is a smart fellow," he thought; "but he had no right to come snoopin' around where I was at work, jist to get points to worry Mr. Farnham with."

The little party in the drawing-room was breaking up. He heard their pleasant last words, as the ladies resumed their wraps and Farnham accompanied them to the door. Mrs. Belding asked him to dinner, "with nobody but ourselves," and he accepted with a pleased eagerness. Sleeny got one more glimpse of the beautiful face under the gray hat and feather, and blessed it as it vanished out of the door. As Farnham came back to the library, he stood for a moment by Sam, and examined what he had done.

"That's a good job. I like your work on the

7

green-house, too.   I know good work when I see it. I worked one winter as a boss carpenter myself."

It seemed to Sleeny like the voice of a brother speaking to him. He thought the presence of the young lady had made everything in the house soft and gentle.

"Where was you ever in that business?" he asked.

"In the Black Hills. I sawed a million feet of lumber and built houses for two hundred soldiers. I had no carpenters; so I had to make some. I knew more about it when I got through than when J began."

Sleeny laughed—a cordial laugh that wagged his golden beard and made his white teeth glisten.

"I'll bet you did!" he replied.

The two men talked a few minutes like old acquaintances; then Sleeny gathered up his tools and slung them over his shoulder, and as he turned to go both put out their hands at the same instant, with an impulse that surprised each of them, and said "Good-morning."

VII.

GHOSTLY COUNSEL.

A MAN whose intelligence is so limited as that of Sam Sleeny is always too rapid and rash in his inferences. Because he had seen Farnham give Maud a handful of roses, he was ready to believe things about their relations that had filled him with fury ; and now, because he had seen the same man talking with a beautiful girl and her mother, the conviction was fixed in his mind that Farnham's affections were placed in that direction, and that he was therefore no longer to be dreaded as a rival. He went home happier, in this belief, than he had been for many a day ; and so prompt was his progress in the work of deceiving himself, that he at once came to the conclusion that little or nothing now stood between him and the crowning of his hopes. His happiness made him unusually loquacious, and at the supper-table he excited the admiration of Matchin and the surprise of Maud by his voluble history of the events of the day. He passed over Offitt's visit in silence, knowing that the Matchins detested him ; but he spoke with energetic emphasis of the beauty of the house, the handsome face and kindly manners of Farnham, and the wonderful beauty and sweetness of Alice Belding.

"Did that bold thing go to call on him alone ?"

cried Miss Maud, thoroughly aroused by this supposed offence against the proprieties of life.

"Why, no, Mattie," said Sam, a little disconcerted.
"Her ma was along."

"Why didn't you say so, then ?" asked the unap-
peased beauty.

"I forgot all about the old lady, though she was
more chinny than the young one. She just seemed
like she was a-practisin' the mother-in-law, so as to
do it without stumblin' when the time come."

"Hullo! Do you think they are strikin' a match ?"
cried Saul, in high glee. "That would be first-rate.
Keep the money and the property all together.
There's too many of our rich girls marryin' out of
the State lately—keeps buildin' dull."

"I don't believe a word of it," Maud interposed.
"He ain't a man to be caught by a simperin' school-
girl. And as to money, he's got a plenty for two.
He can please himself when he marries."

"Yes, but may be he won't please you, Mattie,
and that would be a pity," said the ironical Saul.

The old man laughed loudly at his own sarcasm,
and pushed his chair back from the table, and Maud
betook herself to her own room, where she sat down,
as her custom was, by the window, looking over the
glowing lake, and striving to read her destiny as she
gazed into the crimson and golden skies. She did
not feel at all so sure as she pretended that there was
no danger of the result that Sleeny had predicted;
and now that she was brought face to face with it,
she was confounded at discovering how much it
meant to her. She was carrying a dream in her
heart which would make or ruin her, according as it

should prove true or false. She had not thought of herself as the future wife of Farnham with any clearness of hope, but she found she could not endure the thought of his marrying any one else and passing forever out of her reach. She sat there, bitterly ruminating, until the evening glow had died away from the lake and the night breeze spread its viewless wings and flapped heavily in over the dark ridge and the silent shore. Her thoughts had given her no light of consolation ; her chin rested on her hands, her elbows on her knees ; her large eyes, growing more luminous in the darkness, stared out at the gathering night, scarcely noting that the sky she gazed at had changed from a pompous scene of red and yellow splendor to an infinite field of tender and dark violet, fretted with intense small stars.

"What shall I do ?" she thought. "I am a woman. My father is poor. I have got no chance. Jurildy is happier to-day than I am, and got more sense."

She heard a timid rap at her door, and asked, sharply :

"Who's there ?"

"It's me," said Sleeny's submissive voice.

"What do you want ?" she asked again, without moving.

"Mr. Bott give me two tickets to his séance to-night,"—Sam called it "seeuns,"—"and I thought mebbe you'd like to go."

There was silence for a moment. Maud was thinking : "At any rate it will be better than to sit here alone and cry all the evening." So she said : "I'll come down in a minute." She heard Sam's heavy step descending the stairs, and thought what

a different tread another person had ; and she wondered whether she would ever "do better" than
take Sam Sleeny; but she at once dismissed the
thought. "I can't do that; I can't put my hand in
a hand that smells so strong of sawdust as Sam's.
But he is a good soul, and I am sorry for him, every
time I look in the glass."

Looking in the glass, as usual, restored her good
humor, and she started off to the ghostly rendezvous
with her faithful attendant. They never talked
very much when they were alone together, and this
evening both were thoughtful. Maud had never
taken this commerce with ghosts much to heart.
She had a feeling, which she could hardly have de-
fined, that it was a common and plebeian thing to
believe in it, and if she ever heard it ridiculed she
joined in the cry without mercy. But it was an
excitement and an interest in a life so barren of both
that she could not afford to throw it away. She had
not intelligence enough to be disgusted or shocked
by it. If pressed to explain the amount of her faith
in the whole business, she would probably have said
she thought "there was something in it," and stopped
at that. In minds like hers, there is no clearly
drawn line between the unusual and the supernatu-
ral. An apparent miracle pleased her as it would
please a child, without setting her to find out how it
was done. She would consult a wizard, taking the
chances of his having occult sources of information,
with the same irregular faith in the unlikely with
which some ladies call in homœopathic practitioners.

All the way to the rooms of Bott, she was revolv-
ing this thought in her mind: "Perhaps he could

tell me something about Mr. Farnham. I don't think much of Bott; he has too many knuckles on his hands. I never saw a man with so many knuckles. I wouldn't mention Mr. Farnham to him to save his life, but I might get something out of him without telling him anything. He is certainly a very smart man, and whether it's spirits or not, he knows lots of things."

It was in this mood that she entered the little apartment where Bott held what he called his "Intermundane Séances." The room was small and stuffy. A simulacrum of a chest of drawers in one corner was really Bott's bed, where the seer reposed at night, and which, tilted up against the wall during the day, contained the rank bedclothes, long innocent of the wash-tub. There were a dozen or so of cane-bottom chairs, a little table for a lamp, but no other furniture. At one side of the room was a small closet without a door, but with a dark and dirty curtain hung before its aperture. Around it was a wooden railing, breast high.

A boy with a high forehead, and hair combed behind ears large and flaring like those of a rabbit, sat by the door, and took the tickets of invited guests and the half-dollars of the casuals. The seer received everybody with a nerveless shake of a clammy hand, showed them to seats, and exchanged a word or two about the weather, and the "conditions," favorable or otherwise, to spiritual activity. When he saw Maud and Sam his tallowy face flushed, in spots, with delight. He took them to the best places the room afforded, and stammered his pleasure that they had come.

" Oh! the pleasure is all ours," said Maud, who was always self-possessed when she saw men stammering. " It's a great privilege to get so near to the truth as you bring us, Mr. Bott."

The prophet had no answer ready; he merely flushed again in spots, and some new arrivals called him away.

The room was now pretty well filled with the unmistakable crowd which always attend such meetings. They were mostly artisans, of more intellectual ambition than their fellows, whose love of the marvellous was not held in control by any educated judgment. They had long, serious faces, and every man of them wore long hair and a soft hat. Their women were generally sad, broken-spirited drudges, to whom this kind of show was like an opera or a ball. There were two or three shame-faced believers of the better class, who scoffed a little but trembled in secret, and a few avowed skeptics, young clerks on a mild spree, ready for fun if any should present itself.

Bott stepped inside the railing by the closet, and placing his hands upon it, addressed the assembly. He did not know what peculiar shape the manifestations of the evening might take. They were in search of truth; all truth was good. They hoped for visitors from the unseen speers; he could promise nothing. In this very room the spirits of the departed had walked and talked with their friends; perhaps they might do it again; he knew not. How they mingled in the earth-life, he did not pretend to say; perhaps they materialized through the mejum; perhaps they dematerialized material from the audience which they rematerialized in visible forms; as to that, the opinion of another—he said with a spacious magnanimity—was as good as his. He would now request two of the audience to step up and tie him. One of the long-haired ruminant men stood up, and a young fellow, amid much nudging and giggling among the scorners, was also forced from his chair. They came forward, the believer with a business-like air, which showed practice, and the young skeptic blushing and ill at ease. Bott took a chair inside the curtain, and showed them how to tie him. They bound him hand and foot, the believer testified that the binding was solid, and the skeptic went to his seat, playfully stepping upon the toes of his scoffing friends. The curtain was lowered, and the lamp was turned down.

In a few moments, a scuffling sound was heard in the closet, and Bott's coat came flying out into the room. The believer pulled back the curtain, and Botts sat in his chair, his shirt sleeves gleaming white in the dust. His coat was laid over his shoulders, and almost as soon as the curtain was lowered he yelled for light, and was disclosed sitting tied as before, clothed in his right coat.

Again the curtain went down amid a sigh of satisfaction from the admiring audience, and a choking voice, which tried hard not to sound like Bott's, cried out from the closet: "Turn down the light; we want more power." The kerosene lamp was screwed down till hardly a spark illumined the visible darkness, and suddenly a fiery hand appeared at the aperture of the closet, slowly opening and shutting its long fingers.

A half dozen voices murmured : " A spirit hand "; but Sam Sleeny whispered to Maud : " Them are Bott's knuckles, for coin." The hand was withdrawn and a horrible face took its place—a pallid corpse-like mask, with lambent fire sporting on the narrow forehead and the high cheek-bones. It stayed only an instant, but Sam said, " That's the way Bott will look in——"

" Hush !" said Maud, who was growing too nervous to smile, for fear of laughing or crying.

A sound of sobbing came from a seat to the right of them. A poor woman had recognized the face as that of her husband, who had died in the army, and she was drawing the most baleful inferences from its fiery adjuncts.

A moment later, Bott came out of the closet, crouching so low that his head was hardly two feet from the ground. He had a sheet around his neck, covering his whole person, and a white cap over his head, concealing most of his face. In this constrained attitude he hopped about the clear space in front of the audience with a good deal of dexterity, talking baby-talk in a shrill falsetto. " Howdy, pappa ! Howdy, mamma ! Itty Tudie tum adin !"

A rough man and woman, between joy and grief, were half hysterical. They talked to the toad-like mountebank in the most endearing tones, evidently believing it was their dead baby toddling before them. Two or three times the same horrible imposture was repeated. Bott never made his appearance without somebody recognizing him as a dear departed friend. The glimmering light, the unwholesome excitement, the servile credulity fixed by long habit, seemed to produce a sort of passing dementia upon the regular habitués.

With these performances the first part came to an end. The light was turned on again, and the tying committee was requested to come forward and examine the cords with which Bott still seemed tightly bound. The skeptic remained scornfully in his seat, and so it was left for the believer to announce that not a cord had been touched. He then untied Bott, who came out from the closet, stretching his limbs as if glad to be free, and announced that there would be a short intermission for an interchange of views.

As he came toward Maud, Sam rose and said:

"Whew! he smells like a damp match. I'll go out and smoke a minute, and come back."

Bott dropped into the seat which Sleeny had left.

To one who has never attended one of these queer *cenacula*, it would be hard to comprehend the unhealthy and even nauseous character of the feeling and the conversation there prevalent. The usual decent restraints upon social intercourse seem removed. Subjects which the common consent of civilized creatures has banished from mixed society are freely opened and discussed. To people like the ordinary run of the believers in spiritism, the opera, the ballet, and the annual Zola are unknown, and they must take their excitements where they can find them. The dim light, the unhealthy commerce of fictitious ghosts, the unreality of act and sentiment, the unwonted abandon, form an atmosphere in which these second-hand mystics float

away into a sphere where the morals and the manners
are altogether different from those of their working
days.

Miss Matchin had not usually joined in these
morbid discussions. She was of too healthy an
organization to be tempted by so rank a mental
feast as that, and she had a sort of fierce maiden-
hood about her which revolted at such exposures of
her own thought. But to-night she was sorely perplexed. She had been tormented by many fancies
as she looked out of her window into the deepening
shadows that covered the lake. The wonders she
had seen in that room, though she did not receive
them with entire faith, had somewhat shaken her
nerves; and now the seer sat beside her, his pale
eyes shining with his own audacity, his lank hair
dripping with sweat, his hands uneasily rubbing
together, his whole attitude expressive of perfect
subjection to her will.

"Why isn't this a good chance?" she thought.
"He is certainly a smart man. Horrid as he looks,
he knows lots. May be he could tell me how to
find out."

She began in her airiest manner: "Oh, Mr. Bott,
what a wonderful gift you have got! How you
must look down on us poor mortals!"

Bott grew spotted, and stammered:

"Far from it, Miss Matchin. I couldn't look
down on you."

"Oh, you are flattering. That's not right, because I believe every word you say—and that ain't
true."

She rattled recklessly on in the same light tone.

"I'm going to ask you something very particular.
I don't know who can tell me, if you can't. How
can a young lady find out whether a young gentleman is in love with her or not? Now, tell me the
truth this time," she said with a nervous titter,
"for it's very important."

This question from any one else would not have
disconcerted Bott in the least. Queries as absurd
had frequently been put to him in perfect good
faith, and answered with ready and impudent ignorance. But, at those giggling words of Maud Matchin, he turned livid and purple, and his breath came
heavily. There was room for but one thought in
that narrow heart and brain. He had long cherished
a rather cowardly fondness for Maud, and now that
this question was put to him by the agitated girl, his
vanity would not suffer him to imagine that any one
but himself was the subject of her dreams. There was,
to him, nothing especially out of the way in this sort
of indirect proposal on the part of a young woman.
It was entirely in keeping with the general tone of
sentiment among the people of his circle, which
aimed at nothing less than the emancipation of the
world from its old-fashioned decencies.

But he would not answer hastily ; he had a cow-
ard's caution. He looked a moment at the girl's
brilliant color, her quick, high breathing, her eager
eyes, with a gloating sense of his good luck. But
he wanted her thoroughly committed. So he said,
with an air in which there was already something
offensively protecting :

"Well, Miss Matchin, that depends on the speer.
If the affection be unilateral, it is one thing ; if it

be recippercal, it is another. The currents of soul works in different ways."

"But what I mean is, if a young lady likes a young gentleman pretty well, how is she going to find out for sure whether he likes her?" She went intrepidly through these words, though her cheeks were burning, and her eyes would fall in spite of her, and her head was singing.

There was no longer any doubt in Bott's mind. He was filled with an insolent triumph, and thought only of delaying as long as possible the love chase of which he imagined himself the object. He said, slowly and severely:

"The question is too imperious to be answered in haste. I will put myself in the hands of the sperruts, and answer it as they choose after the intermission."

He rose and bowed, and went to speak a word or two to his other visitors. Sam came back and took his seat by Maud, and said:

"I think the fun is about over. Less go home."

"Go home yourself, if you want to," was the petulant reply. "I am going to stay for the inspirational discourse."

"Oh, my!" said Sam. "That's a beautiful word. You don't know how pretty your mouth looks when you say that." Sam had had his beer, and was brave and good-natured.

Bott retired once more behind the railing, but took his seat in a chair outside the curtain, in full view of the audience. He sat for some minutes motionless, staring at vacancy. He then slowly closed his eyes, and a convulsive shudder ran through his frame. This was repeated at rapid intervals, with more or less violence. He next passed his hands alternately over his forehead, as if he were wiping it, and throwing some invisible, sticky substance, with a vicious snap, to right and left. At last, after a final shudder, which stiffened him into the image of death for a moment, he rose to his feet and, leaning on the railing, began to intone, in a dismal whine, a speech of which we need give only the opening words.

"Dear brothers and sisters of the earth-life! On pearly wings of gossamer-down we float down from our shining speers to bring you messages of the higher life. Let your earth-soul be lifted to meet our sperrut-soul; let your earth-heart blend in sweet accordion with our heaven-heart; that the beautiful and the true in this weary earth-life may receive the bammy influence of the Eden flowrets, and rise, through speers of disclosure, to the plane where all is beautiful and all is true."

He continued in this strain for some time, to the evident edification of his audience, who listened with the same conventional tolerance, the same trust that it is doing your neighbor good, with which the ordinary audience sits under an ordinary sermon. Maud, having a special reason for being alert, listened with a real interest. But during his speech proper he made no allusion to the subject on which she had asked for light. It was after he had finished his harangue, and had gone through an *entr'acte* of sighs and shudders, that he announced himself once more in the hands of the higher intelligences, and ready to answer questions. "It does not need," he whined, "the word of the mouth or the speech of the tongue to tell the sperruts what your souls desire. The burden of your soul is open to the sperrut-eye. There sits in this room a pure and lovely soul in quest of light. Its query is, How does heart meet heart in mutual knowledge?"

Maud's cheek grew pale and then red, and her heart beat violently. But no one noticed her, and the seer went on. "If a true heart longs for another, there is no rest but in knowledge, there is no knowledge but in trewth, there is no trewth but in trust. Oh, my brother, if you love a female, tell your love. Oh, my sister, if you love—hum—if you love—hum—an individual of the opposite sex —oh, tell your love! Down with the shams of a false-hearted society; down with the chains of silence that crushes your soul to the dust! If the object of your hearts' throbs is noble, he will respond. Love claims love. Love has a right to love. If he is base, go to a worthier one. But from your brave and fiery heart a light will kindle his, and dual flames will wrap two chosen natures in high-menial melodies, when once the revelating word is spoke."

With these words he subsided into a deep trance, which lasted till the faithful grew tired of waiting, and shuffled slowly out of the door. When the last guest had gone, he rose from his chair, with no pretence of spiritual dignity, and counted his money and his tickets. He stretched himself in two chairs, drew his fingers admiringly through his lank locks, while a fatuous grin of perfect content spread over his face, as he said aloud to himself, "She has got it bad. I wonder whether she will have the nerve to ask me. I'll wait awhile, anyhow. I'll lose nothing by waiting."

Meanwhile, Maud was walking rapidly home with Sam. She was excited and perplexed, and did not care to answer Sam's rather heavy pleasantries over the evening's performance. He ridiculed the spirit-lights, the voices, and the jugglery, without provoking a reply, and at last he said :

"Well, what do you think of his advising the girls to pop? This ain't leap year!"

"What of that?" she answered, hastily. "I don't see why a girl hasn't as good a right to speak her mind as a man."

"Why, Mattie," said Sam, with slow surprise, "no decent girl would do that."

They had come to Matchin's gate. She slipped in, then turned and said :

"Well, don't be frightened, Mr. Sleeny ; I'm not going to propose to you," and she was gone from his sight.

She went directly to her room, and walked up and down a few moments without taking off her hat, moving with the easy grace and the suppressed passion of an imprisoned panther. Then she lighted her lamp and placed it on her bureau at one side of her glass. She searched in her closet and found a candle, which she lighted and placed on the other side of the glass. She undressed with reckless haste, throwing her clothes about on the floor, and sat down before her mirror with bare arms and shoulders, and nervously loosened her hair, watching every movement with blazing eyes. The thick

8

masses of her blue-black curls fell down her back
and over her sloping shoulders, which glowed with
the creamy light of old ivory. The unequal rays
of the lamp and candle made singular effects of
shadow on the handsome face, the floating hair, and
the strong and wholesome color of her neck and
arms. She gazed at herself with eager eyes and
parted lips, in an anxiety too great to be assuaged
by her girlish pride in her own beauty. "This is
all very well," she said, "but he will not see me
this way. Oh! if I only dared to speak first. I
wonder if it would be as the spirits said. 'If he is
noble he will respond!' He *is* noble, that's sure.
'Love claims love,' they said. But I don't know
as I love him. I *would*, if that would fetch him,
quick enough;" and the hot blood came surging up,
covering neck and brow with crimson.

VIII.

A BUD AND A BLOSSOM.

FARNHAM was sitting the next evening in his library, when Budsey entered and said Mr. Ferguson desired to see him. The gaunt Scotchman came in and said with feverish haste: "The cereus grandiflorus will be goin' to bloom the night. The buds are tremblin' and laborin' now." Farnham put on his hat and went to the conservatory, which was separated from the house by the entire extent of the garden. Arriving there, the gardener took him hurriedly to an inner room, dimly lighted,—a small square piece between the ferns and the grapes,— where the regal flower had a wall to itself. Two or three garden chairs were disposed about the room. Ferguson mounted on one of them, and turned up the gas so that its full light shone upon the plant. The bud was a very large one, perfect and symmetrical; the strong sheath, of a rich and even brown, as yet showed only a few fissures of its surface, but even now a faint odor stole from the travailing sphere, as from a cracked box of alabaster filled with perfume.

The face of the canny Fergus was lighted up with an eager joy. He had watched the growth and progress of this plant from its infancy. He had leaned above its cradle and taken pride in its size and beauty. He had trained it over the wall—from

which he had banished every rival—in large and
graceful curves, reaching from the door of the fern-
ery to the door of the grapery, till it looked, in the
usual half light of the dim chamber, like a well-regu-
lated serpent maturing its designs upon the neighboring paradise; and now the time was come when
he was to see the fruit of his patience and his care.

"Heaven be thankit," he murmured devoutly,
"that I was to the fore when it came."

"I thank you, Fergus, for calling me," said Farnham, smiling. "I know it must have cost you an
effort to divide such a sight with any one."

"It's your siller bought it," the Scotchman answered sturdily; "but there's nobody knows it, or
cares for it, as I do,—and that's the truth."

His glance was fixed upon the bud, which seemed
to throb and stir as he spoke. The soft explosive
force within was at work so strongly that the eye
could watch its operation. The fissures of the
sheath widened visibly and turned white as the two
men looked at them.

"It is a shame to watch this beautiful thing happening for only us," Farnham said to the gardener.
"Go and tell Mrs. Belding, with my compliments,
and ask her and Miss Belding to come down." But
observing his crestfallen expression, he took com-
passion on him and said: "No, you had better remain, for fear something should happen in your
absence. I will go for the ladies."

"I hope ye'll not miss it," said Fergus, but his
eyes and his heart were fixed upon the bud, which
was slowly gaping apart, showing a faint tinge of
gold in its heart.

Farnham walked rapidly up the garden, and found the Beldings at the door, starting for evening service with their prayer-books in their hands.

" Do you wish to see the prettiest thing you ever saw in your lives ? of course I except your mirrors when in action," he began, without salutation. " If so, come this moment to my conservatory. My night-blooming cereus has her coming-out party to-night."

They both exclaimed with delight, and were walking with him toward the garden. Suddenly, Mrs. Belding stopped and said :

" Alice, run and get your sketch-book and pencil. It will be lovely to draw the flower."

" Why, mamma ! we shall not have time for a sketch."

" There, there ! do as I tell you, and do not waste time in disputing."

The young girl hesitated a moment, and then, with instinctive obedience, went off to fetch the drawing materials, while her mother said to Farnham :

" Madame de Veaudrey says Alice is very clever with her pencil ; but she is so modest I shall have to be severe with her to make her do anything. She takes after me. I was very clever in my lessons, but never would admit it."

Alice came down the steps. Farnham, seeing her encumbered by her books, took them from her, and they went down the walks to the conservatory. They found Ferguson sitting, with the same rapt observation, before his tropical darling. As the ladies entered, he rose to give them seats, and

then retired to the most distant corner of the room,
where he spent the rest of the evening entirely un-
aware of any one's presence, and given up to the
delight of his eyes. The bud was so far opened
that the creamy white of the petals could be seen
within the riven sheath, whose strong dark color exquisitely relieved the pallid beauty it had guarded
so long. The silky stamens were still curled about
the central style, but the splendor of color which
was coming was already suggested, and a breath of
intoxicating fragrance stole from the heart of the
immaculate flower.

They spoke to each other in low tones, as if impressed with a sort of awe at the beautiful and mysterious development of fragrant and lovely life going
forward under their sight. The dark eyes of Alice
Belding were full of that vivid happiness which
strange and charming things bring to intelligent
girlhood. She was looking with all her soul, and
her breath was quick and high, and her soft red lips
were parted and tremulous. Farnham looked from
her to the flower, and back again, gazing on both
with equal safety, for the one was as unconscious of
his admiring glances as the other.

Suddenly, the sound of bells floated in from the
neighboring street, and both of the ladies started.
" No, don't you go," said Mrs. Belding to her
daughter. " I must, because I have to see my
'Rescue the Perishing.' But you can just as well
stay here and make your sketch. Mr. Farnham can
take care of you, and I will be back in an hour."

" But, mamma!" cried Miss Alice, too much scandalized to speak another word.

"I won't have you lose this chance," her mother continued. "I am sure Mr. Farnham will not object to taking care of you a little while; and if he hasn't the time, Fergus will bring you home—hm, Fergus?"

"Ay, madam, with right guid will," the gardener said, his hard face softening into a smile.

"There, sit down in that chair and begin your sketch. It is lovely just as it is." She waited until Alice, whose confusion had turned her face crimson, had taken her seat, opened her sketch-book, and taken her pencils in her trembling hands, and then the brisk and hearty woman drew her shawl about her and bustled to the door.

"I will walk to the church door with you," said Farnham, to the infinite relief of Alice, who regained her composure at the instant, and began with interest to sketch the flower. She thought, while her busy fingers were at work, that she had perhaps been too prudish in objecting to her mother's plan. "He evidently thinks nothing of it, and why should I?"

By the time Farnham returned, the cereus had attained its full glory of bloom. Its vast petals were thrown back to their fullest extent, and shone with a luminous beauty in which its very perfume seemed visible; the countless recurved stamens shot forth with the vigorous impulse and vitality of sun rays; from the glowing centre to the dark fringe with which the shattered sheath still accented its radiant outline it blazed forth, fully revealed; and its sweet breath seemed the voice of a pride and consciousness of beauty like that of the goddess on Mount

Ida, calmly triumphant in the certainty of perfect loveliness.

Alice had grown interested in her task, and looked up for only an instant with her frank, clear eyes as Farnham entered. "Now, where shall I sit?" he asked. "Here, behind your right elbow, where I can look over your shoulder and observe the work as it goes on?"

"By no means. My hand would lose all its little cunning in that case."

"Then I will sit in front of you and study the artistic emotions in your face."

"That would be still worse, for you would hide my subject. I am sure you are very well as you are," she added, as he seated himself in a chair beside her, a little way off.

"Yes, that is very well. I have the flower three-quarters and you in profile. I will study the one for a panel and the other for a medal."

Miss Alice laughed gently. She laughed often from sheer good humor, answering the intention of what was said to her better than by words.

"Can you sketch and talk too?" asked Farnham.

"I can sketch and listen," she said. "You will talk and keep me amused."

"Amusement with malice aforethought! The order affects my spirits like a Dead March. How do the young men amuse young ladies nowadays? Do they begin by saying, 'Have you been very gay lately?'"

Again Miss Alice laughed. "She is an easy-laughing girl," thought Farnham. "I like easy-laughing girls. When she laughs, she always blushes a very little. It is worth while talking nonsense to see a girl laugh so pleasantly and blush so prettily."

It is not worth while, however, to repeat all the nonsense Farnham uttered in the next hour. He got very much interested in it himself, and was so eager sometimes to be amusing that he grew earnest, and the gentle laugh would cease and the pretty lips would come gravely together. Whenever he saw this he would fall back upon his trifling again. He had the soldier's fault of point-blank compliment, but with it an open sincerity of manner which relieved his flattery of any offensiveness. He had practised it in several capitals with some success. A dozen times this evening, a neat compliment came to his lips and stopped there. He could hardly understand his own reserve before this laughing young lady. Why should he not say something pretty about her hair and eyes, about her graceful attitude, about the nimble play of her white fingers over the paper? He had uttered frank flatteries to peeresses without rebuke. But he held his hand before this school-girl, with the open dark-brown eyes and a club of yellow hair at the back of her neck. He could not help feeling that, if he talked to her with any forcing of the personal accent, she would stop laughing and the clear eyes would be troubled. He desired anything rather than that, and so the conversation went rattling on as free from personalities as the talk of two light-hearted and clever schoolboys.

At one moment he was describing a bill of fare in a Colorado hotel.

"With nice bread, though, one can always get on," she said.

"True," Farnham answered; "but this bread was of a ghostly pallor and flatness, as if it had been baked by moonlight on a grave-stone."

"The Indian women cook well, do they not?" she asked.

"Some are not so bad as others. One young chief boasted to me of his wife's culinary accomplishments. He had been bragging all the morning about his own exploits, of the men he had killed and the horses he had stolen, and then to establish his standing clearly in my mind, he added: 'My squaw same white squaw—savey pie.'"

"Even there, then, the trail of the pie-crust is over them all."

"No! only over the aristocracy."

"I should like so much to see that wonderful country."

"It is worth seeing," he said, with a curious sinking of the heart, "if you are not under orders."

He could not help thinking what a pleasant thing a journey through that Brobdingnaggian fairy-land would be with company like the young girl before him. Nature would be twice as lovely reflected from those brown eyes. The absurdities and annoyances of travel would be made delightful by that frank, clear laugh. The thought of his poor Nellie flitted by him an instant, too gentle and feeble for reproach. Another stronger thought had occupied his mind.

"You ought to see it. Your mother will need rest before long from her Rescue-the-Perishings,

and you are overworking yourself dreadfully over
that sketch-book. There is a touch of malaria about
the fountain in Bluff Park. Colorado will do you
both no end of good. I feel as if I needed it myself. I haven't energy enough to read Mr. Martin's
'Life of the Prince Consort.' I shall speak to Mrs.
Belding as soon as she returns."

"Do, by all means. I should like to go, but
mamma would not spend three nights in a sleep-
ing-car to see the Delectable Mountains themselves."

He rose and walked about the room, looking at
the flower and the young artist from different points
of view, and seeing new beauties in each continually. There were long lapses of conversation, in
which Alice worked assiduously and Farnham
lounged about the conservatory, always returning
with a quick word and a keen look at the face of
the girl. At last he said to himself: "Look here!
She is not a baby. She is nearly twenty years old.
I have been wondering why her face was so steady
and wise." The thought that she was not a child
filled his heart with pleasure and his face with
light. But his volubility seemed to die suddenly
away. He sat for a good while in silence, and
started a little as she looked up and said:

"Now, if you will be very gentle, you can see my
sketch and tell me what to do next."

It was a pretty and unpretentious picture that she
had made. The flower was faithfully though stiffly
given, and nothing especially remarkable had been
attempted or achieved. Farnham looked at the
sketch with eyes in which there was no criticism.
He gave Alice a word or two of heartier praise for

her work than she knew she deserved. It was
rather more than she expected, and she was not
altogether pleased to be so highly commended,
though she could hardly have said why. Perhaps it was because it made her think less of his
critical faculty. This was not agreeable, for her
admiration of him from her childhood had been one
of the greatest pleasures of her life. She had regarded him as children regard a brilliant and handsome young uncle. She did not expect from him
either gallantry or equality of treatment.

"There! Do not say too much about it—you
will make me ashamed of it. What does it lack?"

"Nothing, except something on the right to balance the other side. You might sketch in roughly
a half-opened flower on the vine about there," indi-
cating the place.

She took her pencils and began obediently to do
what he had suggested. He leaned over her shoulder, so near her she could feel his breath on the
light curls that played about her ear. She wished
he would move. She grew nervous, and at last
said:

"I am tired. You put in that flower."

He took the book and pencils from her, as she
rose from her chair and gave him her place, and
with a few strong and rapid strokes finished the
sketch.

"After all," she said to herself, with hearty ap-
preciation, "men do have the advantage of girls.
He bothered me dreadfully, and I did not bother
him in the least. And yet I stood as near to him
as he did to me."

Mrs. Belding came in a moment later. She was in high spirits. They had had a good meeting—had converted a Jew, she thought. She admired the sketch very much; hoped Alice had been no trouble to Farnham. He walked home with the ladies, and afterward smoked a cigar with great deliberation under the limes.

Mrs. Belding asked Alice how they had got on.

"He did not eat you, you see. You must get out of your ideas of men, especially men of Arthur Farnham's age. He never thinks of you. He is old enough to be your father."

Alice kissed her mother and went to her own room, calculating on the way the difference between her age and Captain Farnham's.

IX.

A DRAMA WITH TWO SPECTATORS.

THE words of Bott lingered obstinately in Maud Matchin's mind. She gave herself no rest from dwelling on them. Her imagination was full, day after day, of glowing pictures of herself and Farnham in tête-à-tête; she would seek in a thousand ways to tell her love—but she could never quite arrange her avowal in a satisfactory manner. Long before she came to the decisive words which were to kindle his heart to flame in the imaginary dialogue, he would himself take fire by spontaneous combustion, and, falling on his knees, would offer his hand, his heart, and his fortune to her in words taken from "The Earl's Daughter" or the "Heir of Ashby."

"Oh, pshaw! that's the way it ought to be," she would say to herself. "But if he won't—I wonder whether I ever could have the brass to do it? I don't know why I shouldn't. We are both human. Bott wouldn't have said that if there was nothing in it, and he's a mighty smart man."

The night usually gave her courage. Gazing into her glass, she saw enough to inspire her with an idea of her own invincibility; and after she had grown warm in bed she would doze away, resolving with a stout heart that she would try her fate in the morning. But when day came, the enterprise no longer

seemed so simple. Her scanty wardrobe struck her
with cowardice as she surveyed it. The broad daylight made everything in the house seem poor and
shabby. When she went down-stairs, her heart
sank within her as she entered the kitchen to help
her mother, and when she sat with the family at the
breakfast-table, she had no faith left in her dreams
of the rosy midnight. This alternation of feeling
bred in her, in the course of a few days, a sort of
fever, which lent a singular beauty to her face, and
a petulant tang to her speech. She rose one morning, after a sleepless night, in a state of anger and
excitement in which she had little difficulty in
charging upon Farnham all responsibility for her
trouble of mind.

"I won't stand it any longer," she said aloud in
her chamber. "I shall go to him this day and have
it out. I shall ask him what he means by treating
me so."

She sat down by her bureau and began to crimp
her hair with grim resolution. Her mother came
and knocked at her door. "I'm not coming to
breakfast, I've got a headache," she said, and added
to herself, "I sha'n't go down and get the smell of
bacon on me this morning."

She continued her work of personal adornment
for two hours, going several times over her whole
modest arsenal of finery before she was ready for
the fray. She then went down in her street costume, and made a hasty meal of bread and butter,
standing by the pantry. Her mother came in and
found her there.

"Why, Mattie, how's your head?"

"I'm going to take a walk and see what that will do."

As she walked rapidly out of Dean Street, the great clock of the cathedral was striking the hour of nine.

"Goodness !" she exclaimed, "that's too early to call on a gentleman. What shall I do ?"

She concluded to spend the time of waiting in the library, and walked rapidly in that direction, the fresh air flushing her cheeks, and blowing the frizzed hair prettily about her temples. She went straight to the reference rooms, and sat down to read a magazine. The girl who had prompted her to apply for a place was there on duty. She gave a little cry of delight when she saw Maud, and said : "I was just crazy to see you. I have got a great secret for you. I'm engaged !"

The girls kissed each other with giggles and little screams, and the young woman told who *he* was—in the lightning-rod business in Kalamazoo, and doing very well ; they were to be married almost immediately.

"You never saw such a fellow, he just won't wait ;" and consequently her place in the library would be vacant. "Now, you must have it, Maud ! I haven't told a soul. Even the Doctor don't know it yet."

Maud left the library and walked up the avenue with an easier mind. She had an excuse for her visit now, and need not broach, unless she liked, the tremendous subject that made her turn hot and cold to think of. She went rustling up the wide thoroughfare at a quick pace ; but before arriving at Farnham's, moved by a momentary whim, she turned down a side street leading to Bishop's Lane. She said to herself, "I will go in by that little gate once, if I never do again." As she drew near, she thought, "I hope Sam isn't there."

Sam was there, just finishing his work upon the greenhouse. Farnham was there also ; he had come down to inspect the job, and he and Sleeny were chatting near the gate as Maud opened it and came in. Farnham stepped forward to meet her. The unexpected rencounter made her shy, and she neither spoke to Sam nor looked toward him, which filled him with a dull jealousy.

"Could I have a few moments' conversation with you, sir ?" she asked, with stiff formality.

"Certainly," said Farnham, smiling. "Shall we go into the house ?"

"Thank you, sir," she rejoined, severely decorous.

They walked up the garden-path together, and Sam looked after them with an unquiet heart.

She was walking beside Farnham with a stately step, in spite of the scabbard-like narrowness of the dress she wore. She was nearly as tall as he, and as graceful as a young pine blown to and fro by soft winds. The carpenter, with his heart heavy with love and longing, felt a bitter sense that she was too fine for him. They passed into the house, and he turned to his work with a sigh, often dropping his busy hands and looking toward the house with a dumb questioning in his eyes. After a half hour which seemed endless to him, they reappeared and walked slowly down the lawn. There was trouble and agitation in the girl's face, and Farnham was serious also. As they came by the rose-house, Maud

9

paused and looked up with a sorrowful smile and a
question. Farnham nodded, and they walked to
the open door of the long, low building. He led
the way in, and Maud, looking hastily around, closed
the door behind them.

"He's goin' to give her some more of them roses,"
said Sam, explaining the matter to himself. But he
worked for some time with his blond beard on his
shoulder in his impatience to see them come out.
At last, he could resist no longer. He knew a point
where he could look through the glass and see whatever was taking place among the roses. He walked
swiftly across the turf to that point. He looked in
and saw Maud, whose back was turned toward him,
talking as if she were pleading for her life, while
Farnham listened with a clouded brow. Sleeny
stood staring with stupid wonder while Maud laid
her hand upon Farnham's shoulder. At that moment
he heard footsteps on the gravel walk at some distance
from him, and he looked up and saw Mrs. Belding
approaching. Confused at his attitude of espionage,
he walked away from his post, and, as he passed her,
Mrs. Belding asked him if he knew where Mr.
Farnham was.

"Yes," he answered, "he's in there. Walk right
in;" and in the midst of his trouble of spirit he
could hardly help chuckling at his own cleverness
as he walked, in his amazement, back to the conservatory.

While she was in the house, Maud had confined
herself to the subject of the vacancy in the library.
She rushed at it, as a hunter at a hedge, to get away
from the other matter which had tormented her for

a week. When she found herself alone with Farnham she saw that it would be "horrid" to say what she had so long been rehearsing. "Now I can get that place, if you will help me. No earthly soul knows anything about it, and Minnie said she would give me a good chance before she let it out."

Farnham tried to show her the difficulties in the way. He was led by her eagerness into a more detailed account of his differences with the rest of the board than he had ever given to any one, a fuller narrative than was perhaps consistent with entire prudence. Whenever he paused, she would insist with a woman's disconcerting directness:

"But they don't know anything about it this time —they can't combine on anybody. You can certainly get one of them."

Farnham still argued against her sanguine hopes, till he at last affected her own spirits, and she grew silent and despondent. As she rose to go, he also took his hat to return to the garden, where he had left Sleeny, and they walked over the lawn together. As they approached the rose-house, she thought of her former visit and asked to repeat it. The warm breath of the flowers saluted her as she crossed the threshold, bringing so vivid a reminiscence of the enchantment of that other day, that there came with it a sudden and poignant desire to try there, in that bewitched atmosphere, the desperate experiment which would decide her fate. There was no longer any struggle in her mind. She could not, for her life, have kept silent now. She walked slowly beside him to the place where the pots of roses stood ranged on their frames, filling the air with dense fragrance. Her hands were icy cold and quick flushes passed through her, while her face reddened and paled like a horizon smitten by heat-lightning in a sultry night of summer. She looked at the moist brick pavement at her feet, her eyelids seemed too heavy to lift, and the long lashes nearly touched her cheeks.

"What sort will you have?" said Farnham, reaching for the gardener's shears.

"Never mind the roses," she said, in a dry voice which she hardly recognized as her own. "I have something to say to you."

He turned and looked at her with surprise. She raised her eyes to his with a great effort, and then, blushing fiery red, she said, in a clear, low voice, "I love you."

Like many another daughter and son of Eve, she was startled at the effect of these momentous words upon herself. Of all forms of speech these three words are the most powerful, the most wonder-working upon the being who utters them. It was the first time they had ever passed her lips, and they exalted and inebriated her. She was suddenly set free from the bashful constraint which had held her, and with a leaping pulse and free tongue she poured out her heart to the astonished and scandalized young man.

"Yes, I love you. You think it's horrid that I should say so, don't you? But I don't care, I love you. I loved you the first time I saw you, though you made me so angry about my glasses. But you were my master, and I knew it, and I never put them on again. And I thought of you day and night, and I longed for the day to come when I might see you once more, and I was glad when I did not get that place, so that I could come again and see you and talk with you. I can tell you over again every word you ever said to me. You were not like other men. You are the first real man I ever knew. I was silly and wild when I wanted to be your secretary. Of course, that wouldn't do. If I am not to be your wife, I must never see you again; you know that, don't you?" and, carried away by her own reckless words, she laid her hand on his shoulder. His frown of amazement and displeasure shook her composure somewhat. She turned pale and trembled, her eyes fell, and it seemed for an instant as if she would sink to the floor at his feet. He put his arm around her, to keep her from falling and pressed her closely to him. She threw her head back upon his shoulder and lifted her face to him. He looked down on her, and the frown passed from his brow as he surveyed her flushed cheeks, her red full lips parted in breathless eagerness; her dark eyes were wide open, the iris flecked with golden sparks and the white as clear and blue-tinged as in the eyes of a vigorous infant; her head lay on his shoulder in perfect content, and she put up her mouth to him as simply and as sure of a response as a pretty child. He was entirely aware of the ridiculousness of his position, but he stooped and kissed her.

Her work seemed all done; but her satisfaction lasted only a second. Her face broke into happy smiles.

"You do love me, do you not?" she asked.

"I certainly do not," he answered; and at that instant the door opened and Mrs. Belding saw this pretty group of apparent lovers on a rich background of Jacqueminot roses.

Startled more at the words of Farnham than at the entry of Mrs. Belding, Maud had started up, like Vivien, "stiff as a viper frozen." Her first thought was whether she had crushed her hat on his shoulder, and her hands flew instinctively to her head-gear. She then walked tempestuously past the astonished lady out into the garden and brushed roughly by Sleeny, who tried to detain her.

"Hold your tongue, Sam! I hate you and all men"; and with this general denunciation, she passed out of the place, flaming with rage and shame.

Mrs. Belding stood for a moment speechless, and then resorted to the use of that hard-worked and useful monosyllable,

"Well!" with a sharp, falling inflection.

"Well!" returned Farnham, with an easy, rising accent; and then both of them relieved the strained situation with a laugh.

"Come, now," said the good-natured woman, "I am a sort of guardian of yours. Give an account of yourself."

"That is easily given," said Farnham. "A young woman, whose name I hardly know, came to me in the garden this morning to ask for help to get some lady-like work to do. After discussing that subject threadbare, she came in here for a rose, and, apropos of nothing, made me a declaration and a proposal of honorable wedlock, *dans toutes les formes.*"

"The forms were evident as I entered," said Mrs. Belding, dryly.

"I could not let her drop on the damp floor," said Farnham, who was astonished to find himself positively blushing under the amused scrutiny of his mother-confessor. " Consider, if you please, my dear madam, that this is the first offer I have ever received, and I was naturally somewhat awkward about declining it. We shall learn better manners as we go along."

"You did decline, then?" said Mrs. Belding, easily persuaded of the substantial truth of the story, and naturally inclined, as is the way of woman, to the man's side. Then, laughing at Arthur's discomfiture, she added, "I was about to congratulate you."

"I deserve only your commiseration."

"I must look about and dispose of you in some way. You are evidently too rich and too fascinating. But I came over to-day to ask you what I ought to do about my Lake View farm. I have two offers for it; if I had but one, I would take either —well, you know what I mean;" and the conversation became practical. After that matter was disposed of, she said, with a keen side-glance at Farnham, "That was a very pretty girl. I hope you will not be exposed to such another attack ; I might not be so near the next time."

"That danger, thanks to you, is over; Mademoiselle will never return," he answered, with an air of conviction.

Mrs. Belding went home with no impression left of the scene she had witnessed but one of amusement. She thought of it only as "a good joke on Arthur Farnham." She kept chuckling to herself over it all day, and if she had had any especial gossip in the town, she would have put on her hat and hurried off to tell it. But she was a woman who lived very much at home, and, in fact, cared little for tattling. She was several times on the point of sharing the fun of it with her daughter, but was prevented by an instinctive feeling that it was hardly the sort of story to tell a young girl about a personal acquaintance. So she restrained herself, though the solitary enjoyment of it irritated her.

They were sitting on the wide porch which ran around two sides of the house just as twilight was falling. The air was full of drowsy calls and twitters from the grass and the trees. The two ladies had been sitting ever since dinner, enjoying the warm air of the early summer, talking very little, and dropping often into long and contented silences. Mrs. Belding had condescended to grenadine in consideration of the weather, and so looked less funereal than usual. Alice was dressed in a soft and vapory fabric of creamy bunting, in the midst of which her long figure lay reclined in an easy chair of Japanese bamboo; she might have posed for a statue of graceful and luxurious repose. There was light enough from the rising moon and the risen stars to show the clear beauty of her face and the yellow lustre of her hair; and her mother cast upon her from time to time a glance of pride and fondness, as if she were a recovered treasure to which the attraction of novelty had just been added anew.

"They say she looks as I did at her age," thought

the candid lady; "but they must flatter me. My
nose was never so straight as that : her nose is Belding all over. I wonder whom she will care about
here ? Mr. Furrey is a nice young man, but she is
hardly polite to him. There he is now."

The young man came briskly up the walk, and
ran up the steps so quickly that he tripped on the
last one and dropped his hat. He cleverly recovered
it, however, and made very elaborate bows to both
the ladies, hoping that he found them quite well.
Mrs. Belding bustled about to give him a chair, at
which Alice knitted her pretty brows a little. She
had scarcely moved her eyelashes to greet her visitor;
but when Mrs. Belding placed a light chair near her
daughter and invited Mr. Furrey to take it, the young
lady rose from her reclining attitude and sat bolt
upright with a look of freezing dignity. The youth
was not at all abashed, but took his seat, with his
hat held lightly by the brim in both hands. He
was elegantly dressed, in as faithful and reverent an
imitation as home talent could produce of the costume of the gentlemen who that year were driving
coaches in New York. His collar was as stiff as tin ;
he had a white scarf, with an elaborate pin con-
structed of whips and spurs and horseshoes. He
wore dog-skin gloves, very tight and red. His hair
was parted in the middle with rigorous impar-
tiality and shed rather rank fragrance on the night.
He began conversation with an easy air, in which
there was something of pleasurable excitement
mixed.

"I come to receive your congratulations, ladies!"

"What, you are engaged?" said Mrs. Belding,

and even the placid face of Miss Alice brightened
with a look of pleased inquiry.

"Oh, dear, no; how could you think so?" he protested, with an arch look at Alice which turned her
to marble again. "I mean I have this day been appointed assistant cashier of our bank!" Napoleon,
informing Madame de Beauharnais * that he was to
command the army of Italy, probably made less ado
about it.

Mrs. Belding made haste to murmur her congratulations. "Very gratifying, I am sure,—at your
age;" to which Alice responded like a chorus, but
without any initiative warmth, "Very gratifying, I
am sure."

Furrey went on at some length to detail all the
circumstances of the event: how Mr. Lathers, the
president of the bank, had sent for him, and how he
complimented him; how he had asked him where
he learned to write such a good hand; and how he
had replied that it came sort of natural to him to
write well, that he could make the American eagle
with pen and ink before he was fifteen, all but the
tail-feathers, and how he discovered a year later that
the tail-feathers had to be made by holding the pen
between the first and second fingers; with much
more to the like innocent purpose, to which Mrs.
Belding listened with nods and murmurs of approval.
This was all the amiable young man needed to en-
courage him to indefinite prattle. He told them all
about the men in the bank, their habits and their

---

* Perhaps Josephine told Napoleon herself, but I think she
was clever enough to let him imagine he owed the appointment to his merits.

loves and their personal relations to him, and how
he seemed somehow to be a general favorite among
them all. Miss Alice sat very still and straight in
her chair, with an occasional smile when the laughter of Mr. Furrey seemed to require it, but with her
eyes turned to the moonlit night in vagrant reverie,
and her mind in those distant and sacred regions
where we cannot follow the minds of pure and
happy girls.

"Now, you would hardly understand, if I did not
tell you," said Mr. Furrey, "how it is that I have
gained the confidence——"

At this moment Alice, who had been glancing
over Mr. Furrey's shoulder for a moment with a
look of interest in her eyes, which he thought was
the legitimate result of his entertaining story, cried:

"Why, there comes Mr. Farnham, mamma."

"So it is," said her mother. "I suppose he
wants to see me. Don't move, Mr. Furrey. Mr.
Farnham and I will go into the house."

"By no means," said that gentleman, who by this
time had mounted the steps. "I was sitting all
alone on my porch and saw by the moon that yours
was inhabited; and so I came over to improve my
mind and manners in your society."

"I will get a chair for you," said Mrs. Belding.

"No, thank you; this balustrade will bear my
weight, and my ashes will drop harmless on the
flower-bed, if you will let me finish my cigar." And
he seated himself between the chair of Furrey and
the willow fabric in which Alice had resumed her
place. This addition to the company was not at all
to the taste of the assistant cashier, who soon took

his leave, shaking hands with the ladies, with his best bow.

"After all, I do prefer a chair," said Farnham, getting down from his balustrade, and throwing away his cigar.

He sat with his back to the moonlight. On his left was Alice, who, as soon as Furrey took his departure, settled back in her willow chair in her former attitude of graceful ease. On the right was Mrs. Belding, in her thin, cool dress of gauzy black. Farnham looked from one to the other as they talked, and that curious exercise, so common to young men in such circumstances, went through his mind. He tried to fancy how Mrs. Belding looked at nineteen, and how Miss Belding would look at fifty, and the thought gave him singular pleasure. His eyes rested with satisfaction on the kindly and handsome face of the widow, her fine shoulders and arms, and comfortable form, and then, turning to the pure and exquisite features of the tall girl, who was smiling so freshly and honestly on him, his mind leaped forward through coming years, and he said to himself: "What a wealth of the woman there is there—for somebody." An aggressive feeling of disapproval of young Furrey took possession of him, and he said, sharply:

"What a very agreeable young man Mr. Furrey is?"

Mrs. Belding assented, and Miss Alice laughed heartily, and his mind was set at rest for the moment.

They passed a long time together. At first Mrs. Belding and Arthur "made the expenses" of the conversation; but she soon dropped away, and Alice, under the influence of the night and the moonlight and Farnham's frank and gentle provocation, soon found herself talking with as much freedom and energy as if it were a girls' breakfast. With far more, indeed,—for nature takes care of such matters, and no girl can talk to another as she can to a man, under favoring stars. The conversation finally took a personal turn, and Alice, to her own amazement, began to talk of her life at school, and with sweet and loving earnestness sang the praises of Madame de Veaudrey.

"I wish you could know her," she said to Farnham, with a sudden impulse of sympathy. He was listening to her intently, and enjoying her eager, ingenuous speech as much as her superb beauty, as the moon shone full on her young face, so vital and so pure at once, and played, as if glad of the privilege, about the curved lips, the flashing teeth, the soft eyes under their long lashes, and the hair over the white forehead, gleaming as crisply brilliant as fine-spun wire of gold.

"By her fruits I know her, and I admire her very much," he said, and was sorry for it the moment afterward, for it checked the course of the young girl's enthusiasm and brought a slight blush to her cheek.

"I ought to have known better," he said to himself with real penitence, "than to utter a stupid commonplace to such a girl when she was talking so earnestly." And he tried to make amends, and succeeded in winning back her attention and her slow unconscious smiles by talking to her of things a

thousand miles away. The moon was silvering the
tops of the linden-trees at the gates before they
thought of the flight of time, and they had quite
forgotten the presence of Mrs. Belding when her
audible repose broke in upon their talk. They
looked at each other, and burst into a frank laugh,
full of confidence and comradeship, which the good
lady heard in her dreams and waked, saying, "What
are you laughing at? I did not catch that last
witticism."

The young people rose from their chairs. "I
can't repeat my own mots," said Arthur: "Miss
Belding will tell you."

"Indeed I shall not," replied Alice. "It was not
one of his best, mamma."

She gave him her hand as he said "Good-night,"
and it lay in his firm grasp a moment without reserve or tremor.

"You are a queer girl, Alice," said Mrs. Belding,
as they walked into the drawing-room through the
open window. "You put on your stiffest company
manners for Mr. Furrey, and you seem entirely at
ease with Mr. Farnham, who is much older and
cleverer, and is noted for his sarcastic criticisms."

"I do not know why it is, mamma, but I do feel
very much at home with Mr. Farnham, and I do
not want Mr. Furrey to feel at home with me."

Upon this, Mrs. Belding laughed aloud. Alice
turned in surprise, and her mother said, "It is too
good to keep. I must tell you. It is such a joke
on Arthur;" and, sitting in a low arm-chair, while
Alice stood before her leaning upon the back of another, she told the whole story of the scene of the

morning in the rose-house. She gave it in the fullest detail, interrupting herself here and there for soft cachinnations, unmindful of the stern, unsmiling silence with which her daughter listened.

She finished, with a loud flourish of merriment, and then asked: "Did you ever hear anything so funny in your life?"

The young lady was turning white and red in an ominous manner, and was biting her nether lip. Her answer to her mother's question was swift and brief:

".I never heard anything so horrid," and she moved majestically away without another word.

Mrs. Belding sat for a moment abashed. "There!" she said to herself, "I knew very well I ought not to tell her. But it was too good to keep, and I had nobody else to tell." She went to bed, feeling rather ill-used. As she passed her daughter's door, she said, "Good-night, Alice!" and a voice not quite so sweet as usual replied, "Good-night, mamma," but the door was not opened.

Alice turned down her light and sat upon a cushioned seat in the embrasure of her open window. She looked up at the stars, which swam and glittered in her angry eyes. With trembling lips and clinched hands she communed with herself. "Why, why, why did mamma tell me that horrid story? To think there should be such women in the world! To take such a liberty with him, of all men! She could not have done it without some encouragement—and he could not have encouraged her. He is not that kind of a vulgar flirt at all. But what do I know about men? They may all be

—but I did not think—what business have I thinking about it? I had better go to bed. I have spent
all the evening talking to a man who—Oh! I wish
mamma had not told me that wretched story. I
shall never speak to him again. It is a pity, too,
for we are such near neighbors, and he is so nice, if
he were not—But I don't care how nice he is, she has
spoiled him. I wonder who she was. Pretty, was
she? I don't believe a word of it—some bold-faced,
brazen creature. Oh! I shall hate myself if I cry;"
but that was past praying for, and she closed her
lattice and went to bed for fear the stars should witness her unwelcome tears.

X.

A WORD OUT OF SEASON.

ARTHUR FARNHAM awoke the next day with a flight of sweet hopes and fancies singing in his heart and brain. He felt cheerfully and kindly toward the whole human race. As he walked down into the city to transact some business he had there with his lawyer, he went out of his way to speak to little children. He gave all his acquaintances a heartier "Good-morning" than usual. He even whistled at passing dogs. The twitter of the sparrows in the trees, their fierce contentions on the grass, amused him. He leaned over the railing of the fountain in the square with the idlers, and took a deep interest in the turtles, who were baking their frescoed backs in the warm sun, as they floated about on pine boards, amid the bubbles of the clear water.

As he passed by the library building, Dr. Buchlieber was standing in the door. "Good luck," he said; "I was just wishing to see you. One of our young women resigned this morning, and I think there may be a chance for our handsome friend. The meeting, you remember, is this afternoon."

Farnham hardly recalled the name of the young lady in whose success he had been so interested, although recent intimate occurrences might have been expected to fix it somewhat permanently in his
10

remembrance. But all female images except one
had become rather vague in his memory. He assented, however, to what the doctor proposed, and
going away congratulated himself on the possibility
of doing Maud a service and ridding himself of the
faintest tinge of remorse. He was not fatuous or
conceited. He did not for a moment imagine that
the girl was in love with him. He attributed her
demonstration in the rose-house to her " congenital
bad breeding," and thought it only one degree worse
than other match-making manœuvres of which he
had been the object in the different worlds he had
frequented. He gave himself no serious thought
about it, and yet he was glad to find an apparent
opportunity to be of use to her. She was poor and
pretty. He had taken an interest in her welfare.
It had not turned out very well. She had flung
herself into his arms and been heartily kissed. He
could not help feeling there was a balance against
him.

As he turned the corner of the street which led
to the attorney's office where he was going, he saw
a man standing by the wall with his hat off, bowing
to him. He returned the unusual salutation and
passed on ; it was some moments before he remembered that it was one of his colleagues on the Library Board. He regretted not having stopped and
made the effort to engage his vote for Maud ; but,
on second thought, he reflected that it would be as
well to rely upon the surprise of the three to prevent a combination at the meeting. When he
reached the entrance of the building where his lawyer's offices were, he turned, with a sense of being

pursued by a shuffling footstep which had hastened
its speed the last few paces, and saw his colleague
coming up the steps after him with a perspiring but
resolute face.

"Hold on, Cap," he said, coming into the shade
of the passage. "I was thinkin' o' comin' to see
you, when I sighted you comin' round the corner."

"I am glad to see you, Mr. Pennybaker," said
Arthur, taking the clumsy hand which was held out
to him.

"Gettin' pretty hot, ain't it?" said Pennybaker,
wiping his brow with his forefinger and dexterously
sprinkling the floor with the proceeds of the action.

"No danger of frost, I think," Arthur assented,
admiring the dexterity of Pennybaker, but congratulating himself that the shake-hands was disposed
of.

"You bet your life. We're going to have it just
sizzling from now on."

"Were you wishing to see me about anything in
particular?" asked Farnham, who saw no other way
of putting an end to a meteorological discussion
which did not interest him.

"Well, yes," answered Pennybaker, getting
around beside Farnham, and gazing at the wall opposite. "I heerd this mornin' that Minnie Bell was
goin' to get married. My daughter is doing some
sewing for her, and it slipped out that way. She
was trying to keep it secret. Some girls is mighty
funny that way. They will do anything to get engaged, and then they will lie like Sam Hill to make
believe they ain't. Well, that makes a vacancy."
He did not turn his head, but he cast a quick glance

sideways at Farnham, who made no answer, and Pennybaker resumed : " So I thought I would come to you, honor bright, and see if we couldn't agree what to do. That's me. I'm open and square like a bottle of bitters."

Farnham gave no indication of his surprise at this burst of candor, but asked :

" What do you propose ?"

" That's it," said Pennybaker, promptly. " I don't propose nothing—I *ex*pose. You hear me— I *ex*pose." He said this with great mystery, one eye being shut fast and the other only half open. He perceived that he had puzzled Farnham, and enjoyed it for a moment by repeating his mot with a chuckle that did not move a muscle of his face. " I'll tell you the whole thing. There's no use, between gentlemen, of playing the thing too fine." He took his knife from one pocket and from another a twist of tobacco, and, cutting off a mouthful, began his story :

" You see, me and Bud Merritt and Joe Dorman have most generally agreed on paternage, and that was all right. You are well fixed. You don't want the bother of them little giblets of paternage. We've 'tended to 'em for what there was in 'em and for the good of the party. Now Bud he wants to be auditor, and he's got Joe to go in with him, because, if he gits there, Joe's brother-in-law, Tim Dolan, will be his debbity. Bud is weak in the Third Ward, and he knows it, and he knows that Jake Runckel can swing that ward like a dead cat ; and so they have fixed it all up to give the next vacancy to Jake for his sister. She's been turned out of the school for some skylarking, and weighs pretty heavy on Jake's hands. Very well. That's the game, and I'm a-kickin'! Do you hear me? I'm a-kickin'!"

Pennybaker pushed up his hat and looked Farnham fairly in the face. The assertion of his independence seemed to give him great gratification. He said once more, slowly closing one eye and settling back in his former attitude against the wall, while he aimed a deluge of tobacco-juice at the base of the wall before him: "I'm a-kickin' like a Texas steer."

He waited a moment to allow these impressive words to have their full effect, while Farnham preserved a serious and attentive face.

"Well, this bein' the case," continued Pennybaker, "I comes to you, as one gentleman to another, and I asks whether we can't agree against this selfish and corrupt game of Merritt and Dorman. For, you see, I don't get a smell out of what they're doin'. I'm out in the cold if their slate goes through."

"I don't see that I can be of any service to you, Mr. Pennybaker. If I have any influence in the matter, it shall be given to Miss Matchin, whom I proposed once before."

"Exactly! Now you're talkin'. Miss Matchin shall have it, on one little proviso that won't hurt you nor me nor nobody. Say the word, and it's a whack."

And he lifted up his hand to strike the bargain.

"What is it?" asked Farnham, in a tone which was severe and contemptuous, in spite of him.

"Namely, just this," answered Pennybaker.

" You ain't on the make ; you're fixed. You don't care about these d—— little things except to help a friend once 'n awhile," he said, in a large and generous way. " But I ain't that kind yet. . I've got to look out for myself—pretty lively, too. Now, I'll tell you what's my racket. You let me perpose Miss Matchin's name and then go and tell her father that I put it through, and it'll be done slick as a whistle. That's all solid, ain't it ?"

Farnham's brow clouded. He did not answer at once. Pennybaker repeated his question a little anxiously :

" That's all solid, ain't it ?"

" You will excuse me, Mr. Pennybaker, if I do not quite understand your racket, as you call it. I do not see how you make anything out of this. Matchin is a poor man. You surely do not intend——"

" To strike Saul for a divvy ? Nothing of the sort," said Pennybaker, without the least offence. " The whole thing lies just here. Among gentlemen there's no use being shy about it. My brother wants to be assessor in Saul Matchin's ward. Saul's got a lot of influence among the boys in the planing-mills, and I want his help. You see ?"

Farnham thought he saw, and, after assenting to Pennybaker's eager demand, " That's all solid?" he walked away, too much relieved by the thought that Maud was provided for to question too closely the morality of the proceeding which the sordid rascal had exposed to him.

In the afternoon, at the meeting of the board, the programme agreed upon was strictly carried out.

Pennybaker proposed Miss Matchin's name as soon as the vacancy was announced, to the amazement of his late confederates. They moved a postponement, but to no purpose; Maud was elected; and the angry politicians had no better revenge than to say spitefully to Pennybaker on the stairs, as they went away, "How much did the Captain give you for that sell-out?"—a jeer which he met by a smile of conscious rectitude and a request to be informed the next time they organized a freeze-out against him. It must be said, however, that he lost no time in going to Matchin, informing him that he had succeeded in carrying Maud in by unheard-of exertions, and demanding and receiving on the spot five per cent of her year's salary, which he called "the usual commission."

Saul announced the appointment that evening at supper. Maud flushed crimson, and the tears started to her eyes. She was about to declare she would not have it, when her father's next words put a different face on the matter. "And it's no thanks to Cap'n Farnham, neither. He tried it oncet, and couldn't make the riffle. But me and Joel Pennybaker got together and done it. And now I hope, Mattie, you'll behave yourself and save money. It's like a fortun' comin' to you, if you're smart."

Maud found no reply ready. She could not wholly believe her father's story. She still fancied the appointment came from Farnham, and there was a certain bitterness in it; but, on the whole, she received it not without a secret complacency. Mrs. Matchin's pleasure was checked by her daughter's morose confusion. Sam made no pretence of being

pleased, but sat, unmoved by Matchin's speech, in
scowling silence, and soon went out without a word
of comment. The scene he had witnessed in the
rose-house had poisoned his mind ; yet, whenever
he looked at Maud, or tried to speak to her, he was
met with an air of such fierce and beautiful defiance,
that his eyes fell and his voice stuck in his throat.
So the piece of good fortune, so anxiously awaited
in the household, brought little delight when it
came. Maud reported for duty next day, and soon
learned the routine of her work ; but she grew more
and more silent at home, and Saul's hope of a wedding in the family died away.

Arthur Farnham walked away from the meeting
with the feeling of a school-boy who has finished a
difficult task and who thinks he deserves some com-
pensating pleasure. The day had been fine and
warm, but the breeze of the late afternoon was already
blowing in from the lake, lending freshness and life
to the air. The sky was filled with soft gray clouds,
which sailed along at a leisurely rate, evidently on
very good terms with the breeze. As Farnham
walked up the avenue, he cast about in his mind
for the sort of dissipation with which he would reward himself for the day's work and he decided for
a ride.

But as he was drawing on his boots, it occurred
to him, for the first time in his life, that it was a
churlish and unneighborly proceeding for him to go
riding alone day after day, and that he would be doing no more than his duty to offer his escort to Miss
Belding. He said Miss Belding to his own thought
—making it as formal and respectful as possible.

So, sending an order to his groom to keep his horse at the stable for a moment, he walked over the lawn to the Belding cottage and asked for the ladies.

"I believe they are upstairs, sir. Walk into the drawing-room, and I will see," said the neat house-maid, smiling at Farnham, as indeed was the general custom of women. He took his seat in the cool and darkened room facing the door-way, which commanded a view of the stairs. He sat in a large willow chair very much at his ease, looking about the pretty salon, enjoying its pictures and ornaments and the fragrance of the roses in the vases, as if he had a personal interest in them. The maid came back and said the ladies would be down in a moment.

She had announced Farnham to Mrs. Belding, who had replied, "Tell him, in a moment." She was in the summer afternoon condition which the ladies call "dressing-sack," and after an inspection at the glass, which seemed unsatisfactory, she walked across the hall to her daughter's room. She found Alice standing by the window, looking out upon the lake.

"There, I am glad you are all dressed. Arthur Farnham has called, and you must go down and excuse me. I said I would come, but it will take me so long to dress, he will get tired of waiting. You run down and see him. I suppose there is nothing particular."

"Oh, mamma," said Alice, "I don't want to see him, and especially not alone."

Mrs. Belding made large eyes in her surprise. "Why, Alice, what has got into you?"

Alice blushed and cast down her eyes. " Mamma," she said, in a low voice, " do not ask me to go down. You know what you told me last night."

"There, that will do," said the mother, with a tone of authority. " Perhaps I was foolish to tell you that silly little story, but I am the judge of who shall visit this house. You are too young to decide these questions for me, and I insist that what I told you shall make no difference in your treatment of Mr. Farnham. You think too much of your own part in the matter. He has come to see me, and not you, and I wish you to go down and make my excuses for keeping him waiting. Will you go?"

" Yes, I will go," said the young girl. The blush had left her cheek and she had become a trifle pale. She had not raised her eyes from the floor during her mother's little speech; and when it was over and her mother had gone back to her room, Alice cast one glance at her mirror, and with a firm face walked down the stairs to the drawing-room. Farnham heard the rustle of her dress with a beating of the heart which filled him with a delicious surprise. "I am not past it, then," was the thought that came instantly to his mind, and in that one second was a singular joy. When she came in sight on the stairs, it was like a sudden enchantment to him. Her beautiful head, crowned with its masses of hair drawn back into a simple Greek knot; her tall, strong figure, draped in some light and clinging stuff which imposed no check on her natural grace and dignity, formed a charming picture as she came down the long stairs ; and Farnham's eyes fastened eagerly upon her white hand as it glided along the

dark walnut baluster. His heart went out to meet
her. He confessed to himself, with a lover's in-
stantaneous conviction, that there was nothing in the
world so utterly desirable as that tall and fair-haired
girl slowly descending the stairs. In the midst of
his tumultuous feeling a trivial thought occurred to
him: "I am shot through the heart by the blind
archer," he said to himself; and he no longer
laughed at the old-fashioned symbol of the sudden
and fatal power of love.

But with all this tumult of joy in the senses waking
up to their allegiance, there came a certain reserve.
The goddess-like creature who had so suddenly become the mistress of his soul was a very serious per-
sonage to confront in her new majesty. He did not
follow the impulse of his heart and rush forward as
she entered the room. He merely rose and bowed.
She made the faintest possible salutation, and, without taking a seat, conveyed her mother's excuses in
a tone of such studied coldness that it amused Farnham, who took it as a school-girl's assumption of a
grand and ceremonious manner suitable to a tête-à-
tête with man.

"Thank you," he said, "but I did not come
especially to see your mother. My object was rather
to see you." She did not smile or reply, and he
went on, with a slight sensation of chill coming
upon him from this stony dignity, which, the more
he observed it, seemed less and less amusing and not
at all artificial. "I came to ask if you would not
like to go to ride this afternoon. It is just gray
enough for comfort."

"I thank you very much for being so kind as to

think of me," she replied, " but it will not be convenient for me to go."

"Perhaps the morning will suit better. I will come to-morrow at any hour you say."

"I shall not be able to go to-morrow either, I think."

Even while exchanging these few words, Alice felt herself growing slightly embarrassed, and it filled her with dismay. "I am a poor creature," she thought, "if I cannot get this self-satisfied gentleman out of the house without breaking down. I can't stand here forever though," and so she took a seat, and as Arthur resumed his willow chair with an air of content, she could not but feel that as yet the skirmish was not in her favor. She called her angry spirit to her aid, and nerved herself to say something which would promptly close the interview.

His next words gave her the opportunity.

" But you surely do not intend to give up riding altogether ?"

"Certainly not. I hope to ride a good deal. Andrews will go with me."

"Ah! Your objection to me as a groom is entirely personal, then."

"Now for it!" she thought to herself, and she said firmly, "Yes."

But the effort was too great, and after the word was launched her mouth broke up into a nervous smile, for which she despised herself, but which she could not control for her life.

Farnham was so pleased with the smile that he cared nothing for the word, and so he continued in a tone of anxious and coaxing good-nature, every word increasing her trouble :

"You are wrong as you can be. I am a much better groom than Andrews. He has rather more style, I admit, on account of his Scotch accent and his rheumatism. But I might acquire these. I will be very attentive and respectful. I will ride at a proper distance behind you, if you will occasionally throw a word and a smile over your shoulder at me."

As he spoke, a quick vision flashed upon him of the loveliness of the head and shoulder, and the coil of fair hair which he should have before him if he rode after her, and the illumination of the smile and the word which would occasionally be thrown back to him from these perfect lips and teeth and eyes. His voice trembled with love and eagerness as he pleaded for the privilege of taking her servant's place. Alice no longer dared to interrupt him, and hardly ventured to lift her eyes from the floor. She had come down with the firm purpose of saying something to him which would put an end to all intimacy, and here, before she had been five minutes in his presence, he was talking to her in a way that delighted her ears and her heart. He went rattling on as if fearful that a pause might bring a change of mood. As she rarely looked up, he could feast his eyes upon her face, where now the color was coming and going, and on her shapely hands, which were clasped in her lap. He talked of Colorado as if it were settled that they were to go there together, and they must certainly have some preliminary training in rough riding ; and then, merely to make conversation, he spoke of other places that should only be visited on horseback, always claiming in all of them his post of groom. Alice felt her trouble and confusion of spirit passing away as the light stream of talk rippled on. She took little part in it at first, but from monosyllables of assent she passed on to a word of reply from time to time; and before she knew how it happened she was engaged in a frank and hearty interchange of thoughts and fancies, which brought her best faculties into play and made her content with herself, in spite of the occasional intrusion of the idea that she had not been true to herself in letting her just anger die so quickly away.

If Farnham could have seen into the proud and honest heart of the young girl he was talking to, he would have rested on the field he had won, and not tempted a further adventure. Her anger against him had been dissipated by the very effort she had made to give it effect, and she had fallen insensibly into the old relation of good neighborhood and unreserved admiration with which she had always regarded him. She had silenced her scruples by the thought that in talking pleasantly with him she was obeying her mother, and that after all it was not her business to judge him. If he could have known his own best interest, he would have left her then, when her voice and her smile had become gay and unembarrassed according to their wont, with her conscience at ease about his faults, and her mind filled with a pleasant memory of his visit.

But such wisdom was beyond his reach. He had felt suddenly, and once for all, in the last hour, the

power and visible presence of his love. He had
never in his life been so moved by any passion as he
was by the joy that stirred his heart when he heard
the rustle of her dress in the hall and saw her white
hand resting lightly on the dark wood of the stairs.
As she walked into the parlor, from her face and
her hair, from every movement of her limbs, from
every flutter of her soft and gauzy garments, there
came to him an assertion of her power over him
that filled him with a delicious awe. She represented to him, as he had never felt it before, the embodied mystery and majesty of womanhood. During all the long conversation that had followed, he
had been conscious of a sort of dual operation of
his mind, like that familiar to the eaters of hash-
ish. With one part of him he had been carrying
on a light and shallow conversation, as an excuse to
remain in her presence and to keep his eyes upon
her, and with all the more active energies of his
being he had been giving himself up to an act of
passionate adoration of her. The thoughts that uttered themselves to him, as he chatted about all
sorts of indifferent things, were something like these:
How can it have ever happened that such beauty,
such dignity, such physical perfection could come
together in one person, and the best and sweetest
heart have met them there? If she knew her
value, her pride would ruin her. In her there is
everything, and everything else beside: Galatea, the
statue, with a Christian soul. She is the best that
could fall to any man, but better for me than for any
one else. Anybody who sees her must love her, but I
was made for nothing else but to love her. This is

what mythologies meant. She is Venus: she loves laughter, and her teeth and lips are divine. She is Diana: she makes the night beautiful; she has the eye and the arm of an athlete goddess. But she is a woman: she is Mrs. Belding's daughter Alice. Thank heaven, she lives here. I can call and see her. To-morrow, I shall ride with her. She will love and marry some day like other women. Who is the man who shall ever kiss her between those straight brows? And fancies more audacious and extravagant fed the fever of his heart as he talked deliberate small talk, still holding his hat and whip in his hand.

He knew it was time he should go, but could not leave the joy of his eyes and ears. At last his thoughts, like a vase too full, ran over into speech. It was without premeditation, almost without conscious intention. The under-tone simply became dominant and overwhelmed the frivolous surface talk. She had been talking of her mother's plans of summer travel, and he suddenly interrupted her by saying in the most natural tone in the world: "I must see your mother before she decides. I hope you will make no plans without me. I shall go where you go. I shall never be away from you again, if I can help it. No, no, do not frown about it. I must tell you. I love you; my whole life is yours."

She felt terribly shocked and alarmed, not so much at his words as at her own agitation. She feared for a moment she could not rise from her seat, but she did so with an effort. He rose and approached her, evidently held in check by her inflexible face; for the crisis had brought a momentary self-control with it, and she looked formidable with her knit brows and closed lips.

"Do not go," he pleaded. "Do not think I have been wanting in respect and consideration. I could not help saying what I did. I cannot live without you any more than I can without light and sunshine. I ought to have waited and not startled you. But I have only begun to live since I loved you, and I feel I must not waste time."

She was deeply disturbed at these wild and whirling words, but still bore herself bravely. She felt her heart touched by the vibration of his ardent speech, but her maiden instinct of self defence enabled her to stand on her guard. Though beaten by the storm of his devotion, she said to herself that she could get away if she could keep from crying or sobbing, and one thought which came to her with the swiftness of lightning gave her strength to resist. It was this: "If I cry, he will take me in his arms, and we shall repeat the tableau mamma saw in the rose-house."

Strong in that stimulating thought, she said: "I am too sorry to hear you say these things. You know how much we have always thought of you. If you forget all this, and never repeat it, we may still be friends. But if you renew this subject, I will never speak to you again alone, as long as I live."

He began to protest; but she insisted, with the calm cruelty of a woman who sees her advantage over the man she loves. "If you say another word, it is the end of our acquaintance, and perhaps it is

11

best that it should end. We can hardly be again as we were."

Farnham was speechless, like one waked in the cold air out of a tropical dream. He had been carried on for the last hour in a whirlwind of emotion, and now he had met an obstacle against which it seemed that nothing could be done. If he had planned his avowal, he might have been prepared for rejection; but he had been hurried into it with no thought of what the result would be, and he was equally unprovided for either issue. In face of the unwavering voice and bearing of Alice, who seemed ten times more beautiful than ever as she stood before him as steady and unresponsive as a young Fate, his hot speech seemed suddenly smitten powerless. He only said:

"It shall be as you wish. If I ever offend you again, I will take my punishment upon myself and get out of your way."

She did not dare to say another word, for fear it would be too kind. She gave him her hand; it was soft and warm as he pressed it; and if he had only known how much softer and warmer her heart was, he would have covered her hand with a thousand kisses. But he bowed and took his leave, and she stood by the lattice and saw him go away, with eyes full of tears and a breast filled with the tenderest ruth and pity—for him and for herself.

XI.

THE SANTA RITA SHERRY.

FARNHAM walked down the path to the gate, then turned to go to his own house, with no very definite idea of what direction he was taking. The interview he had just had was still powerfully affecting his senses. He was conscious of no depression from the prompt and decided refusal he had received. He was like a soldier in his first battle who has got a sharp wound which does not immediately cripple him, the perception of which is lost in the enjoyment of a new, keen, and enthralling experience. His thoughts were full of his own avowal, of the beauty of his young mistress, rather than of her coldness. Seeing his riding-whip in his hand, he stared at it an instant, and then at his boots, with a sudden recollection that he had intended to ride. He walked rapidly to the stable, where his horse was still waiting, and rode at a brisk trot out of the avenue for a few blocks, and then struck off into a sandy path that led to the woods by the river-side.

As he rode, his thoughts were at first more of himself than of Alice. He exulted over the discovery that he was in love as if some great and unimagined good fortune had happened to him. "I am not past it, then," he said to himself, repeating the phrase which had leaped from his heart when he saw Alice descending the stairs. "I hardly

thought that such a thing could ever happen to me.
She is the only one." His thoughts ran back to a
night in Heidelberg, when he sat in the shadow of
the castle wall with a German student of his acquaintance, and looked far over the valley at the
lights of the town and the rippling waves of the
Neckar, silvered by the soft radiance of the summer
moon.

"Poor Hammerstein! How he raved that night
about little Bertha von Eichholz. He called her
Die Einzige something like a thousand times. It
seemed an absurd thing to say; I knew dozens just
like her, with blue eyes and Gretchen braids. But
Hammerstein meant it, for he shot himself the week
after her wedding with the assessor. But mine *is*
the Only One—though she is not mine. I would
rather love her without hope than be loved by any
other woman in the world."

A few days before he had been made happy by
perceiving that she was no longer a child; now he
took infinite pleasure in the thought of her youth;
he filled his mind and his senses with the image of
her freshness, her clear, pure color, the outline of
her face and form. "She is young and fragrant as
spring; she has every bloom and charm of body and
soul," he said to himself, as he galloped over the
shady woodland road. In his exalted mood, he had
almost forgotten how he had left her presence. He
delighted in his own roused and wakened passion,
as a devotee in his devotions, without considering
what was to come of it all. The blood was surging
through his veins. He was too strong, his love was
too new and wonderful to him, to leave any chance

for despair. It was not that he did not consider himself dismissed. He felt that he had played a great stake foolishly, and lost. But the love was there, and it warmed and cheered his heart, like a fire in a great hall, making even the gloom noble.

He was threading a bridle-path which led up a gentle ascent to a hill overlooking the river, when his horse suddenly started back with a snort of terror as two men emerged from the thicket and grasped at his rein. He raised his whip to strike one of them down; the man dodged, and his companion said, "None o' that, or I'll shoot your horse." The sun had set, but it was yet light, and he saw that the fellow had a cocked revolver in his hand.

"Well, what do you want?" he asked.

"I want you to stop where you are and go back," said the man sullenly.

"Why should I go back? My road lies the other way. You step aside and let me pass."

"You can't pass this way. Go back, or I'll make you," the man growled, shifting his pistol to his left hand and seizing Farnham's rein with his right. His intention evidently was to turn the horse around and start him down the path by which he had come. Farnham saw his opportunity and struck the hand that held the pistol a smart blow. The weapon dropped, but went off with a sharp report as it fell. The horse reared and plunged, but the man held firmly to the rein. His companion, joined by two or three other rough-looking men who rushed from the thicket, seized the horse and held him firmly, and pulled Farnham from the saddle. They attempted no violence and no robbery. The man who had held the pistol, a black-visaged fellow with a red face and dyed mustache, after rubbing his knuckles a moment, said: "Let's take it out o' the —— whelp!" But another, to whom the rest seemed to look as a leader, said: "Go slow, Mr. Bowersox; we want no trouble here."

Farnham at this addressed the last speaker and said, "Can you tell me what all this means? You don't seem to be murderers. Are you horse-thieves?"

"Nothing of the kind," said the man. "We are Reformers."

Farnham gazed at him with amazement. He was a dirty-looking man, young and sinewy, with long and oily hair and threadbare clothes, shiny and unctuous. His eyes were red and furtive, and he had a trick of passing his hand over his mouth while he spoke. His mates stood around him, listening rather studidly to the conversation. They seemed of the lower class of laboring men. Their appearance was so grotesque, in connection with the lofty title their chief had given them, that Farnham could not help smiling, in spite of his anger.

"What is your special line of reform?" he asked, —"spelling, or civil service?"

"We are Labor Reformers," said the spokesman. "We represent the toiling millions against the bloated capitalists and grinding monopolies; we believe that man is better——"

"Yes, no doubt," interrupted Farnham; "but how are you going to help the toiling millions by stopping my horse on the highway?"

"We was holding a meeting which was kep'

secret for reasons satisfactory to ourselves. These two gentlemen was posted here to keep out intruders from the lodge. If you had 'a' spoke civil to them, there would have been no harm done. None will be done now if you want to go."

Farnham at once mounted his horse. "I would take it as a great favor," he said, "if you would give me your name and that of the gentleman with the pistol. Where is he, by the way?" he continued. The man they called Bowersox had disappeared from the group around the spokesman. Farnham turned and saw him a little distance away directly behind him. He had repossessed himself of his pistol and held it cocked in his hand.

"What do you want of our names?" the spokesman asked.

Farnham did not again lose sight of Bowersox. It occurred to him that the interview might as well be closed. He therefore said, carelessly, without turning:

"A man has a natural curiosity to know the names of new acquaintances. But no matter, I suppose the police know you," and rode away.

Bowersox turned to Offitt and said, "Why in —— did you let him go? I could have knocked his head off and nobody knowed it."

"Yes," said Offitt, coolly, "and got hung for it."

"It would have been self-defence," said Bowersox. "He hit me first."

"Well, gentlemen," said Offitt, "that closes up Greenwood Lodge. We can't meet in this grass any more. I don't suppose he knows any of us by sight, or he'd have us up to-morrow."

"It was a piece of —— nonsense, comin' out here, anyhow," growled Bowersox, unwilling to be placated. "You haven't done a —— thing but lay around on the grass and eat peanuts and hear Bott chin."

"Brother Bott has delivered a splendid address on 'The Religion of Nature,' and he couldn't have had a better hall than the Canopy to give it under," said Offitt. "And now, gentlemen, we'd better get back our own way."

As Farnham rode home he was not much puzzled by his adventure in the woods. He remembered having belonged, when he was a child of ten, to a weird and mysterious confraternity called "Early Druids," which met in the depths of groves, with ill-defined purposes, and devoted the hours of meeting principally to the consumption of confectionery. He had heard for the past few months of the existence of secret organizations of working-men— wholly outside of the trades-unions and unconnected with them—and guessed at once that he had disturbed a lodge of one of these clubs. His resentment did not last very long at the treatment to which he had been subjected; but still he thought it was not a matter of jest to have the roads obstructed by ruffians with theories in their heads and revolvers in their hands, neither of which they knew how to use. He therefore promised himself to consult with the chief of police the next morning in regard to the matter.

As he rode along, thinking of the occurrence, he was dimly conscious of a pleasant suggestion in something he had seen among the hazel brush, and searching tenaciously in his recollection of the affair, it all at once occurred to him that, among the faces of the men who came out of the thicket in the scuffle, was that of the blonde-bearded, blue-eyed young carpenter who had been at work in his library the day Mrs. Belding and Alice lunched with him. He was pleased to find that the pleasant association led him to memories of his love, but for a moment a cloud passed over him at the thought of so frank and hearty a fellow and such a good workman being in such company. "I must see if I cannot get him out of it," he said to himself, and then reverted again to thoughts of Alice.

Twilight was falling, and its melancholy influence was beginning to affect him. He thought less and less of the joy of his love and more of its hopelessness. By the time he reached his house he had begun to confront the possibility of a life of renunciation, and, after the manner of Americans of fortune who have no special ties, his mind turned naturally to Europe. "I cannot stay here to annoy her," he thought, and so began to plot for the summer and winter, and, in fancy, was at the second cataract of the Nile before his horse's hoofs, ringing on the asphalt of the stable-yard, recalled him to himself.

The next day, he was compelled to go to New York to attend to some matters of business. Before taking the train, he laid his complaint of being stopped on the road before the chief of police, who promised to make vigorous inquisition. Farnham remained several days in New York, and on his return, one warm, bright evening, he found his table prepared and the grave Budsey waiting behind his chair.

He ate his dinner hastily and in silence, with no great zest. "You have not forgot, sir," said Budsey, who was his external conscience in social matters, "that you are going this evening to Mrs. Temple's?"

"I think I shall not go."

"Mr. Temple was here this afternoon, sir, which he said it was most particular. I asked him would he call again. He said no, he was sure of seeing you to-night. But it was most particular, he said."

Budsey spoke in the tone of solemn and respectful tyranny which he always assumed when reminding Farnham of his social duties, and which conveyed a sort of impression to his master that, if he did not do what was befitting, his butler was quite capable of picking him up and deferentially carrying him to the scene of festivity, and depositing him on the door-step.

"What could Temple want to see me about 'most particular'?" Farnham asked himself. "After all, I may as well pass the evening there as anywhere."

Mr. Temple was one of the leading citizens of Buffland. He was the vice-president of the great rolling-mill company, whose smoke darkened the air by day and lighted up the skies at night as with the flames of the nether pit. He was very tall and very slender, with reddish-brown hair, eyes and mustache. Though a man of middle age, his trim figure, his fashionable dress, and his clean shaven cheek and chin gave him an appearance of youth. He was president of the local jockey club, and the joy of

his life was to take his place in the judges' stand,
and sway the destinies of the lean, keen-faced train-
ers who drove the trotting horses. He had the eye
of a lynx for the detection of any crookedness in
driving, and his voice would ring out over the track
like the trump of doom, conveying fines and penal-
ties to the luckless trickster who was trying to get
some unfair advantage in the start. His voice, a
deep basso, rarely was heard, in fact, anywhere else.
Though excessively social, he was also extremely silent. He gave delightful dinner-parties and a great
many of them, but rarely spoke, except to recom-
mend an especially desirable wine to a favored guest.
When he did speak, however, his profanity was
phenomenal. Every second word was an oath. To
those who were not shocked by it there was nothing
more droll and incongruous than to hear this quiet,
reserved, well-dressed, gentleman-like person pouring out, on the rare occasions when he talked freely,
in a deep, measured, monotonous tone, a flood of
imprecations which would have made a pirate hang
his head. He had been, as a boy, clerk on a Mississippi River steamboat, and a vacancy occurring in
the office of mate, he had been promoted to that
place. His youthful face and quiet speech did not
sufficiently impose upon the rough deck-hands of
that early day. They had been accustomed to
harsher modes of address, and he saw his authority
defied and in danger. So he set himself seriously
to work to learn to swear; and though at first it
made his heart shiver a little with horror and his
cheek burn with shame, he persevered, as a matter
of business, until his execrations amazed the rousta-

bouts. When he had made a fortune, owned a line of steamboats, and finally retired from the river, the habit had been fastened upon him, and oaths became to him the only form of emphatic speech. The hardest work he ever did in his life was, while courting his wife, a Miss Flora Ballston, of Cincinnati, to keep from mingling his ordinary forms of emphasis in his asseverations of affection. But after he was married, and thrown more and more into the company of women, that additional sense, so remarkable in men of his mould, came to him, and he never lapsed, in their presence, into his natural way of speech. Perhaps this was the easier, as he rarely spoke at all when they were by—not that he was in the least shy or timid, but because they, as a rule, knew nothing about stocks, or pig-iron, or wine, or trotting horses,—the only subjects, in his opinion, which could interest any reasonable creature.

When Farnham arrived at his house, it was already pretty well filled with guests. Mr. and Mrs. Temple were at the door, shaking hands with their friends as they arrived, she with a pleasant smile and word from her black eyes and laughing mouth, and he in grave and speechless hospitality.

" Good-evening, Mr. Farnham!" said the good-natured lady. "So glad to see you. I began to be alarmed. So did the young ladies. They were afraid you had not returned. Show yourself in the drawing-room and dispel their fears. Oh, Mr. Harrison, I am so glad you resolved to stay over."

Farnham gave way to the next comer, and said to Mr. Temple, who had pressed his hand in silence:

"Did you want to see me for anything special
to-day?"

Mrs. Temple looked up at the word, and her
husband said:

"No; I merely wanted you to take a drive with
me."

Another arrival claimed Mrs. Temple's attention,
and as Farnham moved away, Temple half-whis-
pered in his ear, "Don't go away till I get a chance
to speak to you. There is merry and particular
bloom of h— to pay."

The phrase, while vivid, was not descriptive, and
Farnham could not guess what it meant. Perhaps
something had gone wrong in the jockey club;
perhaps Goldsmith Maid was off her feed; perhaps
pig-iron had gone up or down a dollar a ton.
These were all subjects of profound interest to
Temple and much less to Farnham; so he waited
patiently the hour of revelation, and looked about
the drawing-room to see who was there.

It was the usual drawing-room of provincial cities.
The sofas and chairs were mostly occupied by married women, who drew a scanty entertainment
from gossip with each other, from watching the
proceedings of the spinsters, and chiefly, perhaps,
from a consciousness of good clothes. The married
men stood grouped in corners and talked of their
every-day affairs. The young people clustered together in little knots, governed more or less by natural selection—only the veterans of several seasons
pairing off into the discreet retirement of stairs and
hall angles. At the further end of the long drawing-room, Farnham's eyes at last lighted upon the

object of his quest.   Alice sat in the midst of a
group of young girls who had intrenched themselves
in a corner of the room, and defied all the efforts of
skirmishing youths, intent upon flirtation, to dislodge
them.   They seemed to be amusing themselves
very well together, and the correct young men in
white cravats and pointed shoes came, chatted, and
drifted away.   They were the brightest and gayest
young girls of the place ; and it would have been
hard to detect any local color in them.   Young as
they were, they had all had seasons in Paris and in
Washington ; some of them knew the life of that
most foreign of all capitals, New York.   They nearly
all spoke French and German better than they did
English, for their accent in those languages was
very sweet and winning in its incorrectness, while
their English was high-pitched and nasal, and a little too loud in company.   They were as pretty as
girls are anywhere, and they wore dresses designed
by Mr. Worth, or his New York rivals, Loque and
Chiffon ; but they occasionally looked across the
room with candid and intelligent envy at maidens
of less pretensions, who were better dressed by the
local artists.

Farnham was stopped at some distance from the
pretty group by a buxom woman standing near the
open window, cooling the vast spread of her bare
shoulders in a current of air, which she assisted in
its office with a red-and-gold Japanese fan.

"Captain Farnham," she said, "when are you
going to give that lawn-tennis party you promised
so long ago ?   My character for veracity depends
on it.   I have told everybody it would be soon,

and I shall be disgraced if it is delayed much longer."

"That is the common lot of prophets, Mrs. Adipson," replied Farnham. "You know they say in Wall Street that early and exclusive information will ruin any man. But tell me, how is your club getting on?" he continued disingenuously, for he had not the slightest interest in the club; but he knew that once fairly started on the subject, Mrs. Adipson would talk indefinitely, and he might stand there and torture his heart and delight his eyes with the beauty of Alice Belding.

He carried his abstraction a little too far, however, for the good lady soon perceived, from his wandering looks and vague replies, that she was not holding his attention. So she pettishly released him after following the direction of his eyes, and said, "There, I see you are crazy to go and talk to Miss Dallas. I won't detain you. She *is* awfully clever, I suppose, though she never took the trouble to be brilliant in my presence; and she is pretty when she wears her hair that way—I never liked those frizzes."

Farnham accepted his release with perhaps a little more gratitude than courtesy, and moved away to take a seat which had just been vacated beside Miss Dallas. He was filled with a boyish delight in Mrs. Adipson's error. "That she should think I was worshipping Miss Dallas from afar! Where do women keep their eyes? To think that anybody should look at Miss Dallas when Alice Belding was sitting beside her." It was pleasant to think, however, that the secret of his unhappy love was safe.

Nobody was gossiping about it, and using the name of his beloved in idle conjectures. That was as it should be. His love was sacred from rude comment. He could go and sit by Miss Dallas, so near his beloved that he could see every breath move the lace on her bosom. He could watch the color come and go on her young cheek. He could hear every word her sweet voice uttered, and nobody would know he was conscious of her existence.

Full of this thought, he sat down by Miss Dallas, who greeted him warmly and turned her back upon her friends. By looking over her shining white shoulder, he could see the clear, pure profile of Alice just beyond, so near that he could have laid his hand on the crinkled gold of her hair. He then gave himself up to that duplex act to which all unavowed lovers are prone—the simultaneous secret worship of one woman and open devotion to another. It never occurred to him that there was anything unfair in this, or that it would be as reprehensible to throw the name of Miss Dallas into the arena of gossip as that of Miss Belding. That was not his affair; there was only one person in the universe to be considered by him. And for Miss Dallas's part, she was the last person in the world to suspect any one of being capable of the treason and bad taste of looking over her shoulder at another woman. She was, by common consent, the belle of Buffland. Her father was a widowed clergyman, of good estate, of literary tendencies, of enormous personal vanity, who had abandoned the pulpit in a quarrel with his session several years before, and now occupied himself in writing poems and sketches of an amorous and pietistic nature, which in his opinion embodied the best qualities of Swinburne and Chalmers combined, but which the magazines had thus far steadily refused to print.

He felt himself infinitely superior to the society of Buffland,—with one exception,—and only remained there because his property was not easily negotiable and required his personal care. The one exception was his daughter Euphrasia. He had educated her after his own image. In fact, there was a remarkable physical likeness between them, and he had impressed upon her every trick of speech and manner and thought which characterized himself. This is the young lady who turns her bright, keen, beautiful face upon Farnham, with eyes eager to criticise, a tongue quick to flatter and to condemn, a head stuffed full of poetry and artificial passion, and a heart saved from all danger by its idolatry of her father and herself.

"So glad to see you—one sees so little of you— I can hardly believe my good fortune—how have I this honor?" All this in hard, rapid sentences, with a brilliant smile.

Farnham thought of the last words of Mrs. Adipson, and said, intrepidly, "Well, you know the poets better than I do, Miss Euphrasia, and there is somebody who says, 'Beauty draws us by the simple way she does her hair'—or something like it. That classic fillet was the first thing I saw as I entered the room, and *me voici!*"

We have already said that the fault of Farnham's conversation with women was the soldier's fault of direct and indiscriminate compliment. But this

12

was too much in Euphrasia's manner for her to object to it. She laughed and said, "You deserve a
pensum of fifty lines for such a misquotation. But,
dites-donc, monsieur"—for French was one of her
favorite affectations, and when she found a man to
speak it with, she rode the occasion to death. There
had been a crisis in the French ministry a few days
before, and she now began a voluble conversation
on the subject, ostensibly desiring Farnham's opinion on the crisis, but really seizing the opportunity
of displaying her familiarity with the names of the
new cabinet. She talked with great spirit and ani-
mation, sometimes using her fine eyes point-blank
upon Farnham, sometimes glancing about to observe
the effect she was creating; which gave Farnham
his opportunity to sigh his soul away over her shoulder to where Alice was sweetly and placidly talking
with her friends.

She had seen him come in, and her heart had
stood still for a moment; but her feminine instinct
sustained her, and she had not once glanced in his
direction. But she was conscious of every look and
action of his; and when he approached the corner
where she was sitting, she felt as if a warm and
embarrassing ray of sunshine was coming near her.
She was at once relieved and disappointed when he
sat down by Miss Dallas. She thought to herself:
"Perhaps he will never speak to me again. It is all
my fault. I threw him away. But it was not my
fault. It was his—it was hers. I do not know
what to think. He might have let me alone. I
liked him so much. I have only been a month out
of school. What shall I do if he never speaks to

me again ?" Yet such is the power which, for self-
defence, is given to young maidens that, while these
tumultuous thoughts were passing through her
mind, she talked and laughed with the girls beside
her, and exchanged an occasional word with the
young men in pointed shoes, as if she had never
known a grief or a care.

Mr. Furrey came up to say good-evening, with
his most careful bow. Lowering his voice, he said:
" There's Miss Dallas and Captain Farnham flirting in Italian."

" Are you sure they are flirting ?"

"Of course they are. Just look at them !"

" If you are sure they are flirting, I don't think it
is right to look at them. Still, if you disapprove of
it very much, you might speak to them about it,"
she suggested, in her sweet, low, serious voice.

" Oh, that would never do for a man of my age,"
replied Furrey, in good faith. He was very vain
of his youth.

" What I wanted to speak to you about was this,"
he continued. " There is going to be a Ree-gatta
on the river the day after to-morrow, and I hope
you will grant me the favor of your company. The
Wissagewissametts are to row with the Chippago-
waxems, and it will be the finest race this year.
Billy Raum, you know, is stroke of the———"

Her face was still turned to him, but she had
ceased to listen. She was lost in contemplation of
what seemed to her a strange and tragic situation.
Farnham was so near that she could touch him, and
yet so far away that he was lost to her forever. No
human being knew, or ever would know, that a few

days ago he had offered her his life, and she had refused the gift. Nobody in this room was surprised that he did not speak to her, or that she did not look at him. Nobody dreamed that he loved her, and she would die, she resolved deliberately, before she would let anybody know that she loved him. "For I do love him with my whole heart," she said to herself, with speechless energy, which sent the blood up to her temples, and left her, in another instant, as pale as a lily.

Furrey at that moment had concluded his enticing account of the regatta, and she had quietly declined to accompany him. He moved away, indignant at her refusal, and puzzled by the blush which accompanied it.

"What did that mean?" he mused. "I guess it was because I said the crews rowed in short sleeves."

Farnham also saw the blush, in the midst of a disquisition which Miss Dallas was delivering upon a new poem of François Coppée. He saw the clear, warm color rise and subside like the throbbing of an auroral light in a starry night. He thought he had never seen anything so lovely, but he wondered "what that oaf could have said to make her blush like that. Can it be possible that he——" His brow knitted with anger and contempt.

"*Mais, qu'est-ce que vous avez donc?*" asked Euphrasia.

Farnham was saved from the necessity of an explanation by Mr. Temple, who came up at that moment, and, laying a hand on Arthur's shoulder, said:

"Now we will go into my den and have a glass

of that sherry. I know no less temptation than Tio
Pepe could take you away from Miss Dallas."

"Thank you awfully," said the young lady.
"Why should you not give Miss Dallas herself an
opportunity to decline the Tio Pepe?"

"Miss Dallas shall have some champagne in a few
minutes, which she will like very much better.
Age and wickedness are required to appreciate
sherry."

"Ah! I congratulate your sherry; it is about to
be appreciated," said the deserted beauty, tartly, as
the men moved away.

They entered the little room which Temple called
his den, which was a litter of letter-books, stock-lists,
and the advertising pamphlets of wine-merchants.
The walls were covered with the portraits of trotting horses; a smell of perpetual tobacco was in the
air. Temple unlocked a cupboard, and took out a
decanter and some glasses. He filled two, and gave
one to Arthur, and held the other under his nose.

"Farnham," he said, with profound solemnity,
"if you don't call that the"—(I decline to follow
him in the pyrotechnical combination of oaths with
which he introduced the next words)—"best sherry
you ever saw, then I'm a converted pacer with the
ringbone."

Arthur drank his wine, and did not hesitate to
admit all that its owner had claimed for it. He
had often wondered how such a man as Temple had
acquired such an unerring taste.

"Temple," he said, "how did you ever pick up
this wine; and, if you will excuse the question, how
did you know it when you got it?"

Temple smiled, evidently pleased with the question. "You've been in Spain, haven't you?"

"Yes," said Farnham.

"You know this is the genuine stuff, then?"

"No doubt of it."

"*How* do you know?"

"The usual way—by seeing and drinking it at the tables of men who know what they are about."

"Well, I have never been out of the United States, and yet I have learned about wine in just the same way. I commenced in New Orleans among the old Spanish and French creoles, and have kept it up since, here and there. I can see in five minutes whether a man knows anything about his wine. If he does, I remember every word he says —that is my strong point—head and tongue. I can't remember sermons and speeches, but I can remember every syllable that Sam Ward said one night at your grandfather's ten years ago; and if I have once tasted a good wine, I never forget its fashion of taking hold."

This is an expurgated edition of what he said; his profanity kept up a running accompaniment, like soft and distant rolling thunder.

"I got this wine at the sale of the Marquis of Santa Rita. I heard you speak of him, I don't know how long ago, and the minute I read in the paper that he had turned up his toes, I cabled the consul at Cadiz—you know him, a wild Irishman named Calpin—to go to the sale of his effects and get this wine. He cabled back, 'What shall I pay?' I answered, 'Read your dispatch again: Get means get!' Some men have got no sense. I did not mind the price of the wine, but it riled me to have to pay for the two cables."

He poured out another glass and drank it drop by drop, getting, as he said, "the worth of his money every time."

"Have some more?" he said to Farnham.

"No, thank you."

"Then I'll put it away. No use of giving it to men who would prefer sixty-cent whiskey."

Having done this, he turned again to Farnham, and said, "I told you the Old Boy was to pay. This is how. The labor unions have ordered a general strike; day not fixed; they are holding meetings all over town to-night. I'll know more about it after midnight."

"What will it amount to?" asked Farnham.

"Keen savey?" replied Temple, in his Mississippi River Spanish. "The first thing will be the closing of the mills, and putting anywhere from three thousand to ten thousand men on the streets. Then, if the strike gains the railroad men, we shall be embargoed, —— boiling, and safety-valve riveted down."

Farnham had no thought of his imperilled interests. He began instantly to conjecture what possibility of danger there might be of a disturbance of public tranquillity, and to wish that the Beldings were out of town.

"How long have you known this?" he asked.

"Only certainly for a few hours. The thing has been talked about more or less for a month, but we have had our own men in the unions and did not believe it would come to an extremity. To-day,

however, they brought ugly reports; and I ought
to tell you that some of them concern you."

Farnham lifted his eyebrows inquiringly.

" We keep men to loaf with the tramps and sleep
in the boozing kens. One of them told me to-day
that at the first serious disturbance a lot of bad eggs
among the strikers—not the unionists proper, but a
lot of loose fish—intend to go through some of the
principal houses on Algonquin Avenue, and they
mentioned yours as one of them."

" Thank you. I will try to be ready for them,"
said Farnham. But, cool and tried as was his courage, he could not help remembering, with something
like dread, that Mrs. Belding's house was next to his
own, and that in case of riot the two might suffer
together.

" There is one thing more I wanted to say," Mr.
Temple continued, with a slight embarrassment.
" If I can be of any service to you, in case of a row,
I want to be allowed to help."

" As to that," Farnham said with a laugh, " you
have your own house and stables to look after, which
will probably be as much as you can manage."

" No," said Temple, earnestly, " that ain't the case.
I will have to explain to you"—and a positive blush
came to his ruddy face. " They won't touch me or
my property. They say a man who uses such good
horses and such bad language as I do—that's just
what they say—is one of them, and sha'n't be rack-
eted. I ain't very proud of my popularity, but I
am willing to profit by it and I'll come around and
see you if anything more turns up. Now, we'll go
and give Phrasy Dallas that glass of champagne."

XII.

A HOLIDAY NOT IN THE CALENDAR.

THE next morning while Farnham was at breakfast he received a note from Mr. Temple in these words:

"Strikes will begin to-day, but will not be general. There will be no disturbance, I think. They don't seem very gritty."

After breakfast he walked down to the City Hall. On every street corner he saw little groups of men in rather listless conversation. He met an acquaintance crossing the street.

"Have you heard the news?" The man's face was flushed with pleasure at having something to tell. "The firemen and stokers have all struck, and run their engines into the round-house at Riverley, five miles out. There won't be a train leave or come in for the present."

"Is that all?"

"No, that ain't a start. The Model Oil men have struck, and are all over the North End, shutting up the other shops. They say there won't be a lick of work done in town the rest of the week."

"Except what Satan finds for idle hands," Farnham suggested, and hastened his steps a little to the municipal buildings.

He found the chief of police in his office, suffering from nervousness and a sense of importance.

He began by reminding him of the occurrence of the week before in the wood. The chief waited with an absent expression for the story to end, and then said, "My dear sir, I cannot pay any attention to such little matters with anarchy threatening our city. I must protect life and property, sir—life and property."

"Very well," rejoined Farnham, "I am informed that life and property are threatened in my own neighborhood. Can you detail a few policemen to patrol Algonquin Avenue, in case of a serious disturbance?"

"I can't tell you, my dear sir; I will do the best I can by all sections. Why, man," he cried, in a voice which suddenly grew a shrill falsetto in his agitation, "I tell you I haven't a policeman for every ten miles of street in this town. I can't spare but two for my own house!"

Farnham saw the case was hopeless, and went to the office of the mayor. That official had assumed an attitude expressive of dignified and dauntless energy. He sat in a chair tilted back on its hind feet; the boots of the municipal authority were on a desk covered with official papers; a long cigar adorned his eloquent lips; a beaver hat shaded his eyes.

He did not change his attitude as Farnham entered. He probably thought it could not be changed for the better.

"Good-morning, Mr. Quinlin."

"Good-morning, sirr, to you." This salutation was uttered through teeth shut as tightly as the integrity of the cigar would permit.

" There is a great deal of talk of possible disturbance to-night, in case the strikes extend. My own
neighborhood, I am told, has been directly threatened. I called to ask whether, in case of trouble, I
could rely on any assistance from the city authorities, or whether we must all look out for ourselves."

The mayor placed his thumbs in the arm-holes of
his waistcoat, and threw his head back so that he
could stare at Farnham from below his hat brim.
He then said, in a measured voice, as if addressing
an assembly : " Sirr ! I would have you to know
that the working-men of Buffland are not thieves
and robbers. In this struggle with capital they
have my profound sympathy. I expect their conduct to be that of perr-fect gentlemen. I, at least,
will give no orders which may tend to array one
class of citizens against another. That is my answer, sirr ; I hope it does not disappoint you."

" Not in the least," said Farnham, putting on his
hat. " It is precisely what I should have expected
of you."

" Thank you, sirr. Call again, sirr."

As Farnham disappeared, the chief magistrate of
the city tilted his hat to one side, shut an eye with
profoundly humorous significance, and said to the
two or three loungers who had been enjoying the
scene :

" That is the sort of T-rail I am. That young
gentleman voted agin me, on the ground I wasn't
high-toned enough."

Farnham walked rapidly to the office of the evening newspaper. He found a man in the counting-
room, catching flies and trimming their wings with

a large pair of office shears. He said, " Can you put an advertisement for me in your afternoon editions ?"

The man laid down his shears, but held on to his fly, and looked at his watch.

" Have you got it ready?"

" No, but I will not be a minute about it."

" Be lively ! You haven't got but a minute."

He picked up his scissors and resumed his surgery, while Farnham wrote his advertisement. The man took it, and threw it into a tin box, blew a whistle, and the box disappeared through a hole in the ceiling. A few minutes later the boys were crying the paper in the streets. The advertisement was in these words :

"Veterans, Attention! All able-bodied veterans of the Army of the Potomac, and especially of the Third Army Corps, are requested to meet at seven this evening, at No. — Public Square."

From the newspaper office Farnham went to a gunsmith's. The dealer was a German and a good sportsman, whom Farnham knew very well, having often shot with him in the marshes west of the city. His name was Leopold Grosshammer. There were two or three men in the place when Farnham entered. He waited until they were gone, and then said :

" Bolty, have you two dozen repeating rifles ?"

" Ja wohl! Aber, Herr Gott, was machen Sie denn damit?"

" I don't know why I shouldn't tell you. They think there may be a riot in town, and they tell me at the City Hall that everybody must look out for himself. I am going to try to get up a little company of old soldiers for patrol duty."

"All right, mine captain, and I will be the first freiwilliger. But I don't dink you wants rifles. Revolvers and clubs—like the pleecemen—dat's de dicket."

"Have you got them?"

"Oh, yes, and the belts thereto. I got der gondract to furnish 'em to de city."

"Then you will send them, wrapped up in bundles, to my office in the Square, and come yourself there at seven."

"Freilich," said Leopold, his white teeth glistening through his yellow beard at the prospect of service.

Farnham spent an hour or two visiting the proprietors of the large establishments affected by the strikes. He found, as a rule, great annoyance and exasperation, but no panic. Mr. Temple said, "The poor —— fools! I felt sorry for them. They came up here to me this morning,—their committee, they called it,—and told me they hated it, but it was orders! 'Orders from where?' I asked. 'From the chiefs of sections,' they said; and that was all I could get out of them. Some of the best fellows in the works were on the committee. They put 'em there on purpose. The sneaks and lawyers hung back."

"What will they do if the strike should last?" asked Farnham.

"They will be supported for awhile by the other mills. Our men are the only ones that have struck so far. They were told off to make the move, just as they march out a certain regiment to charge a battery. If we give in, then another gang will strike."

"Do you expect to give in?"

"Between us, we want nothing better than ten days' rest. We want to repair our furnaces, and we haven't a —— thing to do. What I told you this morning holds good. There won't be any riot. The whole thing is solemn fooling, so far."

The next man Farnham saw was in a far less placid frame of mind. It was Jimmy Nelson, the largest grocer in the city. He had a cargo of perishable groceries at the station, and the freight hands would not let them be delivered. "I talked to the rascals," he said. "I asked them what they had against *me;* that they was injuring Trade!" a deity of which Mr. Nelson always spoke with profound respect. "They laughed in my face, sir. They said, "That's just our racket. We want to squeeze you respectable merchants till you get mad and hang a railroad president or two!" Yes, sir; they said that to me, and five thousand dollars of my stuff rotting in the depot."

"Why don't you go to the mayor?" asked Farnham, though he could not suppress a smile as he said it.

"Yes, I like that!" screamed Jimmy. "You are laughing at me. I suppose the whole town has heard of it. Well, it's a fact. I went and asked that infernal scoundrel what he was going to do. He said his function was to keep the peace, and there wasn't a word in the statutes about North Carliny water-melons. If I live till he gets out of office, I'll lick him."

"Oh, I think you won't do that, Jimmy."

"You think I won't!" said Nelson, absolutely incandescent with the story of his wrongs. "I'll swear by Matthew, Mark, Luke, and John, that I will thrash the hide off him next spring—if I don't forget it."

Farnham went home, mounted his horse, and rode about the city to see what progress the strike was making. There was little disorder visible on the surface of things. The "sections" had evidently not ordered a general cessation of labor; and yet there were curious signs of demoralization, as if the spirit of work was partially disintegrating and giving way to something not precisely lawless, but rather listless. For instance, a crowd of workmen were engaged industriously and, to all appearance, contentedly upon a large school-building in construction. A group of men, not half their number, approached them and ordered them to leave off work. The builders looked at each other and then at their exhorters in a confused fashion for a moment, and ended by obeying the summons in a sullen and indifferent manner. They took off their aprons, went to the hydrant and washed their hands, then put on their coats and went home in silence and shamefacedness, amid the angry remonstrances of the master-builder. A little farther on Farnham saw what seemed like a burlesque of the last performance. Several men were at work in a hole in the street; the tops of their heads were just visible above the surface. A half-grown, ruffianly boy, with a boot-black's box slung over his shoulder, came up and shouted, "You —— —— rats, come out of

that, or we'll knock the scalps off'n you." The
men, without even looking to see the source of the
summons, threw down their tools and got out of the
hole. The boy had run away; they looked about
for a moment, as if bewildered, and then one of
them, a gray-headed Irishman, said, "Well, we'd
better be a lavin' off, if the rest is," and they all
went away.

In this fashion it came about that by nightfall all
the squares and public places were thronged with
an idle and expectant crowd, not actively mischiev-
ous or threatening, but affording a vast mass of in-
flammable material in case the fire should start in
any quarter. They gathered everywhere in dense
groups, exchanging rumors and surmises, in which
fact and fiction were fantastically mingled.

"The rolling-mills all close to-morrow," said a
sallow and hollow-eyed tailor. "That'll let loose
twenty thousand men on the town,—big, brawny
fellows. I'm glad my wife is in Clairfield."

"All you know about it! Clairfield is twice as
bad off as here. The machine shops has all struck
there, and the men went through the armory this
afternoon. They're camped all along Delaware
street, every man with a pair of revolvers and a
musket."

"You don't say so!" said the schneider, turning
a shade more sallow. "I'd better telegraph my
wife to come home."

"I wouldn't hurry," was the impassive response.
"You don't know where we'll be to-morrow. They
have been drilling all day at Riverley, three thousand of 'em. They'll come in to-morrow, mebbe,

and hang all the railroad presidents. That may make trouble."

Through these loitering and talking crowds Farnham made his way in the evening to the office which he kept, on the public square of the town, for the transaction of the affairs of his estate. He had given directions to his clerk to be there, and when he arrived found that some half-dozen men had already assembled in answer to his advertisement. Some of them he knew; one, Nathan Kendall, a powerful young man, originally from the north of Maine, now a machinist in Buffland, had been at one time his orderly in the army. Bolty Grosshammer was there, and in a very short time some twenty men were in the room. Farnham briefly explained to them his intention. "I want you," he said, "to enlist for a few days' service under my orders. I cannot tell whether there will be any work to do or not; but it is likely we shall have a few nights of patrol at least. You will get ten dollars apiece anyhow, and ordinary day's wages besides. If any of you get hurt, I will try to have you taken care of."

All but two agreed to the proposition. These two said "they had families and could not risk their skins. When they saw the advertisement they had thought it was something about pensions, or the county treasurer's office. They thought soldiers ought to have the first chance at good offices." They then grumblingly withdrew.

Farnham kept his men for an hour longer, arranging some details of organization, and then dismissed them for twenty-four hours, feeling assured that there would be no disturbance of public tranquillity

13

that night. " I will meet you here to-morrow evening," he said, " and you can get your pistols and
sticks and your final orders."

The men went out one by one, Bolty and Kendall
waiting for a while after they had gone and going
out on the sidewalk with Farnham. They had instinctively appointed themselves a sort of body-
guard to their old commander, and intended to keep
him in sight until he got home. As they reached
the door, they saw a scuffle going on upon the sidewalk. A well-dressed man was being beaten and
kicked by a few rough fellows, and the crowd was
looking on with silent interest. Farnham sprang
forward and seized one of the assailants by the collar ; Bolty pulled away another. The man who had
been cuffed turned to Kendall, who was standing
by to help where help was needed, and cried, " Take
me away somewhere ; they will have my life ;" an
appeal which only excited the jeers of the crowd.

" Kendall, take him into my office," said Farnham, which was done in an instant, Farnham and
Bolty following. A rush was made,—not very
vicious, however,—and the three men got safely
inside with their prize, and bolted the door. A
few kicks and blows shook the door, but there was
no movement to break it down ; and the rescued
man, when he found himself in safety, walked up to
a mirror there was in the room and looked earnestly
at his face. It was a little bruised and bloody, and
dirty with mud, but not seriously injured.

He turned to his rescuers with an air more of
condescension than gratitude. " Gentlemen, I owe
you my thanks, although I should have got the bet-

ter of those scoundrels in a moment. Can you assist
me in identifying them?"

"Oh! it is Mayor Quinlin, I believe," said Farnham, recognizing that functionary more by his voice
than by his rumpled visage. "No, I do not know
who they were. What was the occasion of this
assault?"

"A most cowardly and infamous outrage, sir,"
said the Mayor. "I was walking along the sidewalk to me home, and I came upon this gang of
ruffians at your door. Impatient at being delayed,
—for me time is much occupied,—I rebuked them
for being in me way. One of them turned to me
and insolently inquired, 'Do you own this street, or
have you just got a lien on it?' which unendurable
insult was greeted with a loud laugh from the other
ruffians. I called them by some properly severe
name, and raised me cane to force a passage,—and
the rest you know. Now, gentlemen, is there anything I can do?"

Farnham did not scruple to strike while the iron
was hot. He said: "Yes, there is one thing your
Honor may do, not so much for us as for the cause
of order and good government, violated to-night in
your own person. Knowing the insufficiency of the
means at your disposal, a few of us propose to raise
a subsidiary night-patrol for the protection of life
and property during the present excitement. We
would like you to give it your official sanction."

"Do I understand it will be without expense to
my—to the city government?" Mr. Quinlin was
anxious to make a show of economy in his annual
message.

"Entirely," Farnham assured him.

"It is done, sir. Come to-morrow morning and get what papers you want. The sperrit of disorder must be met and put down with a bold and defiant hand. Now, gentlemen, if there is a back door to this establishment, I will use it to make me way home."

Farnham showed him the rear entrance, and saw him walking homeward up the quiet street; and, coming back, found Bolty and Kendall writhing with merriment.

"Well, that beats all," said Kendall. "I guess I'll write home like the fellow did from Iowa to his daddy, 'Come out here quick. Mighty mean men gits office in this country.'"

"Yes," assented Bolty. "Dot burgermeister ish better as a circus mit a drick mule."

"Don't speak disrespectfully of dignitaries," said Farnham. "It's a bad habit in soldiers."

When they went out on the sidewalk the crowd had dispersed. Farnham bade his recruits good night and went up the avenue. They waited until he was a hundred yards away, and then, without a word to each other, followed him at that distance till they saw him enter his own gate.

XIII.

A BUSY SUNDAY FOR THE MATCHINS.

MATTERS were not going on pleasantly in the Matchin cottage. Maud's success in gaining an eligible position, as it was regarded among her friends, made her at once an object of greater interest than ever ; but her temper had not improved with her circumstances, and she showed herself no more accessible than before. Her father, who naturally felt a certain satisfaction at having, as he thought, established her so well, regarded himself as justified in talking to her firmly and seriously respecting her future. He went about it in the only way he knew. " Mattie," he said one evening, when they happened to be alone together, " when are you and Sam going to make a match ?"

She lifted her eyes to him, and shot out a look of anger and contempt from under her long lashes that made her father feel very small and old and shabby.

"Never !" she said, quietly.

" Come, come, now," said the old man ; " just listen to reason. Sam is a good boy, and with what he makes and what you make——"

" That has nothing to do with it. I won't discuss the matter any further. We have had it all out before. If it is ever mentioned again, Sam or I will leave this house."

" Hoity-toity, Missy ! is that the way you take

good advice——" but she was gone before he could say another word. Saul walked up and down the room a few moments, taking very short steps, and solacing his mind by muttering to himself: "Well, that's what I get by having a scholar in the family. Learning goes to the head and the heels—makes 'em proud and skittish."

He punctually communicated his failure to Sam, who received the news with a sullen quietness that perplexed still more the puzzled carpenter.

On a Sunday afternoon, a few days later, he received a visit from Mr. Bott, whom he welcomed, with great deference and some awe, as an ambassador from a ghostly world of unknown dignity. They talked in a stiff and embarrassed way for some time about the weather, the prospect of a rise in wages, and other such matters, neither obviously taking any interest in what was being said. Suddenly Bott drew nearer and lowered his voice, though the two were alone in the shop.

"Mr. Matchin," he said, with an uneasy grin, "I have come to see you about your daughter."

Matchin looked at him with a quick suspicion.

"Well, who's got anything to say against my daughter?"

"Oh, nobody that I know of," said Bott, growing suspicious in his turn. "Has anything ever been said against her?"

"Not as I know," said Saul. "Well, what *have* you got to say?"

"I wanted to ask how you would like me as a son-in-law?" said Bott, wishing to bring matters to a decision.

Saul stood for a moment without words in his astonishment. He had always regarded Bott as "a professional character," even as a "litrary man"; he had never hoped for so lofty an alliance. And yet he could not say that he wholly liked it. This was a strange creature—highly gifted, doubtless, but hardly comfortable. He was too "thick" with ghosts. One scarcely knew whether he spent most of his time "on earth or in hell," as Saul crudely phrased it. The faint smell of phosphorus that he carried about with him, which was only due to his imperfect ablutions after his séances, impressed Saul's imagination as going to show that Bott was a little too intimate with the under-ground powers. He stood chewing a shaving and weighing the matter in his mind a moment before he answered. He thought to himself, "After all, he is making a living. I have seen as much as five dollars at one of his seeunses." But the only reply he was able to make to Bott's point-blank question was:

"Well, I dunno."

The words were hardly encouraging, but the tone was weakly compliant. Bott felt that his cause was gained, and thought he might chaffer a little.

"Of course," he said, "I would like to have a few things understood, to start with. I am very particular in business matters."

"That's right," said Saul, who began to think that this was a very systematic and methodical man.

"I am able to support a wife, or I would not ask for one," said Bott.

"Exactly," said Saul, with effusion; "that's just what I was saying to myself."

"Oh, you was!" said Bott, scowling and hesitating. "You was, was you?" Then, after a moment's pause, in which he eyed Saul attentively, he continued, "Well—that's so. At the same time, I am a business man, and I want to know what you can do for your girl."

"Not much of anything, Mr. Bott, if you must know. Mattie is makin' her own living."

"Yes. That's all right. Does she pay you for her board?"

"Look here, Mr. Bott, that ain't none of your business yet, anyhow. She don't pay no board while she stays here; but that ain't nobody's business."

"Oh, no offence, sir, none in the world. Only I am a business man, and don't want misunderstandings. So she don't. And I suppose you don't want to part with your last child—now, do you? It's like breaking your heart-strings, now, ain't it?" he said, in his most sentimental lecture voice.

"Well, no, I can't say it is. Mattie's weelome in my house while I live, but of course she'll leave me some day, and I'll wish her joy."

"Why should that be? My dear sir, why should that be?" Bott's voice grew greasy with sweetness and persuasion. "Why not all live together? I will be to you as a son. Maud will soothe your declining years. Let it be as it is, Father Saul."

The old carpenter looked up with a keen twinkle of his eye.

"You and your wife would like to board with us when you are married? Well, mebbe we can arrange that."

This was not quite what Bott expected, but he

thought best to say no more on that subject for the moment.

Saul then asked the question that had all along been hovering on his lips.

"Have you spoke to Mattie yet?"

The seer blushed and simpered, "I thought it my duty to speak first to you; but I do not doubt her heart."

"Oh! you don't," said Saul, with a world of meaning. "You better find out. You'll find her in the house."

Bott went to the house, leaving Saul pondering. Girls were queer cattle. Had Mattie given her word to this slab-sided, lanky fellow? Had she given Sam Sleeny the mitten for him? Perhaps she wanted the glory of being Mrs. Professor Bott. Well, she could do as she liked; but Saul swore softly to himself, "If Bott comes to live offen me, he's got to pay his board."

Meanwhile, the seer was walking, not without some inward perturbation, to the house, where his fate awaited him. It would have been hard to find a man more confident and more fatuous; but even such fools as he have their moments of doubt and faltering when they approach the not altogether known. He had not entertained the slightest question of Maud's devotion to him, the night she asked from him the counsel of the spirits. But he had seen her several times since that, and she had never renewed the subject. He was in two minds about it. Sometimes he imagined she might have changed her purpose; and then he would comfort himself with the more natural supposition that maiden mod-

esty had been too much for her, and that she was
anxiously awaiting his proffer. He had at last
girded up his loins like a man and determined to
know his doom. He had first ascertained the
amount of Maud's salary at the library, and then, as
we see, had endeavored to provide for his subsist-
ence at Saul's expense; and now nothing was wanting but the maiden's consent. He trembled a little,
but it was more with hope than fear. He could not
make himself believe that there was any danger—
but he wished it were over and all were well. He
paused as he drew near the door. He was conscious
that his hands were disagreeably cold and moist.
He took out his handkerchief and wiped them, rubbing them briskly together, though the day was
clear and warm, and the perspiration stood beaded
on his forehead. But there was no escape. He
knocked at the door, which was opened by Maud in
person, who greeted him with a free and open kindness that restored his confidence. They sat down
together, and Maud chatted gayly and pleasantly
about the weather and the news. A New York
girl, the daughter of a wealthy furrier, was reported
in the newspaper as about to marry the third son of
an English earl. Maud discussed the advantages of
the match on either side as if she had been the
friend from childhood of both parties.

Suddenly, while she was talking about the forth-
coming wedding, the thought occurred to Bott,
"Mebbe this is a hint for me," and he plunged into
his avowal. Turning hot and cold at once, and
wringing his moist hands as he spoke, he said, taking
everything for granted:

"Miss Maud, I have seen your father and he gives his consent, and you have only to say the word to make us both happy."

"What?"

Anger, surprise, and contempt were all in the one word and in the flashing eyes of the young woman, as she leaned back in her rocking-chair and transfixed her unhappy suitor.

"Why, don't you understand me? I mean——"

"Oh, yes, I see what you mean. But I *don't* mean; and if you had come to me, I'd have saved you the trouble of going to my father."

"Now, look here," he pleaded, "you ain't a-going to take it that way, are you? Of course, I'd have come to you first if I had 'a' thought you'd preferred it. All I wanted was——"

"Oh," said Maud, with perfect coolness and malice,—for in the last moment she had begun heartily to hate Bott for his presumption,—"I understand what *you* want. But the question is what *I* want —and I don't want you."

The words, and still more the cold monotonous tone in which they were uttered, stung the dull blood of the conjurer to anger. His mud-colored face became slowly mottled with red.

"Well, then," he said, "what did you mean by coming and consulting the sperrits, saying you was in love with a gentleman——"

Maud flushed crimson at the memory awakened by these words. Springing from her chair, she opened the door for Bott, and said, "Great goodness! the impudence of some men! You thought I meant *you?*"

Bott went out of the door like a whipped hound, with pale face and hanging head. As he passed by the door of the shop, Saul hailed him and said with a smile, "What luck?"

Bott did not turn his head. He growled out a deep imprecation and walked away. Matchin was hardly surprised. He mused to himself, "I thought it was funny that Mattie should sack Sam Sleeny for that fellow. I guess he didn't ask the sperrits how the land lay," chuckling over the discomfiture of the seer. Spiritualism is the most convenient religion in the world. You may disbelieve two-thirds of it and yet be perfectly orthodox. Matchin, though a pillar of the faith, always keenly enjoyed the defeat and rout of a medium by his tricksy and rebellious ghosts.

He was still laughing to himself over the retreat of Bott, thinking with some paternal fatuity of the attractiveness and spirit of his daughter, when a shadow fell across him, and he saw Offitt standing before him.

"Why, Offitt, is that you? I did not hear you. You always come up as soft as a spook!"

"Yes, that's me. Where's Sam?"

"Sam's gone to Shady Creek on an excursion with his lodge. My wife went with him."

"I wanted to see him. I think a heap of Sam."

"So do I. Sam is a good fellow."

"Excuse my making so free, Mr. Matchin, but I once thought Sam was going to be a son-in-law of yours."

"Well, betwixt us, Mr. Offitt, I hoped so myself. But you know what girls is. She jest wouldn't."

"So it's all done, is it? No chance for Sam?" Offitt asked eagerly.

"Not as much as you could hold sawdust in your eye," the carpenter answered.

"Well, now, Mr. Matchin, I have got something to say." ("Oh, Lordy," groaned Saul to himself, "here's another one.") "I wouldn't take no advantage of a friend; but if Sam's got no chance, as you say, why shouldn't I try? With your permission, sir, I will."

"Now look ye here, Mr. Offitt. I don't know as I have got anything against you, but I don't know nothing *fur* you. If it's a fair question, how do you make your livin'?"

"That's all right. First place, I have got a good trade. I'm a locksmith."

"So I have heard you say. But you don't work at it."

"No," Offitt answered; and then, assuming a confidential air, he continued, "As I am to be one of the family, I'll tell you. I don't work at my trade, because I have got a better thing. I am a Reformer."

"You don't say!" exclaimed Saul. "I never heard o' your lecturin'."

"I don't lecture. I am secretary of a grand section of Labor Reformers, and I git a good salary for it."

"Oh, I see," said Saul, not having the least idea of what it all meant. But, like most fathers of his kind, he made no objection to the man's proposal, and told him his daughter was in the house. As Offitt walked away on the same quest where Bott had so recently come to wreck, Saul sat smiling, and nursing his senile vanity with the thought that there were not many mechanics' daughters in Buffland that could get two offers in one Sunday from "professional men." He sat with the contented inertness of old men on his well-worn bench, waiting to see what would be the result of the interview.

"I don't believe she'll have him," he thought. "He ain't half the man that Sam is, nor half the scholar that Bott is."

It was well he was not of an impatient temperament. He sat quietly there for more than an hour, as still as a knot on a branch, wondering why it took Offitt so much longer than Bott to get an answer to a plain question ; but it never once occurred to him that he had a right to go into his own house and participate in what conversation was going on. To American fathers of his class, the parlor is sacred when the daughter has company.

There were several reasons why Offitt stayed longer than Bott.

The seer had left Maud Matchin in a state of high excitement and anger. The admiration of a man so splay and ungainly was in itself insulting, when it became so enterprising as to propose marriage. She felt as if she had suffered the physical contact of something not clean or wholesome. Besides, she had been greatly stirred by his reference to her request for ghostly counsel, which had resulted in so frightful a failure and mortification. After Bott had gone, she could not dismiss the subject from her mind. She said to herself, "How

can I live, hating a man as I hate that Captain
Farnham? How can I breathe the same air with
him, blushing like a peony whenever I think of
him, and turning pale with shame when I hear his
name? That ever I should have been refused by a
living man! What *does* a man want," she asked,
with her head thrown back and her nostrils dilated,
"when he don't want me?"

As she was walking to and fro, she glanced out
of the window and saw Offitt approaching from the
direction of the shop. She knew instantly what
his errand would be, though he had never before
said a word to her out of the common. "I wonder
if father has sent him to me—and how many more
has he got in reserve there in the shop? Well, I
will make short work of this one."

But when he had come in and taken his seat, she
found it was not so easy to make short work of him.

Dealing with this one was very different from
dealing with the other—about the difference between handling a pig and a panther. Offitt was a
human beast of prey—furtive, sly, and elusive, with
all his faculties constantly in hand. The sight of
Maud excited him like the sight of prey. His small
eyes fastened upon her; his sinewy hands tingled
to lay hold of her. But he talked, as any casual
visitor might, of immaterial things.

Maud, while she chatted with him, was preparing
herself for the inevitable question and answer.
"What shall I say to him? I do not like him. I
never did. I never can. But what shall I do? A
woman is of no use in the world by herself. He is
not such a dunce as poor Sam, and is not such a

gawk as Bott. I wonder whether he would make me mind? I am afraid he would, and I don't know whether I would like it or not. I suppose if I married him I would be as poor as a crow all my days. I couldn't stand that. I won't have him. I wish he would make his little speech and go."

But he seemed in no hurry to go. He was talking volubly about himself, lying with the marvellous fluency which interest and practice give to such men, and Maud presently found herself listening intently to his stories. He had been in Mexico, it seemed. He owned a silver mine there. He got a million dollars out of it, but took it into his head one day to overturn the Government, and was captured and his money taken; barely escaped the garrote by strangling his jailer; owned the mine still, and should go back and get it some day, when he had accomplished certain purposes in this country. There were plenty of people who wished he was gone now. The President had sent for him to come to Washington; he went, and was asked to breakfast; nobody there but them two; they ate off gold plates like he used to in Mexico; the President then offered him a hundred thousand to leave, was afraid he would make trouble; told the President to make it a million and then he wouldn't. His grandfather was one of the richest men in Europe; his father ran away with his mother out of a palace. "You must have heard of my father, General Offitt, of Georgy? No? He was the biggest slaveholder in the State. I have got a claim against the Government, now, that's good for a million if it's worth a cent; going to Washington next winter to prosecute it."

Maud was now saying to herself, "Why, if half this is true, he is a remarkable man," like many other credulous people, not reflecting that, when half a man says is false, the other half is apt to be also. She began to think it would be worth her while, a red feather in her cap, to refuse such a picturesque person; and then it occurred to her that he had not proposed to marry her, and possibly had no such intention. As his stream of talk, dwelling on his own acts of valor and craft, ran on, she began to feel slightly piqued at its lack of reference to herself. Was this to be a mere afternoon call after all, with no combat and no victory? She felt drawn after awhile to bring her small resources of coquetry into play. She interrupted him with saucy doubts and questions; she cast at him smiles and glances, looking up that he might admire her eyes, and down that her lashes might have their due effect.

He interpreted all these signs in a favorable sense, but still prudently refrained from committing himself, until directly challenged by the blush and simper with which she said:

"I suppose you must have seen a great many pretty ladies in Mexico?"

He waited a moment, looking at her steadily until her eyelids trembled and fell, and then he said, seriously and gravely:

"I used to think so; but I never saw there or anywhere else as pretty a lady as I see at this minute."

This was the first time in her life that Maud had heard such words from a man. Sam Sleeny, with

14

all his dumb worship, had never found words to tell
her she was beautiful, and Bott was too grossly selfish and dull to have thought of it. Poor Sleeny,
who would have given his life for her, had not wit
enough to pay her a compliment. Offitt, whose
love was as little generous as the hunger of a tiger,
who wished only to get her into his power, who
cared not in the least by what means he should accomplish this, who was perfectly willing to have her
find out all his falsehoods the day after her wedding,
relying upon his brute strength to retain her then,
—this conscienceless knave made more progress by
these words than Sam by months of the truest devotion. Yet the impression he made was not altogether pleasant. Thirsting for admiration as she
did, there was in her mind an indistinct consciousness that the man was taking a liberty; and in the
sudden rush of color to her cheek and brow at Offitt's words, there was at first almost as much anger
as pleasure. But she had neither the dignity nor
the training required for the occasion, and all the
reply she found was:

"Oh, Mr. Offitt, how can you say so?"

"I say so," he answered, with the same unsmiling gravity, "because it's the fact. I have been all
over the world. I have seen thousands of beautiful
ladies, even queens and markisses, and I never yet
saw and I never expect to see such beauty as yours,
Miss Maud Matchin, of Buffland."

She still found no means to silence him or defend
herself. She said, with an uneasy laugh, "I am
sure I don't see where the wonderful beauty is."

"That's because your modesty holds over your

beauty. But I see where it is. It's in your eyes, that's like two stars of the night; in your forehead, that looks full of intellect and sense; in your rosy cheeks and smiling lips; in your pretty little hands and feet——" Here she suddenly rolled up her hands in her frilled white apron, and, sitting up straight, drew her feet under her gown. At this performance, they both laughed loud and long, and Maud's nerves were relieved.

"What geese we are," she said at last. "You know I don't believe a word you say."

"Oh, yes, you do. You've got eyes and a looking-glass. Come now, be honest. You know you never saw a girl as pretty as yourself, and you never saw a man that didn't love you on sight."

"I don't know about that."

"Don't all the men you know love you?"

"There is one man I know hates me, and I hate him."

"Who is it? This is very interesting."

Maud was suddenly seized with a desire to tell an adventure, something that might match Offitt's tales of wonder.

"You'll never tell?"

"Hope I may die."

"It's Arthur Farnham!" She had succeeded in her purpose, for Offitt stared at her with looks of amazement. "He once wanted to be rather too attentive to me, and I did not like it. So he hates me, and has tried to injure me."

"And you don't like him very well?"

"I don't. I would owe a good deal to the man who would give him a beating."

"All right. You give me—what?—a kiss, or a lock of your hair, and he shall have his thrashing."

"You do it and bring me the proofs, and we will talk about it."

"Well, I must be off," he said, picking up his hat. He saw on her face a slight disappointment. He put out his hand to take leave. She folded her arms.

"You needn't be in such a hurry," she said, poutingly. "Mother won't be back for ever so long, and I was half asleep over my book when you came in."

"Oh, very well," he said. "That suits me."

He walked deliberately across the room, picked up a chair, and seated himself very near to Maud. She felt her heart beat with something like terror, and regretted asking him to stay. He had been very agreeable, but she was sure he was going to be disagreeable now. She was afraid that if he grew disagreeable she could not manage him as she could the others. Her worst fears were realized with his first words.

"Miss Matchin, if you ask me to stay longer, you must take the consequences. I am going to say to you what I never said to mortal woman before: I love you, and I want you for my wife."

She tried to laugh. "Oh, you do?" but her face grew pale, and her hands trembled.

"Yes, I do; and I am going to have you, too."

He tried to speak lightly, but his voice broke in spite of him.

"Oh, indeed!" she replied, recovering herself with an effort. "Perhaps *I'll* have something to say about that, Mr. Confidence."

"Of course; excuse me for talking like a fool. Only have me, and you shall have everything else. All that wealth can buy shall be yours. We'll leave this dull place and go around the world seeking pleasure where it can be found, and everybody will envy me my beauteous bride."

"That's very pretty talk, Mr. Offitt; but where is all this wealth to come from?"

He did not resent the question, but heard it gladly, as imposing a condition he might meet. "The money is all right. If I lay the money at your feet, will you go with me? Only give me your promise."

"I promise nothing," said Maud; "but when you are ready to travel, perhaps you may find me in a better humor."

The words seemed to fire him. "That's promise enough for me," he cried, and put out his arms toward her. She struck down his hands, and protested with sudden, cattish energy:

"Let me alone. Don't you come so near me. I don't like it. Now you can go," she added. "I have got a lot to think about."

He thought he would not spoil his success by staying. "Good-by, then," he said, kissing his fingers to her. "Good-by for a little while, my own precious."

He turned at the door. "This is between us, ain't it?"

"Yes, what there is of it," she said, with a smile that took all sting from the words.

He walked to the shop, and wrung the old man's hand. His look of exultation caused Saul to say, "All settled, eh?"

"No," said Offitt; "but I have hopes. And now, Mr. Matchin, you know young ladies and the ways of the world. I ask you, as a gentleman, not to say nothing about this, for the present, to nobody."

Saul, proud of his secret, readily promised.

XIV.

CAPTAIN FARNHAM SEES ACTIVE SERVICE AGAIN.

FARNHAM lost no time in calling upon the Mayor
to fulfil his engagement. He found his Honor a
little subdued by the news of the morning. None
of the strikers of the day before had gone back to
work, and considerable accessions were reported
from other trades. The worst symptoms seemed to
be that many shops were striking without orders.
The cessation of work was already greater than
seemed at first contemplated by the leading agitators
themselves. They seemed to be losing their own
control of the workingmen, and a few tonguey va-
grants and convicts from the city and from neighboring towns, who had come to the surface from
nobody knew where, were beginning to exercise a
wholly unexpected authority. They were going
from place to place, haranguing the workmen,
preaching what they called socialism, but what was
merely riot and plunder. They were listened to
without much response. In some places the men
stopped work ; in others they drove out the agitators ; in others they would listen awhile, and then
shout, " Give us a rest !" or " Hire a hall !" or " Wipe
off your chin !" But all the while the crowds gradually increased in the streets and public places ; the
strike, if it promised nothing worse, was taking the

dimensions of a great, sad, anxious holiday. There was not the slightest intention on the part of the authorities to interfere with it, and to do them justice, it is hard to see what they could have done, with the means at their disposal. The Mayor, therefore, welcomed Farnham with great cordiality, made him a captain of police, for special duty, on the spot, and enrolled his list of recruits of the night before as members of the police force of the city, expressly providing that their employment should cost the city nothing, now or hereafter.

Farnham again made his rounds of the city, but found nothing especially noteworthy or threatening. The wide town, in spite of the large crowds in the streets, had a deserted look. A good many places of business were closed. There was little traffic of vehicles. The whistle of the locomotives and the rush of trains—sounds which had grown so familiar in that great railroad centre that the ear ceased to be affected by them—being suddenly shut off, the silence which came in their place was startling to the sense. The voices of the striking employees, who retained possession of the Union Passenger Depot, resounded strangely through the vast building, which was usually a babel of shrill and strident sounds.

On the whole, the feature which most struck him in this violent and unnatural state of things was the singular good-nature of almost all classes. The mass of the workingmen made no threats; the greater number of employers made no recriminations. All hoped for an arrangement, though no one could say how it was to come. The day passed away in fruitless parleys, and at night the fever naturally rose, as is the way of fevers.

When nightfall came, the crowd had become so great in the public square that Farnham thought it might be better not to march his improvised police-men in a body up-town. He therefore dispatched orders to Kendall to send them up with their arms, singly or by twos and threes, to his house. By eight o'clock they were all there, and he passed an hour or so in putting them through a rude form of drill and giving them the instructions which he had prepared during the day. His intention was to keep them together on his own place during the early part of the night, and if, toward midnight, all seemed quiet, to scatter them as a patrol about the neighbor-hood; in case of serious disturbance anywhere else, to be ready to take part in restoring order.

About nine o'clock a man was seen coming rapidly from the house to the rear garden, where Farnham and his company were. The men were dispersed about the place; some on the garden seats, some lying on the grass in the clear moonlight. Farnham was a little apart, talking with Kendall and Gross-hammer. He started up to meet the intruder; it was Mr. Temple.

"What's all this?" said Temple.

"The manly art of self-defence," said Farnham, smiling.

"I see, and I am glad to see it, too," answered Temple, warmly. "One of my men told me an hour ago that in the Tramps' Lodging House, last night, it was the common talk that there would be a rush on the houses in this region to-night. I went

to the Mayor and tried to see him, but he was hiding, I think. I went to the Chief of Police, and
he was in a blue funk. So I thought I would come
up myself and see you. I knew you could raise a
few men among your servants over here, and I
would bring half a dozen, and we could answer for
a few tramps, anyhow. But you are all right, and
there is nothing to do but wait for them."

"Yes, thank you!" said Farnham, "though I am
a thousand times obliged to you for your good-will.
I won't forget it in a hurry, old man. Are you going home now? I will walk a block or two with
you."

"No, I am not going home—not by"—[we draw
the veil over Temple's language at this point]. "I
have come to spend the evening. Have you any
tools for me?"

"Nonsense, my dear fellow! there is not the least
use of it. There is not one chance in a million that
there will be anything to do."

The two men were walking toward the house.
Temple said: "Don't be too sure of it. As I passed
by the corner of the Square ten minutes ago, there
was a fellow in front of Mouchem's gin-mill, a long-
haired, sallow-looking pill, who was making as ugly
a speech to a crowd of ruffians as I ever heard.
One phrase was something like this: 'Yes, my fel-
low-toilers'—he looked like he had never worked a
muscle in his life except his jaw-tackle,—'the time
has come. The hour is at hand. The people rule.
Tyranny is down. Enter in and take possession of
the spoilers' gains. Algonquin Avenue is heaped
with riches wrung from the sweat of the poor.

Clean out the abodes of blood guiltiness.' And you ought to have heard the ki-yi's that followed. That encouraged him, and he went on: 'Algonquin Avenue is a robbers' cave, It's very handsome, but it needs one thing more.' 'What's that?' some fellows yelled. 'An aristocrat hung to every lamp-post.' This was very popular too, you can bet your boots. On that I toddled off, so as to get you a chance to say your peccavy, anyhow."

Walking and talking together, they had passed the house and come to the gate opening on the Avenue.

"You might shut these wide gates," said Temple.

"I do not think they have been shut in ten years," Farnham answered. "Let's try it."

The effort was unsuccessful. The heavy gates would not budge. Suddenly a straggling, irregular cheer was heard from the direction of the Square. "There!" said Temple, "my friend the orator has got off another good thing."

But Farnham, who had stepped outside at the sound and gazed on the moon-lighted avenue, said, "There they come now!"

They both ran back to the house, Farnham blowing his watchman's whistle. "See here," said Temple, "I must have some tools. You have a club and revolver. Give me the club," which he took without more ceremony. The men came up from the garden in an instant, and quickly fell in at Farnham's word of command. Masked by the shadows of the trees and the shrubbery, they were not discernible from the street.

"Remember," said Farnham. "Use your clubs

as much as you see fit, if you come to close quarters;
but do not fire without orders, unless to save your
own lives. I don't think it is likely that these fellows are armed."

The clattering of feet grew louder on the sidewalk, and in a moment the leaders of the gang—it
could hardly be called a mob—stopped by the gates.
"Here's the place. Come along boys!" one of
them shouted, but no one stirred until the whole
party came up. They formed a dense crowd about
the gates and half-filled the wide avenue. There
was evidently a moment of hesitation, and then
three or four rushed through the gate, followed by
a larger number, and at last by the bulk of the
crowd. They had come so near the porch that it
could now be seen by the light of the moon that
few of them carried arms. Some had sticks; one
or two men carried heavy stones in their hands; one
young man brandished an axe; one had a hammer.
There was evidently no attempt at organization
whatever.

Farnham waited until they were only a few feet
away, and then shouted :

"Forward! Guide right! Double time! March!"

The men darted out from the shadow and began
to lay about them with their clubs. A yell of dismay burst from the crowd. Those in front turned
and met those behind, and the whole mass began
striking out wildly at each other. Yelling and curs-
ing, they were forced back over the lawn to the
gate. Farnham, seeing that no shots had been fired,
was confirmed in his belief that the rioters were
without organization and, to a great extent, without

arms. He therefore ordered his men to the right
about and brought them back to the house. This
movement evidently encouraged the mob. Loud
voices were distinctly heard.

"Who's afraid of half a dozen cops?" said a burly
ruffian, who carried a slung-shot. "There's enough
of us to eat 'em up."

"That's the talk, Bowersox," said another. "You
go in and get the first bite."

"That's my style," said Bowersox. "Come
along, Offitt. Where's Bott? I guess he don't feel
very well. Come along, boys! We'll slug 'em this
time!" And the crowd, inspirited by this exhortation and the apparent weakness of the police force,
made a second rush for the house.

Temple was standing next to Farnham. "Arthur," he whispered, "let's change weapons a moment," handing Farnham his club and taking the
revolver from his hand. Farnham hardly noticed
the exchange, so intently was he watching the advance of the crowd, which he saw, in a moment,
was far more serious than the first. They were
coming up more solidly, and the advantage of the
surprise was now gone. He waited, however, until
they were almost as near as they had been before,
and then gave the order to charge, in the same
words as before, but in a much sharper and louder
tone, which rang out like a sudden blast from a
trumpet.

The improvised policemen darted forward and
attacked as vigorously as ever, but the assailants
stood their ground. There were blows given as
well as taken this time. There was even a mo-

ment's confusion on the extreme right of the line, where the great bulk of Bowersox bore down one of the veterans. Farnham sprang forward and struck the burly ruffian with his club ; but his foot slipped on the grass, and he dropped on one knee. Bowersox raised his slung-shot ; a single report of a pistol rang out, and he tumbled forward over Farnham, who sprang to his feet and shouted, " Now, men, drive 'em!" Taking the right himself and profiting by the momentary shock of the shot, they got the crowd started again, and by vigorous clubbing drove them once more into the street.

Returning to the shadow by the house, Farnham's first question was, " Is anybody hurt ?"

" I've got a little bark knocked off," said one quiet fellow, who came forward showing a ghastly face bathed in blood from a wound in his forehead. Farnham looked at him a moment, and then, running to his door, opened it and called Budsey, who had been hiding in the cellar, praying to all his saints.

" Here, Budsey, take this man down to the coachman's house, and then go round the corner and bring Dr. Cutts. If he isn't there, get somebody else. It does not amount to much, but there will be less scar if it is attended to at once."

The man was starting away with Budsey, when Temple said, " Look here! You won't need that arsenal any more to-night. Pass it over," and took the man's belt, with club and pistol, and buckled them around his own slim waist. Handing Farnham his own pistol, he said : " Thanks, Arthur. I owe you one cartridge."

"And I owe you, God knows how much!"

Farnham then briefly announced to his men that the shot which had just been fired was not by a member of the company, and was, therefore, not a disobedience of orders. Catching sight of Bowersox lying motionless on the grass, he ordered,

"Two file-closers from the right, go and bring in that man!"

But at that moment Bowersox moved, sat up and looked about him, and, suddenly remembering where he was, struggled to his feet and half-ran, half staggered to his friends in the street. They gathered about him for a moment, and then two of them were seen supporting him on his way into the town.

Farnham was standing behind his men, and a little apart. He was thinking whether it might not be best to take them at once into the street and disperse the crowd, when he felt a touch at his elbow. He turned, and saw his gardener, Ferguson.

"If I might speak a word, sir!"

"Certainly—what is it? But be quick about it."

"I think all is not right at the Widow Belding's. I was over there but now, and a dozen men—I did not count them,—but—"

"Heavens! why did I not think of that? Kendall, you take command of these men for a moment. Bolty, you and the three files on the left come with me. Come, Temple,—the back way." And he started at a pace so rapid that the others could hardly keep him in sight.

After the first repulse of the crowd, Offitt, Bott, and a few more of the Bread-winners, together with some of the tramps and jail-birds who had come for plunder, gathered together across the street and agreed upon a diversion. It was evident, they said, that Farnham had a considerable police force with him to protect his property; it was useless to waste any more time there; let the rest stay there and occupy the police; they could have more fun and more profit in some of the good houses in the neighborhood. "Yes," one suggested, "Jairus Belding's widder lives just a step off. Lots o' silver and things. Less go there."

They slipped away in the confusion of the second rush, and made their way through the garden to Mrs. Belding's. They tried the door, and, finding it locked, they tore off the shutters and broke the windows, and made their way into the drawing-room, where Mrs. Belding and Alice were sitting.

They had been alarmed by the noise and tumult in front of Farnham's house, and had locked and bolted their own doors in consequence. Passing through the kitchen in their rounds, they found Ferguson there in conversation with the cook. "Why, Fergus!" said the widow: "why are you not at home? They are having lively times over there, are they not?"

"Yes," said the gardener; "but they have a plenty of men with arms, and I thought I'd e'en step over here and hearten up Bessie a bit."

"I'm sure she ought to be very much obliged," responded Mrs. Belding, dryly, though, to speak the truth, she was not displeased to have a man in the house, however little she might esteem his valor.

"I have no doubt he sneaked away from the fuss,"

she said to Alice; "but I would rather have him in the kitchen than nothing."

Alice assented. "That is what they mean by moral support, I suppose."

She spoke with a smile, but her heart was ill at ease. The man she loved was, for all she knew, in deadly danger, and she could not show that she cared at all for him, for fear of showing that she cared too much.

"I am really anxious about Arthur Farnham," continued Mrs. Belding. "I hope he will not get himself into any scrape with those men."

The tumult on the street and on the lawn had as yet presented itself to her in no worse light than as a labor demonstration, involving cheers and rude language. "I am afraid he won't be polite enough to them. He might make them a little speech, complimenting Ireland and the American flag, and then they would go away. That's what your father did, in that strike on the Wabash. It was in the papers at the time. But these soldiers—I'm afraid Arthur mayn't be practical enough."

"Fortunately, we are not responsible for him," said Alice, whose heart was beating violently.

"Why, Alice! what a heartless remark!"

At this instant the windows came crashing in, and a half-dozen ruffians burst into the room. Alice sprang, pale and silent, to the side of her mother, who sat, paralyzed with fright, in her rocking-chair.

A man came forward from the group of assailants. His soft hat was drawn down over his eyes, and a red handkerchief concealed the lower part of his face. His voice was that of Offitt, as he said,

15

" Ladies, we don't want to do no violence; but, in the name of the Revolutionary Committee, we have called to collect an assessment on you." This machinery was an invention of the moment, and was received with great satisfaction by the Bread-winners.

" That's what's the matter," they said, in chorus. " Your assessment, and be lively about it. All you've got handy."

" I have no money in the house," Mrs. Belding cried. " What shall I do ?"

" You forget, mamma," said Alice. " There is some upstairs. If these gentlemen will wait here a moment, I will go and get it."

Offitt looked at her sharply. " Well, run and get it. Bott, you go with her."

Bott turned angrily upon his chief. " What's the use of calling names? What if I said your name was——"

" There, there, don't keep the lady waiting."

Alice turned from the room, closely followed by Bott. Reaching the stairs, she swept up the long flight with the swift grace of a swallow. Bott hurried after her as fast as he could; but she gained her bedroom door enough in advance to shut and lock it between them, leaving him kicking and swearing in the hall. She ran to her open window, which looked toward Farnham's, and sent the voice of her love and her trouble together into the clear night in one loud cry, " Arthur !"

She blushed crimson as the word involuntarily broke from her lips, and cried again as loudly as she could, " Help !"

"I hope he did not hear me at first," she said, covering her face with her hands, and again she cried, "Help!"

"Shut up that noise," said Bott, who was kicking violently at the door, but could not break it down. "Shut up, or I'll wring your neck."

She stopped, not on account of his threats, which suddenly ceased, but because she heard the noise of footsteps on the porch, and of a short but violent scuffle, which showed that aid of some sort had arrived. In a few moments she heard Bott run away from her door. He started toward the stairs, but finding his retreat cut off ran to the front window, closely pursued. She heard a scramble. Then a voice which made her heart beat tumultuously said. "Look out below there."

A moment after, the same voice said, "Have you got him?" and then, "All right! keep him."

A light knock on her door followed, and Farnham said, "Miss Belding."

Alice stood by the door a moment before she could open it. Her heart was still thumping, her voice failed her, she turned white and red in a moment. The strongest emotion of which she was conscious was the hope that Arthur had not heard her call him by his name.

She opened the door with a gravity which was almost ludicrous. Her first words were wholly so.

"Good-evening, Captain Farnham," was all she could find to say. Then, striving desperately to add something more gracious, she stammered, "Mamma will be very——"

"Glad to see me in the drawing-room?" Farnham

laughed. "I have no doubt of it. She is quite safe there; and your visitors have gone. Will you join her now?"

She could not help perceiving the slight touch of sarcasm in his tone. She saw he was hurt by her coldness and shyness, and that made her still more cold and shy. Without another word she walked before him to the drawing-room, where Mrs. Belding still sat in her rocking-chair, moaning and wringing her hands. Mr. Temple was standing beside her trying to soothe her, telling her it was all over. Bolty was tying the arms of one of the ruffians behind him, who lay on the floor on his face. There was no one else in the room.

Alice knelt on the floor by her mother and took her in her arms. "You are not hurt, are you, mamma dear?" she said, in a soft, tender tone, as if she were caressing a crying child.

"Oh, no! I suppose not," said the widow; "but I am not used to such doings at this time of night, and I don't like them. Captain Farnham, how shall I ever thank you? and you, Mr. Temple? Goodness knows what we should have done without you. Alice, the moment you left the room, some of them ran to the sideboard for the silver, another one proposed to set the house afire, and that vile creature with the red handkerchief asked me for my ear-rings and my brooch. I was trying to be as long as I could about getting them off, when these gentlemen came in. I tell you they looked like angels, and I'll tell your wife so when I see her, Mr. Temple; and as for Arthur——"

At this moment Bolty, having finished the last

knot to his satisfaction, rose and touched his prisoner with his foot. "Captain," he said, saluting Farnham, "vot I shall do mit dis schnide?"

"They have got the one I dropped from the window?"

"Jawohl! on de gravel-walk draussen!"

"Very well. Take them both to the stable behind my house for the present, and make them fast together. Then come back here and stand guard awhile with the men on the porch, till I relieve you."

"All right. Git up mid yourself," he said, touching his prostrate foe not so gently, "and vorwaerts."

As they went out, Farnham turned to Mrs. Belding, and said, "I think you will have no more trouble. The men I leave as a guard will be quite sufficient, I have no doubt. I must hurry back and dismiss the friends who have been serenading me."

She gazed at him, not quite comprehending, and then said, "Well, if you must go, good-night, and thank you a thousand times. When I have my wits about me I will thank you better."

Arthur answered laughingly as he shook hands. "Oh, that is of no consequence. It was merely neighborly. You would have done as much for me, I am sure." And the gentlemen took their leave.

When the ladies were alone, Mrs. Belding resumed her story of the great transaction. "Why, it will be something to tell about as long as I live," she said. "You had hardly got upstairs when I heard a noise of fighting outside on the walk and the porch. Then Arthur and Mr. Temple came through that window as if they were shot out of a cannon. The thief who stood by me, the red handkerchief one, did not stop, but burst through the hall into the kitchen and escaped the back way. Then Mr. Temple took another one and positively threw him through the window, while Arthur, with that policeman's club, knocked the one down whom you saw the German tying up. It was all done in an instant, and I just sat and screamed for my share of the work. Then Arthur came and caught me by the shoulder, and almost shook me, and said, 'Where is Alice?' Upon my word, I had almost forgotten you. I said you were upstairs, and one of those wretches was there too. He looked as black as a fury, and went up in about three steps. I always thought he had such a sweet temper, but to-night he seemed just to *love* to fight. Now I think of it, Alice, you hardly spoke to him. You must not let him think we are ungrateful. You must write him a nice note to-morrow."

Alice laid her head upon her mother's shoulder, where her wet eyes could not be seen. "Mamma," she asked, "did he say 'Where is Alice?' Did he say nothing but 'Alice'?"

"Now, don't be silly," said Mrs. Belding. "Of course he said 'Alice.' You wouldn't expect a man to be Miss Beldinging you at such a time. You are quite too particular."

"He called me Miss Belding when he came upstairs," said Alice, still hiding her face.

"And what did you say to him—for saving this house and all our lives?"

The girl's overwrought nerves gave way. She had only breath enough to say, "I said 'Good evening, Captain Farnham!' Wasn't it too perfectly ridiculous?" and then burst into a flood of mingled laughter and tears, which nothing could check, until she had cried herself quiet upon her mother's bosom.

XV.

THE WHIP OF THE SCYTHIANS.

FARNHAM and Temple walked hastily back to where they had left Kendall with the rest of the company. They found him standing like a statute just where he had been placed by Farnham. The men were ranged in the shadow of the shrubbery and the ivy-clad angle of the house. The moon shone full on the open stretch of lawn, and outside the gates. a black mass on the sidewalk and the street showed that the mob had not left the place. But it seemed sluggish and silent.

"Have they done anything new?" asked Farnham.

"Nothin', but fire a shot or two—went agin the wall overhead; and once they heaved a lot of rocks, but it was too fur—didn't git more'n half way. That's all."

"We don't want to stand here looking at each other all night," said Farnham.

"Let's go out and tell them it's bed-time," suggested Temple.

"Agreed!" said Farnham. He turned to his men, and in a voice at first so low that it could not have been heard ten feet away, yet so clear that every syllable was caught by his soldiers, he gave the words of command.

"Company, attention! Right, forward. Fours right. Double time. March!"

The last words rang out clear and loud, and startled the sullen crowd in the street. There was a hurried, irresolute movement among them, which increased as the compact little corps dashed out of the shadow into the clear moonlight, and rushed with the rapid but measured pace of veterans across the lawn. A few missiles were thrown, without effect. One or two shots were heard, followed by a yell in the street—which showed that some rioter in his excitement had wounded one of his own comrades. Farnham and his little band took only a moment to reach the gate, and the crowd recoiled as they burst through into the street. At the first onslaught the rioters ran in both directions, leaving the street clear immediately in front of the gates.

The instant his company reached the middle of the avenue, Arthur, seeing that the greater number of the divided mob had gone to the left, shouted:

"Fours left. March—guide right."

The little phalanx wheeled instantly and made rapid play with their clubs, but only for a moment. The crowd began to feel the mysterious power which discipline backed by law always exerts, and they ran at full speed up the street to the corner and there dispersed. The formation of the veterans was not even broken. They turned at Farnham's order, faced to the rear, and advanced in double time upon the smaller crowd which still lingered a little way beyond the gate.

In this last group there was but one man who

stood his ground and struck out for himself. It was a tall young fellow with fair hair and beard, armed with a carpenter's hammer, with which he maintained so formidable an attitude that, although two or three policemen were opposed to him, they were wary about closing in upon him. Farnham, seeing that this was all there was left of the fight, ordered the men to fall back, and, approaching the recalcitrant, said sharply:

"Drop that hammer, and surrender! We are officers of the law, and if you resist any longer you'll be hurt."

"I don't mind that. I was waiting for *you*," the man said, and made a quick and savage rush and blow at Farnham. In all his campaigns, he had never before had so much use for his careful broadsword training as now. With his policeman's club against the workman's hammer, he defended himself with such address, that in a few seconds, before his men could interfere, his adversary was disarmed and stretched on the sidewalk by a blow over the head. He struggled to rise, but was seized by two men and held fast.

"Don't hit him," said Farnham. "I think I have seen this man somewhere."

"Why," said Kendall, "that's Sam Sleeny, a carpenter in Dean Street. He orter be in better business."

"Yes, I remember," said Farnham; "he is a Reformer. Put him with the others."

As they were tying his hands, Sam turned to Farnham and said, in a manner which was made dignified by its slow, energetic malice, "You've beat me to-night, but I will get even with you yet—as sure as there's a God."

"That's reasonably sure," said Farnham; "but in the meanwhile, we'll put you where you can cool off a little."

The street was now cleared; the last fugitives were out of sight. Farnham returned to his garden, and then divided his men into squads for patrolling the neighborhood. They waited for half an hour, and, finding all was still quiet, then made arrangements for passing the night. Farnham made Temple go into the house with him, and asked Budsey to bring some sherry. "It is not so good as your Santa Rita," he said; "but the exercise in the night air will give it a relish."

When the wine came, the men filled and drank, in sober American fashion, without words; but in the heart of each there was the thought of eternal friendship, founded upon brave and loyal service.

"Budsey," said Farnham, "give all the men a glass of this wine."

"Not this, sir?" said Budsey, aghast.

"I said this," replied Farnham. "Perhaps they won't enjoy it, but I shall enjoy giving it to them."

Farnham and Temple were eating some bread and cheese and talking over the evening, when Budsey came back with something which approached a smile upon his grave countenance.

"Did they like it?" asked Farnham.

"Half of 'em said they was temperance and wouldn't 'ave any. Some of the rest said—you will excuse me, sir—as it was d—— poor cider," and Budsey went out of the room with a suspicious convulsion of the back.

"I'll go on that," said Mr. Temple. "Good-night. I think we will have good news in the morning. There will be an attack made on those men at Riverley to-morrow which will melt them like an iceberg in Tartarus." Mr. Temple was not classical, and, of course, did not say Tartarus.

Farnham was left alone. The reaction from the excitement of the last few hours was settling upon him. The glow of the fight and his success in it were dying away. Midnight was near, and a deep silence was falling upon the city. There was no sound of bells, of steam-whistles, or of rushing trains. The breeze could be heard in the quiet, stirring the young, soft leaves. Farnham felt sore, beaten, discomfited. He smiled a little bitterly to himself when he considered that the cause of his feeling of discouragement was that Alice Belding had spoken to him with coldness and shyness when she opened her door. He could not help saying to himself, "I deserved a kinder greeting than she gave me. She evidently wished me to understand that I am not to be permitted any further intimacy. I have forfeited that by presuming to love her. But how lovely she is! When she took her mother in her arms, I thought of all the Greek heroines I ever read about. Still, 'if she be not fair for me'— if I am not to be either lover or friend—this is no place for me."

The clock on the mantel struck midnight. "A strange night," he mused. "There is one sweet and one bitter thing about it. I have done her a service, and she did not care."

He went to the door to speak to Kendall. "I think our work is over for to-night. Have our prisoners taken down to the Refrigerator and turned over to the ordinary police. I will make charges to-morrow. Then divide the men into watches and make yourself as comfortable as you can. If anything happens, call me. If nothing happens, good-night."

He returned to his library, turned down the gas, threw himself on the sofa, and was soon asleep; even before Alice, who sat, unhappy, as youth is unhappy, by an open window, her eyes full of tears, her heart full of remorse. "It is too wretched to think of," she bemoaned herself. "He is the only man in the world I could ever care for, and I have driven him away. It never can be made right again; I am punished justly. If I thought he would take me, I believe I could go this minute and throw myself at his feet. But he would smile, and raise me up, and make some pretty speech, very gentle, and very dreadful, and bring me back to mamma, and then I should die."

But at nineteen well-nourished maidens do not pass the night in mourning, however heavy their hearts may be, and Alice slept at last, and perhaps was happier in her innocent dreams.

The night passed without further incident, and the next day, though it may have shown favorable signs to practised eyes, seemed very much, to the public, like the day which had preceded it. There were fewer shops closed in the back streets; there

were not so many parties of wandering apostles of
plunder going about to warn laborers away from
their work. But in the principal avenues and in
the public squares there were the same dense
crowds of idlers, some listless and some excited,
ready to believe the wildest rumors and to ap-
plaud the craziest oratory. Speakers were not lack-
ing; besides the agitators of the town, several had
come in from neighboring places, and they were
preaching, with fervor and perspiration, from street
corners and from barrel-heads in the beer-houses,
the dignity of manhood and the overthrow of tyrants.

Bott, who had quite distinguished himself during
the last few days, was not to be seen. He had
passed the night in the station-house, and, on brief
examination before a police-justice at an early hour
of the morning, on complaint of Farnham and Temple, had been, together with the man captured in
Mrs. Belding's drawing-room, bound over to stand
his trial for house-breaking at the next term of
court. He displayed the most abject terror before
his trial, and would have made a full confession of
the whole affair had Offitt not had the address to convey to him the assurance that, if he stood firm, the
Brotherhood of Bread-winners would attend to his
case and be responsible for his safety. Relying
upon this, he plucked up his spirits and bore himself with characteristic impudence in the presence
of the police-justice, insisting upon being called Professor Bott, giving his profession as inspirational
orator, his religion the divinity of humanity. When
bound over for trial, he rose and gained a round of

applause from the idlers in the court-room by shouting, "I appeal from this outrage to the power of the people and the judgment of history."

This was his last recorded oration; for we may as well say at once that, a month later, he stood his trial without help from any Brotherhood, and passed away from public life, though not entirely from public employment, as he is now usefully and unobtrusively engaged in making shoes in the State penitentiary—and is said "to take serious views of life."

The cases of Sleeny and the men who were taken in the street by Farnham's policemen were also disposed of summarily through his intervention. He could not help liking the fair-bearded carpenter, although he had been caught in such bad company, and so charged him merely with riotous conduct in the public streets, for which the penalty was a light fine and a few days' detention. Sleeny seemed conscious of his clemency, but gave him no look or expression of gratitude. He was too bitter at heart to feel gratitude, and too awkward to feign it.

About noon, a piece of news arrived which produced a distinct impression of discouragement among the strikers. It was announced in the public square that the railway blockade was broken in Clairfield, a city to the east of Buffland about a hundred miles. The hands had accepted the terms of the employers and had gone to work again. An orator tried to break the force of this announcement by depreciating the pluck of the Clairfield men. "Why, gentlemen!" he screamed, "a ten-year-old boy in this town has got twice the sand of a Clairfield man. They just *beg* the bosses to kick 'em. When they are fired out of a shop door, they sneak down the chimbley and whine to be took on again. We ain't made of that kind of stuff."

But this haughty style of eloquence did not avail to inspirit the crowd, especially as the orator was just then interrupted to allow another dispatch to be read, which said that the citizens of a town to the south had risen in mass and taken the station there from the hands of the strikers. This news produced a feeling of isolation and discouragement which grew to positive panic, an hour later, on the report that a brigade of regular troops was on its way to Buffland to restore order. The report was of course unfounded, as a brigade of regular troops could not be got together in this country in much less time than it would take to build a city; but even the name of the phantom army had its effect, and the crowds began to disperse from that time. The final blow was struck, however, later in the day.

Farnham learned it from Mr. Temple, at whose counting-room he had called, as usual, for news. Mr. Temple greeted him with a volley of exulting oaths.

"It's all up. You know what I told you last night about the attack that was preparing on River-ley. I went out there myself, this forenoon. I knew some of the strikers, and I thought I would see if the —— —— —— would let me send my horse Blue Ruin through to Rochester to-morrow. He is entered for the races there, you know, and I didn't want, by —— —— ——, to miss my engagements, un-derstand? Well, as I drove out there, after I got about half way, it began to occur to me that I never saw so many women since the Lord made me. The

road was full of them in carts, buggies, horseback,
and afoot. I thought a committee of 'em was
going; but I suppose they couldn't trust a committee, and so they all went. There were so many of
'em I couldn't drive fast, and so I got there about
the same time the head of the column began to ar-
rive. You never saw anything like it in your life.
The strikers had been living out there in a good deal
of style—with sentries and republican government
and all that. By the great hokey-pokey! they
couldn't keep it up a minute when their wives came.
They knew 'em too well. They just bulged in without rhyme or rule. Every woman went for her husband and told him to pack up and go home. Some
of 'em—the artful kind—begged and wheedled and
cried; said they were so tired—wanted their sweet-
hearts again. But the bigger part talked hard sense,
—told 'em their lazy picnic had lasted long enough,
that there was no meat in the house, and that they
had got to come home and go to work. The siege
didn't last half an hour. The men brazened it
out awhile; some were rough; told their wives to
dry up, and one big fellow slapped his wife for crying.
By jingo! it wasn't half a flash before another fellow
slapped *him*, and there they had it, rolling over and
over on the grass, till the others pulled them apart
by the legs. It was a gone case from the start.
They held a meeting off-hand; the women stayed
by to watch proceedings, and, not to make a long
story about it, when I started back a delegation of
the strikers came with me to see the president of
the roads, and trains will run through to-night as
usual. I am devilish glad of it, for my part. There
16

is nothing in Rochester of any force but Rosin-the-
Bow, and my horse can show him the way around
the track as if he was getting a dollar an hour as a
guide."

"That *is* good news certainly. Is it generally
known in the city?"

"I think not. It was too late for the afternoon
papers. I told Jimmy Nelson, and he tore down to
the depot to save what is left of his fruit. He swore
so about it that I was quite shocked."

"What about the mill hands?" asked Farnham.

"The whole thing will now collapse at once.
We shall receive the proposition of the men who
left us to-morrow, and re-engage on our own terms,
next day, as many as we want. We shan't be hard
on them. But one or two gifted orators will have
to take the road. They are fit for nothing but
Congress, and they can't all go from this district.
If I were you, Arthur, by the way, I wouldn't mus-
ter out that army of yours till to-morrow. But I
don't think there will be any more calls in your
neighborhood. You are too inhospitable to visitors."

The sun was almost setting as Farnham walked
through the public square on his way home. He
could hardly believe so sudden a change could have
fallen upon the busy scene of a few hours before.
The square was almost deserted. Its holiday appearance was gone. A few men occupied the
benches. One or two groups stood beneath the
trees and conversed in under-tones. The orators
had sought their hiding-places, unnecessarily—too
fearful of the vengeance which never, in this happy

country, attends the exercise of unbridled "slack jaw." As Arthur walked over the asphalt pavement there was nothing to remind him of the great crowds of the last few days but the shells of the pea-nuts crunching under his feet. It seems as if the American workman can never properly invoke the spirit of liberty without a pocketful of this democratic nut.

As he drew near his house, Farnham caught a glimpse of light drapery upon Mrs. Belding's piazza, and went over to relieve her from anxiety by telling her the news of the day. When he had got half way across the lawn, he saw Alice rise from beside her mother as if to go. Mrs. Belding signed for her to resume her seat. Farnham felt a slight sensation of anger. "It is unworthy of her," he thought, "to avoid me in that manner. I must let her see she is in no danger from me."

He gave his hand cordially to Mrs. Belding and bowed to Alice without a word. He then briefly recounted the news to the elder lady, and assured her that there was no probability of any farther disturbance of the peace.

"But we shall have our policemen here all the same to-night, so that you may sleep with a double sense of security."

"I am sure you are very good," she said. "I don't know what we should have done without you last night, *and* Mr. Temple. When it comes to ear-rings, there's no telling what they wouldn't have done."

"Two of your guests are in jail, with good prospects of their remaining there. The others, I learn, were thieves from out of town; I doubt if we shall capture them."

"For goodness' sake, let them run. I never want to see them again. That ugly creature who went up with Alice for the money—you caught him? I am so glad. The impudence of the creature! going upstairs with my daughter, as if she was not to be trusted. Well," she added candidly, "she wasn't that time, but it was none of *his* business."

Here Alice and Farnham both laughed out, and the sound of the other's voice was very pleasant to each of them, though they did not look toward each other.

"I am beginning to think that the world is growing too wicked for single women," Mrs. Belding continued, philosophically. "Men can take care of themselves in so many ways. They can use a club as you do——"

"Daily and habitually," assented Arthur.

"Or they can make a speech about Ireland and the old flag, as Mr. Belding used to; or they can swear like Mr. Temple. By the way, Alice, you were not here when Mr. Temple swore so at those thieves. I was scandalized, but I had to admit it was very appropriate."

"I was also away from the room," said Farnham; "but I can readily believe the comminatory clauses must have been very cogent."

"Oh, yes! and such a nice woman *she* is."

"Yes, Mrs. Temple is charming," said Farnham, rising.

"Arthur, do not go! Stay to dinner. It will be

ready in one moment. It will strengthen our nerves
to have a man dine with us, especially a liberating
hero like you. Why, you seemed to me last night
like Perseus in the picture, coming to rescue What's-
her-name from the rock."

Farnham glanced at Alice. Her eyes were fixed
upon the ground; her fingers were tightly clasped.
She was wishing with all her energy that he would
stay, waiting to catch his first word of assent, but
unable to utter a syllable.

"Alice," said Mrs. Belding rather sharply, "I
think Arthur does not regard my invitation as quite
sufficient. Will you give it your approval?"

Alice raised her face at these words and looked
up at Farnham. It was a beautiful face at all times,
and now it was rosy with confusion, and the eyes
were timid but kind. She said with lips that
trembled a little: "I should be very glad to have
Captain Farnham stay to dinner."

She had waited too long, and the words were a
little too formal, and Arthur excused himself on the
plea of having to look out for his cohort, and went
home to a lonely dinner.

XVI.

OFFITT DIGS A PIT.

A WEEK had passed by; the great strike was already almost forgotten. A few poor workmen had lost their places. A few agitators had been dismissed for excellent reasons, having no relation with the strike. The mayor had recovered from his panic, and was beginning to work for a renomination, on the strength of his masterly dealing with the labor difficulties, in which, as he handsomely said in a circular composed by himself and signed by his friends, he "nobly accomplished the duty allotted him of preserving the rights of property while respecting the rights of the people, of keeping the peace according to his oath, and keeping faith with the masses, to which he belonged, in their struggle against monopoly."

The rich and prosperous people, as their manner is, congratulated themselves on their escape, and gave no thought to the questions which had come so near to an issue of fire and blood. In this city of two hundred thousand people, two or three dozen politicians continued as before to govern it, to assess and to spend its taxes, to use it as their property and their chattel. The rich and intelligent kept on making money, building fine houses, and bringing up children to hate politics as they did, and in fine to fatten themselves as sheep which should be mutton whenever the butcher was ready. There was hardly a millionaire on Algonquin Avenue who knew where the ward meetings of his party were held. There was not an Irish laborer in the city but knew his way to his ward club as well as to mass.

Among those who had taken part in the late exciting events and had now reverted to private life was Sam Sleeny. His short sentence had expired; he had paid his fine and come back to Matchin's. But he was not the quiet, contented workman he had been. He was sour, sullen, and discontented. He nourished a dull grudge against the world. He had tried to renew friendly relations with Maud, but she had repulsed him with positive scorn. Her mind was full of her new prospects, and she did not care to waste time with him. The scene in the rose-house rankled in his heart; he could not but think that her mind had been poisoned by Farnham, and his hate gained intensity every hour.

In this frame of mind he fell easily into the control of Offitt. That worthy had not come under the notice of the law for the part he took in the attack on the Belding house; he had not been recognized by Farnham's men, nor denounced by his associates; and so, after a day or two of prudential hiding, he came to the surface again. He met Sam at the very door of the House of Correction, sympathized with him, flattered him, gained his full confidence at last, and held him ready for some purpose which was vague even in his own brain. He was determined to gain possession of Maud, and he felt it must be through some crime, the manner of which was not quite clear to him. If he could use Sam to accomplish his purpose and save his own skin, that would be best. His mind ran constantly upon theft, forgery, burglary, and murder; but he could frame no scheme which did not involve risks that turned him sick. If he could hit upon something where he might furnish the brains, and Sam the physical force and the risk! He dwelt upon this day and night. He urged Sam to talk of his own troubles; of the Matchins; at last, of Maud and his love, and it was not long before the tortured fellow had told him what he saw in the rose-house. Strangely enough, the thought of his fiancée leaning on the shoulder of another man did not in the least diminish the ardor of Offitt. His passion was entirely free from respect or good-will. He used the story to whet the edge of Sam's hatred against Farnham.

"Why, Sam, my boy," he would say, "your honor is at stake."

"I would as soon kill him as eat," Sam answered. "But what good would that do me? She cares no more for me than she does for you."

Offitt was sitting alone in his room one afternoon; his eyes were staring blankly at the opposite wall; his clinched hands were cold as ice. He had been sitting in that way motionless for an hour, a prey to a terrible excitement.

It had come about in this way. He had met in one of the shops he frequented a machinist who rented one of Farnham's houses. Offitt had asked him at noon-time to come out and drink a glass of beer with him. The man complied, and was especially careful to bring his waistcoat with him, saying with a laugh, "I lose my shelter if I lose that."

"What do you mean?" asked Offitt.

"I've got a quarter's rent in there for Cap. Farnham."

"Why are you carrying it around all day?"

"Well, you know, Farnham is a good sort of fellow, and to keep us from losing time he lets us come to his house in the evening, after working hours, on quarter-day, instead of going to his office in the day-time. You see, I trot up there after supper and get rid of this wad."

Offitt's eyes twinkled like those of an adder.

"How many of you do this?"

"Oh, a good many,—most everybody in our ward and some in the Nineteenth."

"A good bit of money?" said Offitt carelessly, though his mouth worked nervously.

"You bet your boots! If I had all the cash he takes in to-night, I'd buy an island and shoot the machine business. Well, I must be gettin' back. So long."

Offitt had walked directly home after this conversation, looking neither to the right nor the left, like a man asleep. He had gone to his room, locked his door behind him, and sat down upon the edge of his bed and given himself up to an eager dream of crime. His heart beat, now fast, now slow; a cold sweat enveloped him; he felt from time to time half suffocated.

Suddenly he heard a loud knocking at his door— not as if made by the hand, but as if some one were hammering. He started and gasped with a choking rattle in his throat. His eyes seemed straining from their sockets. He opened his lips, but no sound came forth.

The sharp rapping was repeated, once and again. He made no answer. Then a loud voice said:

"Hello, Andy, you asleep?"

He threw himself back on his pillow and said yawningly, "Yes. That you, Sam? Why don't you come in?"

"'Cause the door's locked."

He rose and let Sleeny in; then threw himself back on the bed, stretching and gaping.

"What did you make that infernal racket with?"

"My new hammer," said Sam. "I just bought it to-day. Lost my old one the night we give Farnham the shiveree."

"Lemme see it." Offitt took it in his hand and balanced and tested it. "Pretty good hammer. Handle's a leetle thick, but—pretty good hammer."

"Ought to be," said Sam. "Paid enough for it."

"Where d'you get it?"

"Ware & Harden's."

"Sam," said Offitt,—he was still holding the hammer and giving himself light taps on the head with it,—"Sam."

"Well, you said that before."

Offitt opened his mouth twice to speak and shut it again.

"What are you doin'?" asked Sleeny. "Trying to catch flies?"

"Sam," said Offitt at last, slowly and with effort, "if I was you, the first thing I did with that hammer, I'd crack Art Farnham's cocoa-nut."

" Well, Andy, go and crack it yourself if you are so keen to have it done. You're mixing yourself rather too much in my affairs, anyhow," said Sam, who was nettled by these too frequent suggestions of Offitt that his honor required repair.

" Sam Sleeny," said Offitt, in an impressive voice, " I'm one of the kind that stands by my friends. If you mean what you have been saying to me, I'll go up with you this very night, and we will together take it out of that aristocrat. Now, that's business."

Sleeny looked at his friend in surprise and with some distrust. The offer was so generous and reckless, that he could not help asking himself what was its motive. He looked so long and so stupidly at Offitt, that the latter at last divined his feeling. He thought that, without telling Sleeny the whole scheme, he would test him one step farther.

" I don't doubt," he said carelessly, " but what we could pay ourselves well for the job,—spoil the 'Gyptians, you know,—forage on the enemy. Plenty of portables in them houses, eh !"

" I never said "—Sam spoke slowly and deliberately—" I wanted to 'sassinate him, or rob him, or burgle him. If I could catch him and lick him, in a fair fight, I'd do it; and I wouldn't care how hard I hit him, or what with."

" All right," said Offitt, curtly. " You met him once in a fair fight, and he licked you. And you tried him another way,—courtin' the same girl,— and he beat you there. But it's all right. I've got nothin' against him, if you hain't. Lemme mark your name on this hammer," and, turning the con-

versation so quickly that Sleeny had no opportunity
to resent the last taunt, he took his knife and began
dexterously and swiftly to cut Sam's initials in the
handle of his hammer. Before, however, he had
half completed his self-imposed task, he exclaimed,
"This is dry work. Let's go out and get some
beer. I'll finish your hammer and bring it around
after supper."

"There's one S on it," said Sam; "that's enough."

"One S enough! It might mean Smith, or
Schneider, or Sullivan. No, sir. I'll put two on
in the highest style of art, and then everybody will
know and respect Sam Sleeny's tool."

They passed out of the room together, and drank
their beer at a neighboring garden. They were both
rather silent and preoccupied. As they parted, Offitt said, " I've got a scheme on hand for raising the
wind, I want to talk to you about. Be at my room
to-night between nine and ten, and wait till I come,
if I am out. Don't fail." Sam stared a little, but
promised, asking no questions.

When Offitt came back, he locked the door again
behind him. He bustled about the room as if preparing to move. He had little to pack; a few shabby
clothes were thrown into a small trunk, a pile of letters and papers were hastily torn up and pitched
into the untidy grate. All this while he muttered
to himself as if to keep himself in company. He
said : " I had to take the other shoot—he hadn't the
sand to help—I couldn't tell him any more. . . . I
wonder if she will go with me when I come to-
night—ready? I shall feel I deserve her anyhow.
She don't treat me as she did him, according to

Sam's story. She makes me keep my distance. She hasn't even shook hands with me since we was engaged. I'll pay her for that after awhile." He walked up and down his room breathing quick and hard. "I shall risk my neck, I know; but it won't be the first time, and I never will have such a reason again. She beats anything I ever saw. I've *got* to have the money—to suit such a woman. . . . I'm almost sorry for Sam—but the Lord made some men to be other men's fools. . . ."

This was the staple of his musings; other things less edifying still may be omitted.

While he was engaged in this manner he heard a timid knock at his door. "Another visitor? I'm getting popular," he said, and went to open the door.

A seedy, forlorn-looking man came in; he took off his shabby hat and held it under his arm.

He said, "Good-evenin'," in a tone a little above a whisper.

"Well, what's the matter?" asked Offitt.

"Have you heered about Brother Bowersox?"

"Never mind the brothering—that's played out. What is there about Bowersox?"

"He's dangerous; they don't think he'll live through the night."

"Well, what of it?"

This was not encouraging, but the poor Bread-winner ventured to say, "I thought some of the Brothers——"

But Offitt closed the subject by a brutal laugh. "The Brothers are looking out for themselves these times. The less said about the Brotherhood the better. It's up the spout, do you hear "

The poor fellow shrunk away into his ragged clothes, and went out with a submissive " Good-evenin'."

" I'll never found another Brotherhood," Offitt said to himself. " It's more trouble than it brings in."

It was now growing dark. He took his hat and went down the stairs and out into the street. He entered a restaurant and ordered a beefsteak, which he ate, paid for, and departed after a short chat with the waiter, whom he knew. He went around the corner, entered another eating-house, called for a cup of coffee and a roll. There also he was careful to speak with the man who served him, slapping him on the shoulder with familiarity. He went into a drug store a little later and bought a glass of soda-water, dropping the glass on the marble floor, and paying for it after some controversy. He then walked up to Dean Street. He found the family all together in the sitting-room. He chatted awhile with them, and asked for Sleeny.

" I don't really know where Sam is. He ain't so reg'lar in his hours as he used to be," said Saul. " I hope he ain't gettin' wild."

" I hope not," said Offitt, in a tone of real distress—then, after a pause, " You needn't mention my havin' asked for him. He may be sensitive about it."

As he came away, Maud followed him to the door. He whispered, " Be ready, my beauty, to start at a moment's notice. The money is on the way. You shall live like a queen before many days are gone."

" We shall see," she answered, with a smile, but shutting the door between them.

He clinched his fists and muttered, "I'll figure it all up and take my pay, Missy. She's worth it. I will have to do some crooked things to get her; but by ——, I'd kill a dozen men and hang another, just to stand by and see her braid her hair."

Returning to his house, he ran nimbly up the stairs, half fearing to find Sleeny there, but he had not yet arrived. He seized the hammer, put it in his pocket, and came down again. Still intent upon accounting for as much of the evening as possible, he thought of a variety-show in the neighborhood, and went there. He spoke to some of the loafers at the door. He then walked to the box-office and asked for a ticket, addressing the man who sold it to him as "Jimmy," and asking how business was. The man handed him his ticket without any reply, but turned to a friend beside him, and said, "Who is that cheeky brother that knows me so well?"

"Oh! that's a rounder by the name of Offitt. He is a sort of Reformer—makes speeches to the puddlers on the rights of man."

"Seems rather fresh," said Jimmy.

"A little brine wouldn't hurt him."

Offitt strolled into the theatre, which was well filled. The curtain was down at the moment, and he walked the full extent of the centre aisle to the orchestra, looking about him as if in search of some one. He saw one or two acquaintances and nodded to them. He then walked back and took a seat near the door. The curtain rose, and the star of the evening bounded upon the stage,—a strapping young woman in the dress of an army officer. She was greeted with applause before she began her

song, and with her first notes Offitt quietly went
out. He looked at the clock on the City Hall, and
saw that he had no more time to kill. He walked,
without hurrying or loitering, up the shady side of
the street till he came to the quarter where Farnham
lived. He then crossed into the wide avenue, and,
looking swiftly about him, approached the open
gates of Farnham's place. Two or three men were
coming out, one or two were going in. He waited
till the former had turned down the street, and the
latter were on the door-step. He then walked
briskly up the path to the house; but instead of
mounting the steps, he turned to the left and lay
down under the library windows behind a clump of
lilacs.

"If they catch me here," he thought, "they can
only take me for a tramp and give me the grand
bounce."

The windows opened upon a stone platform a few
feet from the ground. He could hear the sound of
voices within. At last he heard the men rise, push
back their chairs, and say "Good-night." He heard
their heavy shoes on the front steps. "Now for it,"
he whispered. But at that moment a belated tenant
came in. He wanted to talk of some repairs to his
house. Offitt lay down again, resting his head on
his arm. The soft turf, the stillness, the warmth of
the summer night lulled him into drowsiness. In
spite of the reason he had for keeping awake, his
eyes were closing and his senses were fading, when
a shrill whistle startled him into broad wakefulness.
It was the melancholy note of a whippoorwill in
the branches of a lime-tree in the garden. Offitt

listened for the sound of voices in the library. He
heard nothing. "Can I have slept through——no,
there is a light." A shadow fell across the window.
The heavy tread of Budsey approached. Farnham's
voice was heard: "Never mind the windows, Budsey. I will close them and the front door. I will
wait here awhile; somebody else may come. You
can go to bed."

"Good-night, sir."

"Good-night."

Offitt waited only a moment. He rose and looked
cautiously in at the window. Farnham was seated
at his desk. He had sorted, in the methodical way
peculiar to men who have held command in the
army, the papers which he had been using with his
tenants and the money he had received from them.

They were arranged on the desk before him in
neat bundles, ready to be transferred to the safe,
across the room. He had taken up his pen to make
some final indorsement.

Offitt drew off his shoes, leaped upon the platform, and entered the library as swiftly and noise-
lessly as a panther walking over sand.

17

XVII.

IN AND OUT OF WINDOWS.

ALICE BELDING was seated before her glass braiding her long hair. Her mother had come in from her own room, as her custom often was, to chat with her daughter in the half hour before bed-time. It gratified at once her maternal love and her pride to watch the exquisite beauty of her child, as she sat, dressed in a white wrapper that made her seem still taller than she was, brushing and braiding the luxuriant tresses that gave under the light every tint and reflection of which gold is capable. The pink and pearl of the round arm as the loose sleeve would slip to the elbow, the poise of the proud head, the full white column of the neck, the soft curve of cheek and chin,—all this delighted her as it would have delighted a lover. But with all her lightheadedness, there was enough of discretion, or perhaps of innate New England reserve, to keep her from ever expressing to Alice her pleasure in her beauty. So the wholesome-minded girl never imagined the admiration of which she was the object, and thought that her mother only liked to chat a little before sleeping. They talked of trivial matters, of the tea at Mrs. Hyson's, of Formosa Hyson's purple dress which made her sallower than ever, of rain and fair weather.

"I think," said Mrs. Belding, " that Phrasy Dal-

las gets more and more stylish every day. I don't
wonder at Arthur Farnham's devotion. That would
make an excellent match—they are both so dreadfully clever. By the way, he has not been here
this week. And I declare! I don't believe you
have ever written him that note of thanks."

"No," said Alice, smiling—she had schooled herself by this time to speak of him carelessly. "I
was too much frightened to thank him on the spot,
and now it would be ancient history. We must
save our thanks till we see him."

"I want to see him about other things. You
must write and ask him to dinner to-morrow or next
day."

"Don't you think he would like it better if *you*
would write?"

"There you are again—as if it mattered. Write
that 'Mamma bids me.' There, your hair is braid-
ed. Write the note now, and I will send it over in
the morning before he gets away."

Alice rose and walked to her escritoire, her long
robe trailing, her thick braids hanging almost to the
floor, her fair cheek touched with a delicate spot of
color at the thought of writing a formal note to the
man she worshipped. She took a pen and wrote
"My dear Mr. Farnham," and the conventional address made her heart flutter and her eyes grow dim.
While she was writing, she heard her mother say:

"What a joke!"

She looked up, and saw that Mrs. Belding, having
pushed open the shutters, had picked up her opera-
glass and was looking through it at something out
of the window.

" Do you know, Alice," she said, laughing, " since that ailantus tree was cut down, you can see straight into his library from here.   There he is now, sitting at his desk."

" Mamma !" pleaded Alice, rising and trying to take the glass away from her.   " Don't do that, I beg !"

" Nonsense," said her mother, keeping her away with one hand and holding the glass with the other. " There comes Budsey to close the blinds.   The show is over.   No; he goes away, leaving them open."

" Mamma, I will leave the room if——"

" My goodness! look at that!" cried the widow, putting the glass in her daughter's hand and sinking into a chair with fright.

Alice, filled with a nameless dread, saw her mother was pale and trembling, and took the glass.   She dropped it in an instant, and leaning from the window sent forth once more that cry of love and alarm, which rang through the stillness of night with all the power of her young throat:

" Arthur !"

She turned, and sped down the stairs, and across the lawn like an arrow shot for life or death from a long-bow.

Farnham heard the sweet, strong voice ringing out of the stillness like the cry of an angel in a vision, and raised his head with a startled movement from the desk where he was writing.   Offitt heard it, too, as he raised his hand to strike a deadly blow ; and though it did not withhold him from his murderous purpose, it disturbed somewhat the precision of his hand. The hammer descended a little to the right of where he had intended to strike. It made a deep and cruel gash, and felled Farnham to the floor, but it did not kill him. He rose, giddy and faint with the blow and half-blinded with the blood that poured down over his right eye. He clapped his hand, with a soldier's instinct, to the place where his sword-hilt was not, and then staggered, rather than rushed, at his assailant, to grapple him with his naked hands. Offitt struck him once more, and he fell headlong on the floor, in the blaze of a myriad lights that flashed all at once into deep darkness and silence.

The assassin, seeing that his victim no longer moved, threw down his reeking weapon, and, seizing the packages of money on the desk, thrust them into his pockets. He stepped back through the open window and stooped to pick up his shoes. As he rose, he saw a sight which for an instant froze him with terror. A tall and beautiful form, dressed all in white, was swiftly gliding toward him over the grass. It drew near, and he saw its pale features set in a terrible expression of pity and horror. It seemed to him like an avenging spirit. He shut his eyes for a moment in abject fright, and the phantom swept by him and leaped like a white doe upon the platform, through the open window, and out of his sight. He ran to the gate, quaking and trembling, then walked quietly to the nearest corner, where he sat down upon the curb-stone and put on his shoes.

Mrs. Belding followed, as rapidly as she could, the swift flight of her daughter; but it was some minutes after the young girl had leaped through the

window that her mother walked breathlessly through
the front door and the hall into the library. She
saw there a sight which made her shudder and turn
faint. Alice was sitting on the floor, holding in her
lap the blood-dabbled head of Farnham. Beside
her stood a glass of water, a pitcher, and several
towels. Some of them were red and saturated,
some were still fresh and neatly folded. She was
carefully cleansing and wiping the white forehead
of the lifeless man of the last red drop.

"Oh, Alice, what is this?" cried her mother.

"He is dead!" she answered, in a hoarse, strained
voice. "I feared so when I first came in. He was
lying on his face. I lifted him up, but he could not
see me. I kissed him, hoping he might kiss me
again. But he did not. Then I saw this water on
the stand over there. I remembered there were always towels there in the billiard-room. I ran and
got them, and washed the blood away from his face.
See, his face is not hurt. I am glad of that. But
there is a dreadful wound in his head." She dropped
her voice to a choking whisper at these words.

Her mother gazed at her with speechless consternation. Had the shock deprived her of reason?

"Alice," she said, "this is no place for you. I
will call the servants and send for a surgeon, and
you must go home."

"Oh, no, mamma. I see I have frightened you,
but there is no need to be frightened. Yes, call
the servants, but do not let them come in here for
awhile, not till the doctors come. They can do no
good. He is dead."

Mrs. Belding had risen and rung the bell violently.

"Do, mamma, see the servants in the hall outside. Don't let them come in for a moment. Do! I pray! I pray! I will do anything for you."

There was such intensity of passion in the girl's prayer that her mother yielded, and when the servants came running in, half-dressed, in answer to the bell, she stepped outside the door and said, "Captain Farnham has been badly hurt. Two of you go for the nearest doctors. You need not come in at present. My daughter and I will take care of him."

She went back, closing the door behind her. Alice was smiling. "There, you are a dear! I will love you forever for that! It is only for a moment. The doctors will soon be here, and then I must give him up."

"Oh, Alice," the poor lady whimpered, "why do you talk so wildly? What do you mean?"

"Don't cry, mamma! It is only for a moment. It is all very simple. I am not crazy. He was my lover!"

"Heaven help us!"

"Yes, this dear man, this noble man offered me his love, and I refused it. I may have been crazy then, but I am not now. I can love him now. I will be his widow—if I was not his wife. We will be two widows together—always. Now you know I am doing nothing wrong or wild. He is mine.

"Give me one of those towels," she exclaimed, suddenly. "I can tie up his head so that it will stop bleeding till the doctors come."

She took the towels, tore strips from her own dress, and in a few moments, with singular skill and tenderness, she had stopped the flow of blood from the wound.

"There! He looks almost as if he were asleep, does he not? Oh, my love, my love!"

Up to this moment she had not shed one tear. Her voice was strained, choked, and sobbing, but her eyes were dry. She kissed him on his brow and his mouth. She bent over him and laid her smooth cheek to his. She murmured:

"Good-by, good-by, till I come to you, my own love!"

All at once she raised her head with a strange light in her eyes. "Mamma!" she cried, "see how warm his cheek is. Heaven is merciful! perhaps he is alive."

She put both arms about him, and, gently but powerfully lifting his dead weight of head and shoulders, drew him to her heart. She held him to her warm bosom, rocking him to and fro. "Oh, my beloved!" she murmured, "if you will live, I will be so good to you."

She lowered him again, resting his head on her lap. A drop of blood, from the napkin in which his head was wrapped, had touched the bosom of her dress, staining it as if a cherry had been crushed there. She sat, gazing with an anguish of hope upon his pale face. A shudder ran through him, and he opened his eyes—only for a moment. He groaned, and slowly closed them.

The tears could no longer be restrained. They fell like a summer shower from her eyes, while she sobbed, "Thank God! my darling is not dead."

Her quick ear caught footsteps at the outer door.

"Here, mamma, take my place. Let me hide before all those men come in."

In a moment she had leaped through the window, whence she ran through the dewy grass to her home.

An hour afterward her mother returned, escorted by one of the surgeons. She found Alice in bed, peacefully sleeping. As Mrs. Belding approached the bedside, Alice woke and smiled. "I know without your telling me, mamma. He will live. I began to pray for him,—but I felt sure he would live, and so I gave thanks instead."

"You are a strange girl," said Mrs. Belding, gravely. "But you are right. Dr. Cutts says, if he escapes without fever, there is nothing very serious in the wound itself. The blow that made that gash in his head was not the one which made him unconscious. They found another, behind his ear; the skin was not broken. There was a bump about as big as a walnut. They said it was concussion of the brain, but no fracture anywhere. By the way, Dr. Cutts complimented me very handsomely on the way I had managed the case before his arrival. He said there was positively a professional excellence about my bandage. You may imagine I did not set him right."

Alice, laughing and blushing, said, "I will allow you all the credit."

Mrs. Belding kissed her, and said, "Good-night," and walked to the door. There she paused a moment, and came back to the bed. "I think, after all, I had better say now what I thought of keeping till to-morrow. I thank you for your confidence to-night, and shall respect it. But you will see, I am sure, the necessity of being very circum-spect, under the circumstances. If you should want to do anything for Arthur while he is ill, I should feel it my duty to forbid it."

Alice received this charge with frank, open eyes. "I should not dream of such a thing," she said. "If he had died, I should have been his widow; but, as he is to live, he must come for me if he wants me. I was very silly about him, but I must take the consequences. I can't now take advantage of the poor fellow, by saving his life and establish-ing a claim on it. So I will promise anything you want. I am so happy that I will promise easily. But I am also very sleepy."

The beautiful eyelids were indeed heavy and drooping. The night's excitement had left her wearied and utterly content. She fell asleep even as her mother kissed her forehead.

The feeling of Offitt as he left Algonquin Avenue and struck into a side street was one of pure exul-tation. He had accomplished the boldest act of his life. He had shown address, skill, and courage. He had done a thing which had appalled him in the contemplation, merely on account of its physical difficulties and dangers. He had done it success-fully. He had a large amount of money in his pocket—enough to carry his bride to the ends of the earth. When it was gone—well, at worst, he could leave her, and shift for himself again. He had not a particle of regret or remorse; and, in fact, these sentiments are far rarer than moralists would have us believe. A ruffian who commits a crime usually glories in it. It exalts him in his own eyes, all the more that he is compelled to keep silent about it. As Offitt walked rapidly in the direction of Dean Street, the only shadow on his exultation was his sudden perception of the fact that he had better not tell Maud what he had done. In all his plans he had promised himself the pleasure of telling her that she was avenged upon her enemy by the hands of her lover; he had thought he might extort his first kiss by that heroic avowal; but now, as he walked stealthily down the silent street, he saw that nobody in the universe could be made his confidant.

"I'll never own it, in earth or hell," he said to himself.

When he reached Matchin's cottage, all was dark and still. He tried to attract Maud's attention by throwing soft clods of earth against her window, but her sleep was too sound. He was afraid to throw pebbles for fear of breaking the panes and waking the family. He went into the little yard adjoining the shop, and found a ladder. He brought it out, and placed it against the wall. He perceived now for the first time that his hands were sticky. He gazed at them a moment. "Oh, yes," he said to himself, "when he fell I held out my hands to keep his head from touching my clothes. Careless trick! Ought to have washed them, first thing." Then, struck by a sudden idea, he went to the well-curb, and slightly moistened his fingers. He then rubbed them on the door-knob, and the edge of the door of the cottage, and pressed them several times in different places on the ladder. "Not a bad scheme," he said, chuckling. He then went again to the well, and washed his hands thoroughly, afterward taking a handful of earth, and rubbing them till they were as dirty as usual.

After making all these preparations for future contingencies, he mounted the ladder, and tried to raise the window. It was already open a few inches to admit the air, but was fastened there, and he could not stir it. He began to call and whistle in as low and penetrating a tone as he could manage, and at last awoke Maud, whose bed was only a few feet away. She started up with a low cry of alarm, but saw in a moment who it was.

"Well, what on earth are you doing here? Go away this minute, or I'll call my father."

"Let me in, and I will tell you."

"I'll do nothing of the sort. Begone this instant."

"Maud, don't be foolish," he pleaded, in real alarm, as he saw that she was angry and insulted. "I have done as you told me. I have wealth for us both, and I have"—he had almost betrayed himself, but he concluded—"I have come to take you away forever."

"Come to-morrow, at a decent hour, and I will talk to you."

"Now, Maud, my beauty, don't believe I am humbugging. I brought a lot of money for you to look at—I knew you wanted to be sure. See here!" He drew from his pocket a package of bank bills—he saw a glittering stain on them. He put them in the other pocket of his coat and took out another package. "And here's another, I've got a dozen like them. Handle 'em yourself." He put them in

through the window. Maud was so near that she
could take the bills by putting out her hand. She
saw there was a large amount of money there—more
than she had ever seen before.

"Come, my beauty," he said, "this is only spend-
ing-money for a bridal tour. There are millions behind it. Get up and put on your dress. I will wait
below here. We can take the midnight train east,
be married at Clairfield, and sail for Paris the next
day. That's the world for you to shine in. Come!
Waste no time. No tellin' what may happen to-
morrow."

She was strongly tempted. She had no longer
any doubt of his wealth. He was not precisely a
hero in appearance, but she had never insisted upon
that—her romance having been always of a practical kind. She was about to assent—and to seal her
doom—when she suddenly remembered that all her
best clothes were in her mother's closet, which was
larger than hers, and that she could not get them
without passing through the room where her parents were asleep. That ended the discussion. It
was out of the question that she should marry this
magnificent stranger in her every-day dress and cot-
ton stockings. It was equally impossible that she
should give that reason to any man. So she said,
with dignity:

"Mr. Offitt, it is not proper for me to continue
this conversation any longer. You ought to see it
ain't. I shall be happy to see you to-morrow."

Offitt descended the ladder, grinding out curses
between his set teeth. A hate, as keen as his passion, for the foolish girl fired him. "Think," he

hissed, "a man that killed, half an hour ago, the biggest swell in Buffland, to be treated that way by a carpenter's wench. Wait awhile, Miss; it'll come my innings." He lifted up the ladder, carried it carefully around the house, and leaned it against the wall under the window of the room occupied by Sleeny.

He hurried back to his lodging in Perry Place, where he found Sam Sleeny lying asleep on his bed. He was not very graciously greeted by his drowsy visitor.

"Why didn't you stay out all night?" Sam growled. "Where have you been, anyhow?"

"I've been at the variety-show, and it was the boss fraud of the season."

"You stayed so long you must have liked it."

"I was waiting to see just how bad a show could be and not spoil."

"What did you want to see me about to-night?"

"The fact is, I expected to meet a man around at the Varieties who was to go in with us into a big thing. But he wasn't there. I'll nail him to-morrow, and then we can talk. It's big money, Sammy, and no discount. What would you think of a thousand dollars a month?"

"I'd a heap rather see it than hear you chin about it. Give me my hammer, and I'll go home."

"Why, I took it round to your shop this evening, and I tossed it in through the window. I meant to throw it upon the table, but it went over, I think from the sound, and dropped on the floor. You will find it among the shavings, I reckon."

"Well, I'm off," said Sam, by way of good-night.
"All right. Guess I'll see you to-morrow."

Offitt waited till he could hear the heavy tread of
Sleeny completing the first flight of stairs and going
around to the head of the second. He then shut
and locked his door, and hung his hat over the key-
hole. He turned up his lamp and sat down by the
table to count his night's gains. The first package
he took from his pocket had a shining stain upon the
outside bill. He separated the stained bill carefully
from the rest, and held it a moment in his hand as
if in doubt. He walked to his wash-stand, but at
the moment of touching his pitcher he stopped short.
He took out his handkerchief, but shook his head
and put it back. Finally, he lighted a match, applied it to the corner of the bill, and watched it take
fire and consume, until his fingers were scorched by
the blaze. "Pity!" he whispered—"good money
like that."

He seated himself again and began with a fierce,
sustained delight to arrange and sort the bank-bills,
laying the larger denominations by themselves,
smoothing them down with a quick and tender touch,
a kindling eye and a beating heart. In his whole
life, past and future, there was not such another moment of enjoyment. Money is, of course, precious
and acceptable to all men except idiots. But, if it
means much to the good and virtuous, how infinitely
more it means to the thoroughly depraved—the instant gratification of every savage and hungry devil
of a passion which their vile natures harbor. Though
the first and principal thing Offitt thought of was
the possession of Maud Matchin, his excited fancy

did not stop there. A long gallery of vicious pictures stretched out before his flaming eyes, as he
reckoned up the harvest of his hand. The mere
thought that each bill represented a dinner, where
he might eat and drink what he liked, was enough
to inebriate a starved rogue whose excesses had always been limited by his poverty.

When he had counted and sorted his cash, he
took enough for his immediate needs and put it in
his wallet. The rest he made up into convenient
packages, which he tied compactly with twine and
disposed in his various pockets. "I'll chance it,"
he thought, after some deliberation. "If they get
me, they can get the money, too. But they sha'n't
get it without me."

He threw himself on his bed, and slept soundly
till morning.

XVIII.

OFFITT PLANS A LONG JOURNEY.

The bright sun and the morning noises of the city waked Offitt from his sleep. As he dressed himself the weight of the packages in his pockets gave him a pleasant sensation to begin the day with. He felt as if he were entering upon a new state of existence—a life with plenty of money. He composed in his mind an elaborate breakfast as he walked down-stairs and took his way to a restaurant, which he entered with the assured step of a man of capital. He gave his order to the waiter with more decision than usual, and told him in closing "not to be all day about it, either."

While waiting for his breakfast, he opened the morning "Bale Fire" to see if there was any account of "The Algonquin Avenue Tragedy." This was the phrase which he had arranged in his mind as the probable head-line of the article. He had so convinced himself of the efficacy of his own precautions, that he anticipated the same pleasure in reading the comments upon his exploit that an author whose incognito is assured enjoys in reading the criticisms of his anonymous work. He was at first disappointed in seeing no allusion to the affair in the usual local columns; but at last discovered in a corner of the paper this double-leaded postscript:

"We stop the press to state that an appalling crime was last night committed in Algonquin Avenue. The mansion of

18

Arthur Farnham, Esq., was entered by burglars between ten
and eleven o'clock, and that gentleman assaulted and probably
murdered.

"Full particulars in a later edition."

"LATER. Captain Farnham is still living, and some hopes
are entertained of his recovery. The police have found the
weapon with which the almost fatal blow was struck—a carpenter's hammer marked with a letter S. It is thought this
clew will lead to the detection of the guilty parties."

Offitt was not entirely pleased with the tone of
this notice. He had expected some reference to the
address and daring of the burglar. But he smiled
to himself, "Why should I care for Sam's reputation?" and ate his breakfast with a good appetite.
Before he had finished, however, he greatly modi-
fied his plan, which was to have the threads of
evidence lead naturally, of themselves, to the conviction of Sleeny. He determined to frighten Sam,
if possible, out of the city, knowing that his flight
would be conclusive evidence of guilt. He swal-
lowed his coffee hurriedly and walked down to Dean
Street, where by good fortune he found Sam alone
in the shop. He was kicking about a pile of shavings on the floor. He turned as Offitt entered and
said : "Oh, there you are. I can't find that hammer anywhere."

Offitt's face assumed a grieved expression. "Come,
come, Sam, don't stand me off that way. I'm your
friend, if you've got one in the world. You mustn't
lose a minute more. You've got time now to catch
the 8.40. Come, jump in a hack and be off."

His earnestness and rapidity confused Sleeny,
and drove all thoughts of the hammer from his

mind. He stared at Offitt blankly, and said, "Why, what are you givin' me now?"

"I'm a-givin' you truth and friendship, and fewest words is best. Come, light out, and write where you stop. I'll see you through."

"See here," roared Sam, "are you crazy or am I? Speak out! What's up?"

"Oh! I've got to speak it out, raw and plain, have I? Very well! Art. Farnham was attacked and nearly murdered last night, and if you didn't do it who did? Now come, for the Lord's sake, get off before the police get here. I never thought you had the sand—but I see you've got too much. Don't lose time talking any more. I'm glad you've killed him. You done just right—but I don't want to see you hung for it."

His excitement and feigned earnestness had brought the tears to his eyes. Sam saw them and was convinced.

"Andy," he said solemnly, "I know you're my friend, and mean right. I'll swear before God it wasn't me, and I know nothing about it, and I won't run away."

"But how will we prove it," said Offitt, wringing his hands in distress. "Where was you last night from ten to eleven?"

"You know where I was—in your room. I went there just after nine and fell asleep waiting for you."

"Yes, of course, but who knows it? Sam, I believe you are innocent since you say so. But see the circumstances. You *have* talked about goin' for him. You *have* had a fight with him, and got put in jail for it, and—" he was about to mention the hammer, but was afraid—"I wish you would take my advice and go off for a week or so till the truth comes out. I'll lend you all the money you want. I'm flush this week."

"No, Andy," said Sleeny, "nobody could be kinder than you. But I won't run away. They can't put a man where he wasn't."

"Very well," replied Offitt, "I admire your pluck, and I'll swear a blue streak for you when the time comes. And perhaps I had better get away now so they won't know I've been with you."

He went without a moment's delay to the chief of police and told him that he had a disagreeable duty to perform; that he knew the murderer of Captain Farnham; that the criminal was an intimate friend of his, a young man hitherto of good character named Sleeny.

"Ah-ha!" said the chief. "That was the fellow that Captain Farnham knocked down and arrested in the riot."

"The same," said Offitt. "He has since that been furious against the Captain. I have reasoned with him over and over about it. Yesterday he came to see me; showed me a hammer he had just bought at Ware & Harden's; said he was going to break Arthur Farnham's skull with it. I didn't believe he would, he had said it so often before. While we were talking, I took the hammer and cut his initial on it, a letter S." The chief nodded, with a broad smile. "He then left me, and when I came back to my room a little before midnight, I found him there. He looked excited, and wanted me to go and get a drink with him. I declined, and he went off. This morning when I heard about the murder I said: 'He's the man that did the deed.'"

"You have not seen him since last night?"

"No; I suppose, of course, he has run away."

"Where did he live?"

"Dean Street, at Matchin's the carpenter."

The chief turned to his telegraphic operator and rapidly gave orders for the arrest of Sleeny by the police of the nearest station. He also sent for the clerks who were on duty the day before at Ware & Harden's.

"Mr. ——, I did not get your name," he said to Offitt, who gave him his name and address. "You have acted the part of a good citizen."

"The most painful act of my life," Offitt murmured.

"Of course. But duty before everything. I will have to ask you to wait a little while in the adjoining room till we see whether this man can be found."

Offitt was shown into a small room, barely furnished, with two doors; the one through which he had just come, and one opening apparently into the main corridor of the building. Offitt, as soon as he was alone, walked stealthily to the latter door and tried to open it. It was locked, and there was no key. He glanced at the window; there was an iron grating inside the sash, which was padlocked. A cold sweat bathed him from head to foot. He sank into a chair, trembling like a leaf. He felt for his handkerchief to wipe his wet forehead. His hand touched one of the packages of money. He bounded from his chair in sudden joy. "They did not search me, so they don't suspect. It is only to make sure of my evidence that they keep me here." Nevertheless, the time went heavily. At last an officer came in and said he was to come to the police justice's for the preliminary examination of Sleeny.

"They have caught him, then ?" he asked, with assumed eagerness and surprise. "He had not got away ?"

"No," the man answered curtly.

They came to the court-room in a few steps. Sam was there between two policemen. As Offitt entered, he smiled and slightly nodded. One or two men who had been summoned as witnesses were standing near the justice. The proceedings were summary.

One of the policemen said that he had gone to Matchin's shop to arrest the prisoner; that the prisoner exhibited no surprise; his first words were, "Is Mr. Farnham dead yet ?"

Offitt was then called upon, and he repeated, clearly and concisely, the story he had told the chief of police. When he had concluded he was shown the hammer which had been picked up on the floor at Farnham's, and was asked, "Is that the hammer you refer to ?"

"Yes, that is it."

These words were the signal for a terrible scene.

When Sleeny saw Offitt step forward and begin to give his evidence, he leaned forward with a smile of pleased expectation upon his face. He had such confidence in his friend's voluble cleverness that he had no doubt Offitt would "talk him free" in a few minutes. He was confused a little by his opening words, not clearly seeing his drift; but as the story went on, and Offitt's atrocious falsehood became clear to his mind, he was dumb with stupefaction, and felt a strange curiosity wakening in him to see how the story would end. He did not, for the moment, see what object Offitt could have in lying so, until the thought occurred to him : "May be there's a reward out !" But when the blood-stained hammer was shown and identified by Offitt, all doubt was cleared away in a flash from the dull brain of Sleeny. He saw the whole horrible plot of which he was the victim.

He rose from his seat before the officer could stop him, and roared like a lion in the toils, in a voice filled equally with agony and rage :

"You murdering liar ! I'll tear your heart out of you !"

There was a wide table and several chairs between them, but Sleeny was over them in an instant. Offitt tried to escape, but was so hemmed in, that the infuriated man had him in his hands before the officers could interpose. If they had delayed a moment longer all would have been over, for already Sleeny's hands were at the throat of his betrayer. But two powerful policemen with their clubs soon separated the combatants, and Sleeny was dragged back and securely handcuffed.

Offitt, ghastly pale and trembling, had sunk upon a bench. The justice, looking at him narrowly, said : " The man is going to faint; loosen his collar."

"No," said Offitt, springing to his feet. "I am perfectly well."

In his struggle with Sleeny a button of his coat

had been torn away. He asked a by-stander for a pin, and carefully adjusted the garment. The thought in his mind was, "I don't mind being killed; but I thought he might tear off my coat, and show them my money." From this moment he kept his hand in such position that he might feel the packages in his pockets.

Sleeny was still panting and screaming execrations at Offitt. The justice turned to him with sternness, and said, "Silence there! Have you not sense enough to see how your ferocious attack on the witness damages you? If you can't restrain your devilish temper while your friend is giving his evidence, it will be all the worse for you."

"Judge," cried Sam, now fairly beside himself, "that's the murderer! I know it. I can prove it. He ain't fit to live. I'll break his neck yet!"

Offitt raised his hands and eyes in deprecating sorrow.

"This is the wild talk of a desperate man," said the justice. "But you may as well tell us how you passed last evening."

"Certainly," said Offitt, consulting his memory. "Let me see. I took supper about seven at Duffer's; I went to Glauber's drug-store next and got a glass of soda water; if they don't know me, they'll remember my breaking a glass; then I made a visit at Mr. Matchin's on Dean Street; then I went to the Orleans theatre; I come out between the acts and got a cup of coffee at Mouchem's—then I went back and stayed till the show was over, that was about half-past eleven. Then I went home and found Mr. Sleeny there."

"You had better go with Mr. Fangwell, and let him verify this statement," said the justice.

He then called the policeman who arrived first at Farnham's house the night before. He told his story and identified the hammer which had been shown to Offitt. A young man from Ware & Harden's swore that he had sold the hammer the day before to Sleeny, whom he knew. The justice held this evidence sufficient to justify Sleeny's detention.

"I should think so," said some of the by-standers. "If it don't hang him, there's a loud call for Judge Lynch."

"Silence!" said the justice. "The prisoner will be taken for the present to the city jail."

Sam was led out, and Offitt accompanied the chief of police back to the room he had just quitted. He remained there several hours which seemed to him interminable. At last, however, the detective who had been sent to inquire as to the truth of the account he had given of himself, returned with a full confirmation of it, and Offitt was suffered to go, on his own engagement to give further evidence when called upon.

He left the City Hall with a great load off his mind. It was not without an effort that he had sworn away the character, the freedom, and perhaps the life of his comrade. If he could have accomplished his purpose without crushing Sleeny he would have preferred it. But the attack which his goaded victim had made upon him in the court-room was now a source of lively satisfaction to him. It created a strong prejudice against the prisoner; it caused the justice at once to believe him guilty, and

gave Offitt himself an injured feeling that was extremely comforting in view of what was to happen
to Sleeny.

He went along the street tapping his various
pockets furtively as he walked. He was hungry.
His diverse emotions had given him an appetite.
He went into an eating-house and commanded a
liberal supper. He had an odd fancy as he gave
his order. "That's the sort of supper I would
have, if it was my last—if I was to be hanged to-
morrow." He thought of Sleeny and hoped they
would treat him well in jail. He felt magnani-
mously toward him. "Who would have thought,"
he mused, "that Sam had such a devil of a temper?
I most hope that Farnham won't die—it would be
rough on Sam. Though perhaps that would be
best all round," he added, thinking of Sam's purple
face in the court-room and the eager grip of his
fingers.

He came out of the eating-house into the gathering twilight. The lamps were springing into light
in long straight lines down the dusky streets. The
evening breeze blew in from the great lake temper-
ing the stale heat of the day. Boys were crying
the late editions of the newspapers with "Full account arrest o' the Farnham burglar!" He bought
one, but did not stop to open it. He folded it into
the smallest possible compass, and stuffed it into
his pocket, "along with the other documents in the
case," as he chuckled to himself; "I'll read all about
it in the train to-morrow—business before pleasure,"
he continued, pleased with his wit.

Every moment he would put his hand into his

side pocket and feel the package containing the largest bills. He knew it was imprudent—that it might attract the attention of thieves or detectives; but to save his life he could not have kept from doing it. At last he scratched his hand on the pin which was doing duty for the button he had lost in his scuffle with Sleeny. "Ah!" he said to himself, with humorous banter, "it won't do to be married in a coat with the buttons off."

He went into a little basement shop where a sign announced that "Scouring and Repairing" were done. A small and bald Hamburger stepped forward, rubbing his hands. Offitt told him what he wanted, and the man got a needle and thread and selected from a large bowl of buttons on a shelf one that would suit. While he was sewing it on, he said:

"Derrible news apout Gabben Farnham."

"Yes," said Offitt. "Is he dead?"

"I don't know off he ish tet. Dey say he ish oud mid his het, und tat looksh mighty pad. But one ting ish goot; dey cotch de murterer."

"They have?" asked Offitt, with languid interest. "What sort of fellow is he?"

"Mutter Gottes!" said the little German. "De vorst kind. He would radder gill a man as drink a glass bier. He gome mighty near gillin' his pest vrient to-day in de gourt-house droben, ven he vas dellin' vat he knowed apout it alleweil."

"A regular fire-eater," said Offitt. "So you've finished, have you? How much for the job!"

The German was looking at a stain on the breast of the coat.

"Vot's dish?" he said. "Looksh like baint Yust lemme take your coat off a minute and I gleans dot up like a nudel soup."

"Say, mind your own business, won't you?" growled Offitt. "Here's your money, and when I want any of your guff I'll let you know."

He hurried out, leaving the poor German amazed at the ill result of his effort to turn an honest penny and do a fellow-creature a service.

"Vunny beebles!" he said to himself. "But I got a kevarter off a tollar for a den-cent chob."

Offitt came out of the shop and walked at a rapid pace to Dean Street. He was determined to make an end at once of Maud's scruples and coquetry. He said to himself: "If we are both alive to-morrow, we shall be married." He believed if he could have her to himself for half an hour, he could persuade her to come with him. He was busy all the way plotting to get her parents out of the house. It would be easy enough to get them out of the room; but he wanted them out of hearing, out of reach of a cry for help even.

He found them all together in the sitting-room. The arrest of Sleeny had fallen heavily upon them. They had no doubt of his guilt, from the reports they had heard, and their surprise and horror at his crime were not lessened but rather increased by their familiar affection for him.

"To think," said Saul to his wife, "that that boy has worked at the same bench, and slept in the same house with me for so many years, and I never knowed the Satan that was in him!"

"It's in all of us, Saul," said Mrs. Matchin, trying to improve the occasion for the edification of her unbelieving husband.

Maud had felt mingled with her sorrow a suspicion of remorse. She could not help remembering that Sam considered Farnham his rival, with how little reason she knew better than any one. She could understand how her beauty might have driven him to violence; but when the story of the robbery transpired also—as it did in the course of the morning,—she was greatly perplexed. When she joined in the lamentations of her parents and said she never could have believed that of Sam Sleeny, she was thinking of the theft, and not of the furious assault. When they had all, however, exhausted their limited store of reflections, a thing took place which increased the horror and the certainty of Mr. and Mrs. Matchin, and left Maud a prey to a keener doubt and anxiety than ever. Late in the afternoon a sharp-faced man, with a bright eye and a red mustache, came to the house and demanded in the name of the law to be shown Sam's bedroom. He made several notes and picked up some trifling articles, for which he gave Mr. Matchin receipts. Coming out of the room, he looked carefully at the door-knob. " Seems all right," he said. Then turning to Matchin, he said, with professional severity, " What door did he generally come in by ?"

" Sometimes one and sometimes another," said Saul, determined not to give any more information than he must.

" Well, I'll look at both," the detective said.

The first one stood his scrutiny without effect,

but at the second his eye sparkled and his cheek flushed with pleasure, when he saw the faint, reddish-brown streaks which Offitt had left there the night before.   He could not express his exultation; turning to Saul, "There's where he came in last night, any way."

"He didn't do no such a thing," replied Saul. "That door I locked myself last night before he came in."

"Oh, you did? So you're sure he came in at the other door, are you. We will see if he could get in any other way."

Walking around the corner, he saw the ladder where Offitt had left it.

"Hello! that's his window, ain't it?"

Without waiting for an answer the detective ran up the ladder, studying every inch of its surface as he ran. He came down positively radiant, and slapped Saul heartily on the shoulder.

"All right, old man. I'll trouble you to keep that ladder and that door just as they are. They are important papers. Why, don't you see?" he continued—"bless your innocent old heart, he comes home with his hands just reg'larly dripping with murder. He fumbles at that door, finds it locked, and so gets that ladder, histes it up to the window, and hops into bed as easy as any Christian school-boy in town, and he thinks he's all right—but he never thinks of Tony Smart, your humble servant."

This view of the case was perfectly convincing to Saul and also to his wife when he repeated it at the supper-table; but it struck Maud with a sudden chill. She remembered that when she had dismissed Offitt from that midnight conference at her casement, he had carefully taken the ladder away from her window, and had set it against the house some distance off. She had admired at the time his considerate chivalry, and thought how nice it was to have a lover so obedient and so careful of her reputation. But now, the detective's ghastly discovery turned her thought in a direction which appalled her. Could it be possible—and all that money—where did it come from? As she sat with her parents in the gathering darkness, she kept her dreadful anxiety to herself. She had been hoping all day to see her lover—now she feared to have him come, lest her new suspicions might be confirmed. She quickly resolved upon one thing: she would not go away with him that night—not until this horrible mystery was cleared up. If she was worth having she was worth waiting for a little while.

They all three started as the door opened and Offitt came in. He wasted no time in salutations, but said at once, " It's a funny thing, but I have got a message for each of you. The district attorney saw me coming up this way, Mr. Matchin, and asked me to tell you to come down as quick as you can to his office—something very important, he said. And, stranger than that, I met Mr. Wixham right out here by the corner, and he asked me if I was comin' here, and if I would ask you, Mrs. Matchin, to come right up to their house. Jurildy is sick and wants to see you, and he has run off for the doctor."

Both the old people bustled up at this authoritative summons, and Offitt as they went out said,

"I'll stay a while and keep Miss Maud from gettin' lonesome."

"I wish you would," said Mrs. Matchin. "The house seems creepy-like with Sam where he is."

Maud felt her heart sink at the prospect of being left alone with the man she had been longing all day to see. She said, "Mother, I think I ought to go with you!"

"No, indeed," her mother replied. "You ain't wanted, and it wouldn't be polite to Mr. Offitt."

The moment they were gone, Offitt sprang to the side of Maud, and seized her hands.

"Now, my beauty, you will be mine. Put on your hat and we will go."

She struggled to free her hands.

"Let go," she said, "you hurt me. Why are you in such a terrible hurry?"

"Why can you ask? Your parents will be back in a few minutes. Of course you know that story was only to get them out of our way. Come, my beautiful Maud! my joy, my queen! To-morrow New York! next day the sea, and then Europe and love and pleasure all your life."

"I want to talk with you a minute," said Maud, in a voice which trembled in spite of her efforts. "I can't talk in the dark. Wait here, till I get a lamp."

She slipped from the room before he could prevent her and left him pacing the floor in a cold rage. It was only a moment, however, until she returned, bringing a lamp, which she placed on a table, and then asked him to be seated, in a stiff, formal way, which at once irritated and enchanted him. He sat

down and devoured her with his eyes. He was angry when she went for the lamp; but, as its light
fell on her rich, dark hair, her high color, and her
long, graceful figure, as she leaned back in her chair,
he felt that the tenderest conversation with her in
the darkness would lose something of the pleasure
that the eyes took in her. This he said to her, in
his coarse but effective way.

She answered him with coquettish grace, willing
to postpone the serious talk she dreaded. so. But
the conversation was in stronger hands than hers,
and she found herself forced, in a few minutes, to
either go with him, or give a reason why.

"The fact is, then," she stammered, with a great
effort, "I don't know you well enough yet. Why
cannot you wait a while?"

He laughed.

"Come with me, and you will know me better in
a day than you would here in a year. Do not waste
these precious moments. Our happiness depends
upon it. We have everything we can desire. I
cannot be myself here. I cannot disclose my rank
and my wealth to these people who have only known
me as an apostle of labor. I want to go where you
will be a great lady. Oh, come!" he cried, with an
outburst of pent-up fire, throwing himself on the
floor at her feet, and laying his head upon her knee.
She was so moved by this sudden outbreak, which
was wholly new to her experience, that she almost
forgot her doubts and fears. But a remnant of
practical sense asserted itself. She rose from her
chair, commanded him once more to be seated, and
said:

19

"I am afraid I am going to offend you, but I must ask you something."

"Ask me anything," he said, with a smile, "except to leave you."

She thought the phrase so pretty that she could hardly find courage to put her question. She blushed and stammered, and then, rushing at it with desperation, she said :

"That money—where did you get it ?"

"I will tell you when we are married. It is a secret."

He tried still to smile, but she saw the laughter dying away from his face.

Her blood turned cold in her veins, but her heart grew stronger, and she determined to know the worst. She was not a refined or clever woman; but the depth of her trouble sharpened her wits, and she instinctively made use of her woman's wiles to extort the truth from the man who she knew was under the spell of her beauty, whatever else he was.

"Come here !" she said. Her face was pale, but her lips were smiling. "Get down there where you were !" she continued, with tender imperiousness. He obeyed her, hardly daring to trust his senses. "Now put your hands between my hands," she said, still with that pale, singular smile, which filled him with unquiet transports, "and tell me the truth, you bad boy !"

"The truth," with a beating of the heart which made his utterance thick, "the truth is, that you are the most glorious woman in the world, and that you will be mine to-morrow."

"Perhaps," she almost whispered. "But you

must tell me something else. I am afraid you are
a naughty boy, and that you love me too much. I
once told you I had an enemy, and that I wanted
somebody to punish him. Did you go and punish
him for me—tell me that?"

Her voice was soft and low and beguiling. She
still smiled on him, leaving one hand in his, while
she raised the forefinger of the other in coquettish
admonition. The ruffian at her feet was inebriated
with her beauty and her seductive playfulness. He
thought she had divined his act—that she considered
it a fine and heroic test of love to which she had subjected him. He did not hesitate an instant, but said:
"Yes, my beauty, and I am ready to do the same
for anybody who gives you a cross look."

Now that she had gained the terrible truth, a
sickening physical fear of the man came over her,
and she felt herself growing faint. His voice
sounded weak and distant as he said:

"Now you will go with me, won't you?"

She could make no answer. So he continued:

"Run and get your hat. Nothing else. We can
buy all you want. And hurry. They may come
back any moment."

She perceived a chance of escape and roused herself. She thought if she could only get out of the
room she might save herself by flight or by outcry.

"Wait here," she whispered, "and be very quiet."

He kissed his fingers to her without a word. She
opened the door into the next room, which was the
kitchen and dining-room of the family, and there,
not three feet from her, in the dim light, haggard
and wan, bareheaded, his clothes in rags about him,
she saw Sam Sleeny.

XIX.

A LEAP FOR SOMEBODY'S LIFE.

WHEN Sleeny was led from the room of tne police justice in the afternoon, he was plunged in a sort of stupor. He could not recover from the surprise and sense of outrage with which he had listened to Offitt's story. What was to happen to him he accepted with a despair which did not trouble itself about the ethics of the transaction. It was a disaster, as a stroke of lightning might be. It seemed to him the work had been thoroughly and effectually done. He could see no way out of it; in fact, his respect for Offitt's intelligence was so great that he took it for granted Andy had committed no mistakes, but that he had made sure of his ruin. He must go to prison; if Farnham died, he must be hanged. He did not weary his mind in planning for his defence when his trial should come on. He took it for granted he should be convicted. But if he could get out of prison, even if it were only for a few hours, and see Andy Offitt once more—he felt the blood tingling through all his veins at the thought. This roused him from his lethargy and made him observant and alert. He began to complain of his handcuffs; they were in truth galling his wrists. It was not difficult for him to twist his hands so as to start the blood in one or two places. He showed these quietly to the policemen, who sat

with him in a small anteroom leading to the portion
of the city jail, where he was to be confined for the
night. He seemed so peaceable and quiet that they
took off the irons, saying good-naturedly, "I guess
we can handle you." They were detained in this
room for some time waiting for the warden of the
jail to come and receive their prisoner. There were
two windows, both giving view of a narrow street,
where it was not bright at noonday, and began to
grow dark at sunset with the shade of the high
houses and the thick smoke of the quarter. The
windows were open, as the room was in the third
story, and was therefore considered absolutely safe.
Sleeny got up several times and walked first to
one window and then to another, casting quick but
searching glances at the street and the walls. He
saw that some five feet from one of the windows a
tin pipe ran along the wall to the ground. The
chances were ten to one that any one risking the
leap would be dashed to pieces on the pavement below. But Sleeny could not get that pipe out of his
head. "I might as well take my chance" he said
to himself. "It would be no worse to die that way
than to be hanged." He grew afraid to trust himself in sight of the window and the pipe: it exercised so strong a fascination upon him. He sat down
with his back to the light and leaned his head on his
hands. But he could think of nothing but his leap
for liberty. He felt in fancy his hands and knees
clasping that slender ladder of safety; he began to
think what he would do when he struck the sidewalk, if no bones were broken. First, he would
hide from pursuit, if possible. Then he would go

to Dean Street and get a last look at Maud, if he
could; then his business would be to find Offitt.
"If I find him," he thought, "I'll give them something to try me for." But finally he dismissed the
matter from his mind,—for this reason. He remembered seeing a friend, the year before, fall from
a scaffolding and break his leg. The broken bone
pierced through the leg of his trousers. This
thought daunted him more than death on the gal-
lows.

The door opened, and three or four policemen
came in, each leading a man by the collar, the ordinary riffraff of the street, charged with petty offen-
ces. One was very drunk and abusive. He attracted
the attention of everybody in the room by his antics.
He insisted on dancing a breakdown which he called
the "Essence of Jeems' River"; and in the scuffle
which followed, first one and then the other policeman in charge of Sleeny became involved. Sleeny
was standing with his back to the window, quite
alone. The temptation was too much for him. He
leaped upon the sill, gave one mighty spring, caught
the pipe, and slid safely to the ground. One or two
passers-by saw him drop lightly to the sidewalk, but
thought nothing of it. It was not the part of the
jail in which prisoners were confined, and he might
have been taken for a carpenter or plumber who
chose that unusual way of coming from the roof.
His hat blew off in his descent, but he did not waste
time in looking for it. He walked slowly till he
got to the corner, and then plunged through the
dark and ill-smelling streets of the poor and crowded quarter, till he came by the open gate of a coal-

yard. Seeing he was not pursued he went in, concealed himself behind a pile of boards and lay there until it was quite dark.

He then came out and walked through roundabout ways, avoiding the gas-lights and the broad thoroughfares, to Dean Street. He climbed the fence and crept through the garden to the back door of the house. He had eaten nothing since early morning, and was beginning to be hungry. He saw there were no lights in the rear of the house, and thought if he could enter the kitchen he might get a loaf of bread without alarming the household. He tried the back door and found it fastened. But knowing the ways of the house, he raised the cellar door, went down the steps, shut the door down upon himself, groped his way to the inner stairs, and so gained the kitchen. He was walking to the cupboard when the door opened and he saw Maud coming toward him.

She did not seem in the least startled to see him there. In the extremity of her terror, it may have seemed to her that he had been sent especially to her help. She walked up to him, laid her hands on his shoulders and whispered, "Oh, Sam, I am so glad to see you. Save me! Don't let him touch me! He is in there."

Sam hardly knew if this were real or not. A wild fancy assailed him for an instant—was he killed in jumping from the window? Surely this could never happen to him on the earth; the girl who had always been so cold and proud to him was in his arms, her head on his shoulder, her warm breath on his cheek. She was asking his help against some danger.

"All right, Mattie," he whispered. "Nobody shall hurt you. Who is it?" He thought of no one but the police.

"Offitt," she said.

He brushed her aside as if she had been a cobweb in his path, and with a wild cry of joy and vengeance he burst through the half-open door. Offitt turned at the noise, and saw Sam coming, and knew that the end of his life was there. His heart was like water within him. He made a feeble effort at defence; but the carpenter, without a word, threw him on the floor, planted one knee on his chest, and with his bare hands made good the threat he uttered in his agony in the court-room, twisting and breaking his neck.

Sleeny rose, pulled the cover from the centre-table in the room, and threw it over the distorted face of the dead man.

Maud, driven out of her wits by the dreadful scene, had sunk in a rocking-chair, where, with her face in her hands, she was sobbing and moaning. Sam tried to get her to listen to him.

"Good-by, Mattie, I shall never see you again, I suppose. I must run for my life. I want you to know I was innocent of what they charged me with——"

"Oh, I know that, Sam," she sobbed.

"God bless you, Mattie, for saying so. I don't care so much for what happens, now. I am right glad I got here to save you from that——" he paused, searching for a word which would be descriptive and yet not improper in the presence of a lady, but his vocabulary was not rich and he said at last, " that snide. But I should have done that to him anyhow; so don't cry on that account. Mattie, will you tell me good-by ?" he asked with bashful timidity.

She rose and gave him her hand ; but her eyes happening to wander to the shapeless form lying in the corner, she hid her face again on his shoulder and said with a fresh burst of tears. " Oh, Sam, stay with me a little while. Don't leave me alone."

His mind travelled rapidly through the incidents that would result from his staying—prison, trial, and a darker contingency still, rearing its horrible phantom in the distance. But she said, " You will stay till father comes, won't you ?" and he answered simply :

" Yes, Mattie, if you want me to."

He led her to a seat and sat down beside her, to wait for his doom.

In a few minutes, they heard a loud altercation outside the door. The voice of Saul Matchin was vehemently protesting, " I tell ye he ain't here," and another voice responded,

" He was seen to climb the fence and to enter the house. We've got it surrounded, and there's no use for you to get yourself into trouble aidin' and abettin'."

Sam walked to the door and said to the policeman, with grim humor, " Come in ! you'll find two murderers here, and neither one will show any fight."

The policemen blew their whistles to assemble the rest, and then came in warily, and two of them seized him at once.

"It's all very well to be meek and lowly, my friend," said one of them, "but you'll not play that on us twice—least ways," he added with sarcastic intention, "not twice the same day. See here, Tony Smart," addressing a third, who now entered, "lend a hand with these bracelets," and in a moment Sam was handcuffed and pinioned.

"Where's the other one you was talking about?" asked the policeman.

Sam pointed with his foot in the direction where Offitt lay. The policeman lifted the cloth, and dropped it again with a horror which his professional phlegm could not wholly disguise.

"Well, of all the owdacious villains ever I struck —— Who do you think it is?" he asked, turning to his associates.

"Who?"

"The witness this afternoon,—Offitt. Well, my man," he said, turning to Sam, "you wanted to make a sure thing of it, I see. If you couldn't be hung for one, you would for the other."

"Sam!" said Saul Matchin who, pale and trembling, had been a silent spectator of the scene so far, "for heaven's sake, tell us what all this means."

"Mind now," said the officer, "whatever you say will be reported."

"Very well, I've got nothing to hide," said Sam. "I'll tell you and Mother Matchin" (who had just come in and was staring about her with consternation, questioning Maud in dumb show) "the whole story. I owe that to you for you've always used me well. It's a mighty short one. That fellow Offitt robbed and tried to murder Captain Farnham last night, and then swore it onto me. I got away from the officers to-night, and come round here and found him 'saulting Mattie, and I twisted his neck for him. If it's a hanging matter to kill snakes, I'll have to stand it—that's all."

"Now, who do you think is going to believe that ?" said the captain of the squad.

Maud rose and walked up to where Sam was standing and said, " I know every word he has said is true. That man was the burglar at Captain Farnham's. He told me so himself to-night. He said he had the money in his pocket and wanted to make me go with him."

She spoke firmly and resolutely, but she could not bring herself to say anything of previous passages between them ; and when she opened her lips to speak of the ladder, the woman was too strong within her, and she closed them again. " I'll never tell that unless they go to hang Sam, and then I won't tell anybody but the Governor," she swore to herself.

" It's easy to see about that story," said the officer still incredulous.

They searched the clothing of Offitt, and the face of the officer, as one package of money after another was brought to light, was a singular study. The pleasure he felt in the recovery of the stolen goods was hardly equal to his professional chagrin at having caught the wrong man. He stood for a moment silent, after tying up all the packages in one.

" It's no use dodging," he said at last. " We have been barking up the wrong tree."

"I don't know about that," said the one called
Tony Smart. "Who has identified this money?
Who can answer for this young lady? How about
them marks on the door and the ladder? Anyhow
there's enough to hold our prisoner on."

"Of course there is," said the captain. "He
hadn't authority to go twisting people's necks in
this county."

At this moment the wagon which had been sent
for arrived. The body of Offitt was lifted in. The
captain gathered up the money, notified Matchin
that he and his family would be wanted as witnesses
in the morning, and they all moved toward the door.
Sam turned to say "Farewell." Pinioned as he
was, he could not shake hands, and his voice faltered
as he took leave of them. Maud's heart was not
the most feeling one in the world, but her emotions
had been deeply stirred by the swift succession of
events; and as she saw this young fellow going so
bravely to meet an unknown fate, purely for her
sake, the tears came to her eyes. She put out her
hand to him; but she saw that his hands were
fastened and, seized with sudden pity, she put her
arms about his neck and kissed him, whispering,
"Keep up a good heart, Sam!" and he went away,
in all his danger and ignominy happier than he had
been for many a day.

The probabilities of the case were much discussed
that night at police head-quarters, in conferences
from which the reporters were rigorously excluded,
and the next morning the city newspapers revelled
in the sensation. They vied with each other in in-
venting attractive head-lines and startling theories.

The *Bale-Fire* began its leader with the impressive sentence: " Has a carnival of crime set in amongst us? Last night the drama of Algonquin Avenue was supplemented by the tragedy of Dean Street, and the public, aghast, demands ' What next?' A second murder was accomplished by hands yet dripping with a previous crime. The patriotic witness who, yesterday, with a bleeding heart, denounced the criminality of his friend, paid last night with his life for his fidelity." In another column it called for a "monument, by popular subscription, for Andrew Jackson Offitt, who died because he would not tell a lie." On the other hand, *The Morning Astral*, representing the conservative opinion of the city, called for a suspension of judgment on the part of its candid readers ; said that there were shady circumstances about the antecedents of Offitt, and intimated that documents of a compromising character had been found on his person ; congratulated the city on the improved condition of Captain Farnham ; and, trusting in the sagacity and diligence of the authorities, confidently awaited from them a solution of the mystery. Each of them, nevertheless, gave free space and license to their reporters, and Offitt was a saint, a miscreant, a disguised prince, and an escaped convict, according to the state of the reporter's imagination or his digestion ; while the stories told of Sleeny varied from cannibalism to feats of herculean goodness. They all agreed reasonably well, however, as to the personal appearance of the two men, and from this fact it came about that, in the course of the morning, evidence was brought forward, from a totally unexpected

quarter, which settled the question as to the burglary at Farnham's.

Mrs. Belding had been so busy the day before, in
her constant attendance upon Farnham, that she had
paid no attention to the story of the arrest. She
had heard that the man had been caught and his
crime clearly established, and that he had been sent
to jail for trial. Her first thought was, "I am glad
I was not called upon to give evidence. It would
have been very disagreeable to get up before a
court-room full of men and say I looked with an
opera-glass out of my daughter's window into a
young man's house. I should have to mention
Alice's name, too,—and a young girl's name cannot
be mentioned too seldom in the newspapers. In
fact, twice in a life-time is often enough, and one
of them should be a funeral notice."

But this morning, after calling at Farnham's and
finding that he was getting on comfortably, she sat
down to read the newspapers. Alice was sitting
near her, with hands and lap full of some feminine handiwork. A happy smile played about
her lips, for her mother had just repeated to her
the surgeon's prediction that Captain Farnham
would be well in a week or two. "He said the
scalp wound was healing ' by the first intention,'
which I thought was a funny phrase. I thought
the maxim was that second thoughts were best."
Alice had never mentioned Farnham's name since
the first night, but he was rarely out of her mind,
and the thought that his life was saved made every
hour bright and festal. "He will be well," she
thought. "He will have to come here to thank

mamma for her care of him. I shall see him again
and he shall not complain of me. If he should
never speak to me again, I shall love him and be
good to him always." She was yet too young and too
innocent to know how impossible was the scheme of
life she was proposing to herself, but she was thoroughly happy in it.

Mrs. Belding, as she read, grew perplexed and
troubled. She threw down one newspaper and took
up another, but evidently got no more comfort out
of that. At last she sighed and said, " Oh, dear !
Oh, dear ! I shall have to go down there after all.
They have got the wrong man !"

Alice looked up with wondering eyes.

" These accounts all agree that the assassin is a
tall, powerful young man, with yellow hair and
beard. The real man was not more than medium
height, very dark. Why, he was black and shiny
as a cricket. I must go and tell them. I wonder
who the lawyer is that does the indicting of people ?"

"It must be the prosecuting attorney, Mr. Dalton," said Alice. "I heard he was elected this
spring. You know him very well. You meet him
everywhere."

" That elegant young fellow who leads germans ?
Well, if that is not too absurd ! I never should
have thought of him, outside of a dress-coat. I
don't mind a bit going to see *him*. Order the carriage, while I get my things on."

She drove down to the City Hall, and greatly astonished Mr. Dalton by walking into his office and
requesting a moment's private conversation with
him. Dalton was a dapper young man, exceedingly

glib and well dressed, making his way in political and official, as he had already made it in social life. He greeted Mrs. Belding with effusion, and was anxious to know how he might serve her, having first cleared the room of the half-dozen politicians who did their lounging there.

"It is a most delicate matter for a lady to appear in, and I must ask you to keep my name as much in reserve as possible."

"Of course, you may count upon me," he answered, wondering where this strange exordium would lead to.

"You have got the wrong man. I am sure of it. It was not the blonde one. He was black as a cricket. I saw him as plainly as I see you. You know we live next door to Captain Farn-ham——"

"Ah!" Dalton cried. "Certainly. I understand. This is most important. Pray go on."

With a few interruptions from him, full of tact and intelligence, she told the whole story, or as much of it as was required. She did not have to mention Alice's name, or the opera-glass; though the clever young man said to himself, "She is either growing very far-sighted, or she was scouring the heavens with a field-glass that night—perhaps looking for comets."

He rang his bell and gave a message to an usher who appeared. "I will not ask you to wait long," he said, and turned the conversation upon the weather and social prospects for the season. In a few minutes the door opened, and Sleeny was brought into the room by an officer.

"Was this the man you saw, Mrs. Belding?" asked Dalton.

"Not the slightest resemblance. This one is much taller, and entirely different in color."

"That will do"; and Sleeny and the officer went out.

"Now may I ask you to do a very disagreeable thing? To go with me to the Morgue and see the remains of what I am now sure is the real criminal?" Dalton asked.

"Oh, mercy! I would rather not. Is it necessary?"

"Not positively necessary, but it will enable me to dismiss the burglary case absolutely against young Sleeny."

"Very well. I'll go. I am so glad," she said to herself, "that I did not bring Alice."

They went in her carriage to the Morgue. Dalton said, "I want to make it as easy as I can for you. Please wait a moment in your carriage." He went in and arranged that the face of Offitt, which was horrible, should be turned away as much as possible; the head, and shoulders and back being left exposed, and the hat placed on the head. He then brought Mrs. Belding in.

"That is the man," she said, promptly, "or at least some one exactly like him."

"Thank you," he said, reconducting her to her carriage. "The first charge against Sleeny will be dismissed, though of course he must be held for this homicide."

A few weeks later Sleeny was tried for the killing
20

of Offitt, on which occasion most of the facts of this
history were given in evidence. Mrs. Belding had
at last to tell what she knew in open court, and she
had an evil quarter of an hour in the hands of Mr.
Dalton, who seemed always on the point of asking
some question which would bring her opera-glass
into the newspapers; but he never proceeded to
that extremity, and she came away with a better
opinion of the profession than she had ever before
entertained. "I suppose leading germans human-
izes even a lawyer somewhat," she observed, philosophically.

Maud Matchin was, however, the most important
witness for the defence. She went upon the stand
troubled with no abstract principles in regard to the
administration of justice. She wanted Sam Sleeny
to be set free, and she testified with an eye single to
that purpose. She was perhaps a trifle too zealous
—even the attorney for the defence bit his lip occasionally at her dashing introduction of wholly irrelevant matter in Sleeny's favor. But she was
throughout true to herself also, and never gave the
least intimation that Offitt had any right to consider
himself a favored suitor. Perhaps she had attained
the talent, so common in more sophisticated circles
than any with which she was familiar, of forgetting
all entanglements which it is not convenient to remember, and of facing a discarded lover with a visage of insolent unconcern and a heart unstirred by a
memory.

The result of it all was, of course, that Sleeny was
acquitted, though it came about in a way which may
be worth recording. The jury found a verdict of

" justifiable homicide," upon which the judge very
properly sent them back to their room, as the verdict was flatly against the law and the evidence.
They retired again, with stolid and unabashed patience, and soon reappeared with a verdict of acquit-
tal, on the ground of " emotional insanity." But
this remarkable jury determined to do nothing by
halves, and fearing that the reputation of being
queer might injure Sam in his business prospects,
added to their verdict these thoughtful and considerate words, which yet remain on the record, to the
lasting honor and glory of our system of trial by
jury:

" And we hereby state that the prisoner was perfectly sane up to the moment he committed the
rash act in question, and perfectly sane the moment
after, and that, in our opinion, there is no probability that the malady will ever recur."

After this memorable deliverance, Sam shook
hands cordially and gravely with each of the judicious jurymen, and then turned to where Maud was
waiting for him, with a rosy and happy face and a
sparkling eye. They walked slowly homeward together through the falling shadows.

Their lives were henceforth bound together for
good or evil. We may not say how much of good
or how much of evil was to be expected from a
wedlock between two natures so ill-regulated and
untrained, where the woman brought into the part-
nership the wreck of ignoble ambitions and the man
the memory of a crime.

XX.

"NOW, DO YOU REMEMBER?"

FARNHAM'S convalescence was rapid. When the
first danger of fever was over, the wound on the
head healed quickly, and one morning Mrs. Belding
came home with the news that he was to drive out
that afternoon. Alice sat in the shade by the front
porch for an hour, waiting to see him pass, and
when at last his carriage appeared, she rose and
waved her handkerchief by way of greeting and
congratulation. He bowed as he went by, and
Alice retired to her own room, where she used her
handkerchief once more to dry her wet and happy
eyes.

It was not long after, that Farnham came to dine
with them. They both looked forward to this dinner as an occasion of very considerable importance.
Each felt that much depended upon the demeanor of
the other. Each was conscientiously resolved to do
and to say nothing which should pain or embarrass
the other. Each was dying to fall into the other's
arms, but each only succeeded in convincing the
other of his or her entire indifference and friendship.

As Farnham came in, Mrs. Belding went up to
him with simple kindliness, kissed him, and made
him sit down. " You dear boy," she said, " you do

not know how glad I am to see you here once more."

Alice looked on, almost jealous of her mother's privilege. Then she advanced with shy grace and took Arthur's hand, and asked: "Do you begin to feel quite strong again?"

Farnham smiled, and answered, "Quite well, and the strength will soon come. The first symptom of returning vitality, Mrs. Belding, was my hostility to gruel and other phantom dishes. I have deliberately come to dinner to-day to dine."

"I am delighted to hear of your appetite," said Mrs. Belding; "but I think you may bear a little watching at the table yet," she added, in a tone of kindly menace. She was as good as her word, and exercised rather a stricter discipline at dinner than was agreeable to the convalescent, regulating his meat and wine according to ladylike ideas, which are somewhat binding on carnivorous man. But she was so kindly about it, and Alice aided and abetted with such bashful prettiness, that Farnham felt he could endure starvation with such accessories. Yet he was not wholly at ease. He had hoped, in the long hours of his confinement, to find the lady of his love kinder in voice and manner than when he saw her last; and now, when she was sweeter and more tender than he had ever seen her before, the self-tormenting mind of the lover began to suggest that if she loved him she would not be so kind. He listened to the soft, caressing tones of her voice as she spoke to him, which seemed to convey a blessing in every syllable; he met the wide, clear beauty of her glance, so sweet and bright that his own eyes could hardly support it; he saw the ready smile that came to the full, delicate mouth whenever he spoke; and instead of being made happy by all this, he asked himself if it could mean anything except that she was sorry for him, and wanted to be very polite to him, as she could be nothing more. His heart sank within him at the thought; he became silent and constrained; and Alice wondered whether she had not gone too far in her resolute kindness. "Perhaps he has changed his mind," she thought, "and wishes me not to change mine." So these two people, whose hands and hearts were aching to come together, sat in the same drawing-room talking of commonplace things, while their spirits grew heavy as lead.

Mrs. Belding was herself conscious of a certain constraint, and to dispel it asked Alice to sing, and Farnham adding his entreaties, she went to the piano, and said, as all girls say, "What shall I sing?"

She looked toward Farnham, but the mother answered, "Sing 'Douglas' ——"

"Oh, no, Mamma, not that."

"Why not? You were singing it last night. I like it better than any other of your songs."

"I do not want to sing it to-night."

Mrs. Belding persisted, until at last Alice said, with an odd expression of recklessness, "Oh, very well, if you must have it, I will sing it. But I hate these sentimental songs, that say so much and mean nothing." Striking the chords nervously she sang, with a voice at first tremulous but at last full of

strong and deep feeling, that wail of hopeless love
and sorrow :

> " Could you come back to me, Douglas, Douglas,
>   In the old likeness that I knew,
> I would be so faithful, so loving, Douglas,
>   Douglas, Douglas, tender and true."

There had been tears of vexation in her eyes
when her mother had forced her to sing this song
of all others; but after she had begun, the music
took her own heart by storm, and she sang as she
had never sung before—no longer fearing, but hoping that the cry of her heart might reach her lover
and tell him of her love. Farnham listened in
transport; he had never until now heard her sing,
and her beautiful voice seemed to him to complete
the circle of her loveliness. He was so entranced
by the full rich volume of her voice, and by the
rapt beauty of her face as she sang, that he did not
at first think of the words; but the significance of
them seized him at last, and the thought that she
was singing these words to him ran like fire through
his veins. For a moment he gave himself up to the
delicious consciousness that their souls were floating
together upon that tide of melody. As the song
died away and closed with a few muffled chords, he
was on the point of throwing himself at her feet,
and getting the prize which was waiting for him.
But he suddenly bethought himself that she had
sung the song unwillingly and had taken care to
say that the words meant nothing. He rose and
thanked her for the music, complimented her singing warmly, and bidding both ladies good night,
went home, thrilled through and through with a

deeper emotion than he had yet known, but pain-
fully puzzled and perplexed.

He sat for a long time in his library, trying to
bring some order into his thoughts. He could not
help feeling that his presence was an embarrassment
and a care to Alice Belding. It was evident that
she had a great friendship and regard for him,
which he had troubled and disturbed by his ill-
timed declaration. She could no longer be easy and
natural with him; he ought not to stay to be an annoyance to her. It was also clear that he could not
be himself in her presence; she exercised too powerful an influence upon him to make it possible that
he could go in and out of the house as a mere friend
of the family. He was thus driven to the thought
which always lay so near to the surface with him,
as with so many of his kind; he would exile himself for a year or two, and take himself out of her
way. The thought gave him no content. He could
not escape a keen pang of jealousy when he thought
of leaving her in her beautiful youth to the society
of men who were so clearly inferior to her.

"I am inferior to her myself," he thought with
genuine humility; "but I feel sure I can appreciate
her better than any one else she will ever be likely
to meet."

By and by he became aware that something was
perplexing him, which was floating somewhere below the surface of his consciousness. A thousand
thoughts, more or less puzzling, had arisen and been
disposed of during the hour that had elapsed since
he left Mrs. Belding's. But still he began to be
sure that there was one groping for recognition

which as yet he had not recognized. The more he dwelt upon it, the more it seemed to attach itself to the song Alice had sung, but he could not give it any definiteness. After he had gone to bed, this undefined impression of something significant attaching itself to the song besieged him, and worried him with tantalizing glimpses, until he went to sleep.

But Farnham was not a dreamer, and the morning, if it brought little comfort, brought at least decision. He made up his mind while dressing that he would sail by an early steamer for Japan. He sent a telegram to San Francisco, as soon as he had breakfasted, to inquire about accommodations, and busied himself during the day with arranging odds and ends of his affairs. Coming and going was easy to him, as he rarely speculated and never touched anything involving anxious risks. But in the afternoon an irresistible longing impelled him to the house of his neighbor.

"Why should I not allow myself this indulgence?" he thought. "It will be only civil to go over there and announce my departure. As all is over, I may at least take this last delight to my eyes and heart. And I want to hear that song again."

All day the song had been haunting him, not on account of anything in itself, but because it vaguely reminded him of something else—something of infinite importance, if he could only grasp it. It hung about him so persistently, this vague glimmer of suggestion, that he became annoyed, and said at last to himself, "It is time for me to be changing my climate, if a ballad can play like that on my nerves."

He seized his hat and walked rapidly across the lawn, with the zest of air and motion natural to a strong man in convalescence. The pretty maid-servant smiled and bowed him into the cool, dim drawing-room, where Alice was seated at the piano. She rose and said instinctively to the servant, "Tell mamma Captain Farnham is here," and immedi-ately repented as she saw his brow darken a little. He sat down beside her, and said:

"I come on a twofold errand. I want to say good-by to you, and I want you to sing 'Douglas' for me once more."

"Why, where are you going?" she said, with a look of surprise and alarm.

"To Japan."

"But not at once, surely?"

"The first steamer I can find."

Alice tried to smile, but the attempt was a little woful.

"It will be a delightful journey, I am sure," she faltered, "but I can't get used to the idea of it, all at once. It is the end of the world."

"I want to get there before the end comes. At the present rate of progress there is not more than a year's purchase of bric-à-brac left in the empire. I must hurry over and get my share. What can I do for you?" he continued, seeing that she sat silent, twisting her white fingers together. "Shall I not bring you the loot of a temple or two? They say the priests have become very corruptible since our missionaries got there—the false religion tumbling all to pieces before the true."

Still she made no answer, and the fixed smile on

her face looked as if she hardly heard what he was
saying. But he went on in the same light, banter-
ing tone.

"Shall I bring you back a Jinrickishaw ?"

"What in the world is that—but, no matter what
it is—tell me, are you really going so soon ?"

If Farnham had not been the most modest of men,
the tone in which this question was asked would
have taught him that he need not exile himself. But
he answered seriously :

"Yes, I am really going."

"But why ?" The question came from unwilling
lips, but it would have its way. The challenge was
more than Farnham could endure. He spoke out
with quick and passionate earnestness :

"Must I tell you then ? Do you not know ? I
am going because you send me."

"Oh, no," she murmured, with flaming cheeks
and downcast eyes.

"I am going because I love you, and I cannot
bear to see you day by day, and know that you are not
for me. You are too young and too good to understand what I feel. If I were a saint like you, perhaps I might rejoice in your beauty and your grace
without any selfish wish—but I cannot. If you are
not to be mine, I cannot enjoy your presence.
Every charm you have is an added injury, if I am
to be indifferent to you."

Her hands flew up and covered her eyes. She
was so happy that she feared he would see it and
claim her too soon and too swiftly.

He mistook the gesture, and went on in his error.

"There! I have made you angry, or wounded

you again. It would be so continually, if I should stay. I should be giving you offence every hour in the day. I cannot help loving you, any more than I can help breathing. This is nothing to you or worse than nothing, but it is all my life to me. I do not know how it will end. You have filled every thought of my mind, every vein of my body. I am more you than myself. How can I separate myself from you?"

As he poured out these words, and much more, hot as a flood of molten metal, Alice slowly recovered her composure. She was absolutely and tranquilly happy—so perfectly at rest that she hardly cared for the pain her lover was confessing. She felt she could compensate him for everything, and every word he said filled her with a delight which she could not bear to lose by replying. She sat listening to him with half-shut eyes, determined not to answer until he had made an end of speaking. But she said to herself, with a tenderness which made her heart beat more than her lover's words, "How surprised he will be when I tell him he shall not go."

The rustling of Mrs. Belding's ample approach broke in upon her trance and Farnham's litany. He rose, not without some confusion, to greet her, and Alice, with bright and even playful eyes, said, "Mamma, what do you think this errant young cavalier has come to say to us?"

Mrs. Belding looked with puzzled inquiry from one to the other.

"Simply," continued Alice, "that he is off for

Japan in a day or two, and he wants to know if we have any commissions for him."

"Nonsense! Arthur, I won't listen to it. Come over to dinner this evening and tell me all about it. I've got an appointment this very minute at our Oriental Gospel rooms and cannot wait to talk to you now. But this evening, you must tell me what it all means, and I hope you will have changed your mind by that time."

The good lady did not even sit down, but rustled briskly away. Perhaps she divined more of what was toward than appeared—but she did as she would have wished to be done by, when she was young, and left the young people to their own devices.

Farnham turned to Alice, who was still standing, and said, "Alice, my own love, can you not give me one word of hope to carry with me? I cannot forget you. My mind cannot change. Perhaps yours may, when the ocean is between us, and you have time to reflect on what I have said. I spoke too soon and too rashly. But I will make amends for that by long silence. Then perhaps you will forgive me—perhaps you will recall me. I will obey your call from the end of the world."

He held out his hand to her. She gave him hers with a firm warm grasp. He might have taken courage from this, but her composure and her inscrutable smile daunted him.

"You are not going yet," she said. "You have forgotten what you came for."

"Yes—that song. I must hear it again. You must not think I am growing daft, but that song has haunted me all day in the strangest way. There is something in the way *you* sing it—the words and your voice together—that recall some association too faint for me to grasp. I can neither remember what it is, nor forget it. I have tried to get it out of my mind, but I have an odd impression that I would better cherish it—that it is important to me—that life or death are not more important. There! I have confessed all my weakness to you, and now you will say that I need a few weeks of salt breeze."

"I will sing you the song first. Perhaps we may pluck out its mystery."

She preluded a moment and sang, while Farnham waited with a strained sense of expectancy, as if something unspeakably serious was impending. She sang with far more force and feeling than the night before. Her heart was full of her happy love, as yet unspoken, and her fancy was pleased with the thought that, under the safe cover of her music, she could declare her love without restraint. She sang with the innocent rapture of a mavis in spring, in notes as rich and ardent as her own maiden dreams. Farnham listened with a pleasure so keen that it bordered upon pain. When she came to the line,

"I would be so tender, so loving, Douglas,"

he started and leaned forward in his chair, holding his hands to his temples, and cried,

"Can't you help me to think what that reminds me of ?"

Alice rose from the piano, flushing a pink as sweet and delicate as that of the roses in her belt. She came forward a few paces and then stopped, bent slightly toward him, with folded hands. In her long, white, clinging drapery, with her gold hair making the dim room bright, with her red lips parted in a tender but solemn smile, with something like a halo about her of youth and purity and ardor, she was a sight so beautiful that Arthur Farnham as he gazed up at her felt his heart grow heavy with an aching consciousness of her perfection that seemed to remove her forever from his reach. But the thought that was setting her pulses to beating was as sweetly human as that of any bride since Eve. She was saying to herself in the instant she stood motionless before him, looking like a pictured angel, "I know now what he means. He loves me. I am sure of him. I have a right to give myself to him."

She held out her hands. He sprang up and seized them.

"Come," she said, "I know what you are trying to remember, and I will make you remember it."

He was not greatly surprised, for love is a dream, and dreams have their own probabilities. She led him to a sofa and seated him beside her. She put her arms around his neck and pressed his head to her beating heart, and said in a voice as soft as a mother's to an ailing child, "My beloved, if you will live, I will be so good to you." She kissed him and said gently,

"Now do you remember?"

THE END.

Americans in Fiction

A series of reprints of 19th century American novels important to the study of American folklore, culture and literary history